SEX AN...

The truth is we overseas wives have little to do but amuse ourselves and pass time in these beautiful surroundings with parties, flirtations, even passionate affairs.

The pool looks particularly inviting with the sun sparkling on the surface. I like to be stretched out beside it, improving my tan. I can still get away with a brief bikini rather well at my age, even if my breasts and buttocks are a bit much to be decently covered by such tiny scraps of material. I enjoy revealing myself and men like eyeing my endowments, so we all gain. Even at school my tits were large, firm and shapely. I've always been proud to have them admired, uncovered and fondled . . .

Also by Lesley Asquith

In the Mood

Also available from Headline

Cremorne Gardens
The Temptations of Cremorne
Sweet Sensations
Amorous Liaisons
Hidden Rapture
Learning Curves
My Duty, My Desire
Love in the Saddle
Bare Necessities
The Story of Honey O
Saucy Habits
Bedroom Eyes
Secret Places
Night Moves
Eroticon Dreams
Eroticon Desires
Intimate Positions
Play Time
Carnal Days
Carnal Nights
Hot Type
The Sensual Mirror
French Frolics
Claudine
Wild Abandon
Fondle in Flagrante
After Hours
French Thrills
A Slave to Love
Kiss of Death
Amorous Appetites
The Blue Lantern

Sex and Mrs Saxon

Lesley Asquith

Copyright © 1993 Lesley Asquith

The right of Lesley Asquith to be identified as the Author of
the Work has been asserted by her in accordance with the
Copyright, Designs and Patents Act 1988.

First published in 1993
by HEADLINE BOOK PUBLISHING PLC

10 9 8 7 6 5 4 3 2

All rights reserved. No part of this publication may be
reproduced, stored in a retrieval system, or transmitted,
in any form or by any means without the prior written
permission of the publisher, nor be otherwise circulated
in any form of binding or cover other than that in which
it is published and without a similar condition being
imposed on the subsequent purchaser.

All characters in this publication are fictitious
and any resemblance to real persons, living or dead,
is purely coincidental.

ISBN 0-7472-3967-3

Printed and bound in Great Britain by
HarperCollins Manufacturing, Glasgow

HEADLINE BOOK PUBLISHING PLC
Headline House
79 Great Titchfield Street
London W1P 7FN

Sex and Mrs Saxon

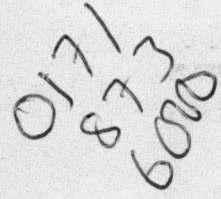

Chapter One
AFRICA

Four so-called ladies sit down to coffee and I alone of them would never claim the distinction. Certainly I'm the only one who doesn't believe beyond doubt she is a true-blue gentlewoman. Born to it.

Cynthia is actually a lady by title on account of her husband's silly knighthood. Midge and Molly are just plain haughty and vindictive. I put up with them only because of Harry's business interests. To hear them carry on about people you would assume it was their only pleasure in life. I think there's enough to be going on with seeing to myself, without bothering or even caring what others may get up to. Good luck to them, I say, if they do no real harm. My own life wouldn't stand much of an investigation at all. What a field day these three with me now would have if they knew even the half of it!

This lovely tropical morning it is my turn to entertain. East Africa really is beautiful. My houseboy has been up since dawn cleaning, polishing and baking, plus providing an extra service for me. Cato has made the house shine. We four females are on the verandah at ease, a cooling breeze wafting pleasantly from the lake. The coffee and pastries have been enjoyed and complimented, for which I accept praise due entirely to my accomplished servant. Then the gossip gets under way.

As usual it is about how the others in our community behave. I refrain from joining in. Instead I prefer to look out across my garden, a riot of colour. Matthew, the old Kikuyu gardener, is rolling the tennis court in a far corner, warned not to disturb such fine ladies with the clatter of his grass-cutter or even dare show his ragged figure near us. The flame trees are a picture, and the plumage of the exotic birds fluttering about the jacaranda gorgeous. The water sprinklers whirl jewelled droplets in three cascades over the sweep of lawn, transformed into chandeliers by the bright morning sun.

It is indeed beautiful and luxurious. The truth is we overseas wives have little to do but amuse ourselves and pass time pleasantly between home leaves with golf, parties and flirtations, even passionate affairs which, if discovered, scandalise and delight everyone. I sit back, barely listening to my guests, pleased with my flower arrangements, which I bung in various vases and pots without the supposed flair of Cynthia. I would very much like a gin and tonic, and I know the same goes for poor puffy-eyed Midge, but it is simply not done. Too early in the day or some such nonsense.

The pool looks particularly inviting with the sunshine sparkling on the surface. I'd like to be stretched out beside it, improving my tan. I can still get away with wearing a brief bikini rather well at my age, even if my breasts and buttocks are a bit much to be decently covered by such tiny scraps of material. I enjoy revealing myself. Men like eyeing my endowments, so we all gain. Even at school my tits were large, firm and shapely. I've always been proud to have them admired, uncovered, fondled and whatever. Harry says they are two sizes too big for my figure, which is still trim and slim apart from my breasts and a rather curvaceous bottom. Mind you, he isn't complaining.

Cato comes up silently to remove the cups and plates.

Sex and Mrs Saxon

I normally thank him politely but with these three present I remain silent, coward that I am. My guests act as if servants were invisible. Never, never, my dear, show the slightest interest in staff. They will without exception bore you with family troubles, sickness, and beg loans continuously for medicine, blankets or whatever, all of which goes on women and drink. And they take so many brides that babies are always arriving to add to their burdens. Cato has three wives already, pretty brown things little more than children themselves.

He is tall, handsome and perfectly proportioned, a Banyarwanda of about twenty, trained superbly by a French connoisseur on diplomatic duty in Zaire with the United Nations. Cato later crossed into East Africa and I am indeed lucky to have such a gem. He cooks, cleans and launders better than any woman I've known. The only drawback is he doesn't attempt to speak English and my Swahili has never got beyond the greeting 'Jambo'. My husband talks to him in French, in which both are fluent. Cato and I get on by my simply leaving all the household responsibilities in his hands. I'm sure in his tribal custom he considers women, including myself, as inferior beings. I suspect too that he understands every word I say but doesn't let on.

He is ideal for these morning sessions, immaculate in white shirt and shorts, his splendid looks and figure shown to advantage. But among other things he is also a skilled voyeur, gliding up barefoot to catch one unawares. I like to relax in the altogether after a bath or shower and before dressing. In the supposed privacy of my bedroom, of course. It's cool and comfortable in the tropic day and I might sit so, reading or writing letters. I've always enjoyed going naked with the air on my bare body and my breasts loose. Cato's silent arrivals always catch me unawares. I'd be nude, perhaps reclining on my bed or dusting talcum between the moist cleavage of my breasts (they do nestle close and cling together, inclined to get sweaty in the heat) when he would appear with a freshly pressed, always crisp and perfectly ironed dress for me to wear.

It happened time after time. Lack of communication made it difficult for me to tell him to stop. I didn't inform my husband as I had no wish to drag him into it, to order Cato to cease creeping up on Madam when she was stark naked. I felt, too, he was not so innocent as he appeared, always on the scene when I was undressed. Next thing he'd be beside me with a coffee, drink, the morning paper or some such relevant item, surveying my completely exposed white charms.

I got the feeling he approved of my well-developed breasts and buttocks. Judging by the buxomness of most African girls their men like them that way. My pubic hair, a thick thatch covering a prominent cunt mound, was what fascinated him most. He always stared at it more than at my big bosom, but then African men are no strangers to bare tits. However, I believe their women don't have bushy pussies and that was why he seemed so intrigued by mine.

The discussion around me had turned to European girls who had taken up with African boyfriends. How those three harpies ranted on about 'letting down the side'. It would never have happened in colonial times, they all agreed. I cringed with embarrassment and not only because Cato was hovering near, taking it all in with the semblance of an amused grin.

There was the added fact of his being in my bed with me less than an hour previously, fucking me even at the moment of my visitors' arrival. The sheets were still warm when he went out to open the door of the car that brought them. I hastily made up my face and hair, zipping myself into a dress to go to greet my guests.

* * *

Sex and Mrs Saxon

It is several weeks now since Cato became my lover. Once more he had silently entered my room while I was stripped, about to dress for a barbecue party at a friend's villa. He hung several freshly ironed articles of clothing in my wardrobe innocently enough, then turned to eye me with a very different expression from his usual stare of curiosity.

'Massage?' he inquired surprisingly. 'Madam would like relaxing massage? I was trained very expert. Taught good way. Always do for Frenchman—'

I'll just bet you did, I thought, having heard of his previous employer, an effete bachelor. Meantime I was still standing naked before the young negro. That he was horny for me and taking the chance while my husband was away on business I had no doubt. The front of his shorts bulged quite amazingly. He had also never bothered to speak English before. His lust transferred itself to me through his dark eyes, which were trained on my body like searchlights.

'Very good massage,' he repeated. 'Make Madam feel nice—'

And what would he feel while he was about it, I wondered? He had never touched me before, not even in serving me in the course of his duties.

'I have an appointment,' I said, but his offer was tempting. Deep within my stomach I felt a distinct stir of arousal, a churning feeling I rarely hesitated to encourage and then relieve by one way or another. I decided to let him massage me, but that would be all. Cato, suspecting my hesitation, spoke up in a sharper tone. I'm sure that was how his French master liked him to take charge at such a moment.

'Lay on bed,' he ordered. 'On stomach first.'

I did as bid, wondering just what I had let myself in for, my cheek resting on the pillows, back and bum upwards to him. Cato had my bottle of suntan oil open and poured a liberal amount down my spine. Then he leaned over me, his two large hands splayed and fingers spread widely. He started on my shoulders, rubbing and kneading, squeezing the nape of my neck. The feeling was of utter and immediate relaxation, plus a pleasing thrill by being stretched out naked before his wide eyes. His hands were both gentle and rough in turn, smoothing and soothing my skin, now pummelling and pressing. He took his time in attending to my neck, shoulders and back, massaging his way down to my hips.

This is it, I considered, as he arrived at my taut buttocks. Instead he ignored them and went on down to start on my ankles, working his way up to the backs of my knees and upper thighs. He was certainly very thorough and expert. I felt a warm glow spread throughout my body. Then I shuddered as cool oil was dripped down between the cleft of my bum cheeks.

His big palms spread to cover both fleshy globes, fingers digging in as he kneaded them. I felt myself being thrust against the mattress, my cunt rubbing against the crumpled sheet below me. A muffled involuntary sigh escaped my lips, I was being worked up to a strong arousal. My legs parted of their own accord. His fingers slipped sensuously down between my open cheeks, stroking the outer lips of my displayed cunt most teasingly, making them pout under his light caress. A finger moved back to pause at my anus before entering that orifice just the merest fraction. I drew in breath. I groaned and writhed my bottom. Never mind your French boss loving this treatment, I thought. It's having the same effect upon me!

Much more and I would have climaxed helplessly under his touch, my body shaking and my hips undulating. But the hand between my legs withdrew.

'Turn,' he said, and I obeyed, rolling over on to my back, heavy breasts lolling before him, my legs parted widely and my aroused cunt throbbing for entry by something, anything. Oil was dripped over my breasts and he began to massage and squeeze them in circular movements. I unashamedly moaned in pleasure and arched my back, thrusting my tits up to him. He pinched my nipples, pulled on them, stiffening and doubling their size and prominence.

More oil was poured, this time directly on to my mound, anointing the hair, trickling down to the puckered cunt lips most sensuously. His finger traced it down and entered, seeking and finding my clitoris, fluttering on it. Enough was enough.

'Get on me and do it,' I ground out between clenched teeth, my cunt thrusting up to meet his fingering. 'Go on, put it in. Fuck me!'

To be seduced so by my servant was no mean feat. He had accomplished it as cleverly as the most sophisticated lecher could have done. Despite offers, mainly from my husband's business associates or others high in their government, I had never had a black man in all my years in Africa. Of course, I remembered the talk as a girl about their size and virility, and had wondered! But such a relationship in a small community would be asking for trouble. This was not the same, however. Cato was here and now, his touch on my clitoris making me mad with high arousal. I wanted his prick deep in me.

He in turn regarded me with a superior male look, as if my plea for him to mount me was expected and natural for a woman, even his white employer. He drew off his shirt and shorts, all he was wearing. Bolt upright was the longest and stiffest penis I had ever seen, reaching up his belly past his navel and curved in its iron rigidity. His whole body was magnificent when naked: supple, muscled and athletic.

As he got between my thighs I opened wide for him, actually sighing with relief as the great shaft went in, parting my labia and penetrating easily, aided by my own copious lubrication and the suntan oil. I could feel the actual shape of his prick in my channel, its purple knob pressing far back against the furthest recess of my palpitating cunt. Again I groaned with pleasure, lifting to meet his thrusts.

Usually I like my lovers to take their time, starting off slowly with easy fucking movements that can arouse me to several climaxes before the frenzy of urgency brings a last shuddering orgasm. Cato and I just fucked that first time, wantonly and without finesse, as a dog will take a bitch on heat with rapid poking strokes. I don't know how many times he made me come. I was heaving under his thrusts, grappling his body with my arms and legs, gasping, groaning and shouting until I finally slumped back utterly sated and exhausted by his youthful virility. I hadn't been fucked and pleasured so by a new lover for years.

But I immediately went in dread that he might boast of his conquest. Such talk soons spreads among servants and becomes common knowledge. But no one seems the wiser and the routine of the house goes on as before except for our regular lovemaking. When I entertain as now he must wonder how I can act the lady when he's seen me acting like the biggest whore of a township bargirl. Each morning when Harry leaves for work, Cato brings in my breakfast tray and allows me a decent interval to enjoy it. When he returns he joins me naked in bed, bringing me to ecstatic heights with his ever-rigid length, always making me want more of him. I kiss my black lover with passion, allowing him anything, encouraging and suggesting new and delightful sexual treats for us to enjoy. Our sessions grow longer through my demands. Some mornings very little housework gets done before noon!

Cato has been good for me, no doubt. I bloom, sexy bit that I am. At forty-three ought I to know better? When he joins me in my bed, perhaps not long after Harry has had me, I enjoy the thought that two men want me. The way I feel, I NEED two men. Harry doesn't go without, in fact our lovemaking, always regular, has increased quite considerably. I can't seem to get enough, living the way I am with a built-in lover. I only wish I could have both of them bed me at the same time.

Cato also takes me on his own initiative over and above our now-usual breakfast sessions. I'm sure his wives are having a thin time of it while our passion and the novelty lasts. One lunchtime in the first week I felt his eyes on me while he served the meal. When Harry left to return to his office in town, Cato walked through to the bedroom and waited there. I knew well what he wanted – me! I went through to tell him it wasn't on. One of his wives was actually clearing the table. Despite protests I was fucked there and then across the bed, skirt up and my knickers down. As ever he brought me to a strong climax, but I was left with an uneasy feeling that I had started something beyond my power to control.

Another early afternoon I was undressed and about to don my golfing outfit when Cato appeared with that look. Two of his wives were in the passageway polishing the tiled floor. It meant nothing to him. I was fucked in a most urgent manner across the bed, our naked bodies slap, slapping in the sweaty heat as he rode me. From my laid-back position on the bed I could watch our black and white forms coupling in the dressing table mirror. Then, his ardour somewhat satisfied, in a more leisurely fashion he fondled me, sucked upon my nipples and had me aroused for more. His lengthy shaft grew rigid again in my hand and I guided it to my cunt. At such times I can't seem to help myself. Deeply penetrated once more, this time he played with me, long strokes and short, withdrawal when I wanted more, looking down upon me almost with a superior smile as I begged him to fuck me harder. This teasing went on until well in the afternoon, until we glistened with sweat. His virility and long-lasting powers are amazing.

When I finally left the room, Cato's third wife had joined the others in waxing the floor. They were on their knees and grinned up at me with perfect white teeth, well aware their strong young husband had been 'serving' Madam. I flushed with embarrassment thinking how they would have heard my groans and pleas while that 'serving' was taking place. I'm very vocal when aroused. Cynthia and co., my trio of friends sitting across from me now, were kept waiting at the first tee for over an hour that day. I arrived still somewhat flustered and told them I'd had a pressing servant problem, which of course they fully understood. They even went so far as to sympathise with me.

Chapter Two
SCOTLAND

The year was 1938 and I was sixteen. The early months of winter were harsh. Each day I walked the three miles to school in darkness and it was dark again when I arrived home. My two sisters were already away from the family working for a living. Unlike them, my mother determined I should continue schooling and do better than a housemaid's job in some mansion. With March the last snow melted. I discovered with the advent of spring I had grown inches in all the right dimensions.

My breasts had become heavy, full, round and firm, as big as my mother's, who was a splendidly built figure of a woman. My nipples now projected half-an-inch from the aureole, soft pink against the surrounding darker circle as round as the top of a teacup. I inspected myself with pleasure, stroking my tits until they seemed to swell and the nipples stiffened and grew longer. Above my cunt a prominent pubic mound was covered in a growth of curling hair. It was a virgin's cunt, a mere slit with no lips, despite an increasing urge for fulfilment. I was a girl in a woman's body with strange desires frustrating and unsettling me.

Father earned his living as a labourer in a quarry near the coast in the Scottish lowlands. He shovelled sand all day and we, his brood, were brought up in a wooden company cottage with a corrugated tin roof,

Sex and Mrs Saxon

a wonderful thing when tucked up snug on a stormy night listening to the downpour. Mother's dream was to live in a 'real' brick house and have nice things, but she kept the little cottage spotless and as comfortable as was possible. She was strict but caring, always there was good plain food and plenty of it; delicious thick soups and porridge was our staple diet. The way I grew, it was obvious I thrived on it. Money was the scarcest for us and I wore my older sisters' handed-down clothes, which made me determined to have nice things one day, no matter what I might have to do to get them.

There were two bedrooms and before sisters Isobel and Jennifer left home we three girls shared one. We always knew when father's sexual demands were being met. The walls were mere paperboard. Consequently on frequent nights we lay abed listening to their brass bed rattling as the marriage rites of grown-ups were enacted. Mother would complain bitterly not to make it last all night, but often her tone would change and we would hear her sigh and mutter pleasurably until her groans increased. The coupling would increase in frenzy then and the whole room shook.

Jennifer, the bold one, would sit up in bed to listen, stifling her giggles. She had 'done it' herself, she claimed, and had explained to me in detail what it was like. Isobel, the oldest and a prude, would cover her ears with the pillow, shocked and ashamed. I found nothing disgusting in what my parents were doing. That's what the secret parts between our legs were for and I considered it natural and exciting, looking forward to experiencing getting fucked. I often imagined it, especially when my fingers were busy pleasuring myself. But my favourite way of masturbating, which I discovered for myself, was to lie face down in bed, the hard pillow between my thighs, and thrust my cunt against it until reaching an orgasm I would have to stifle for fear of discovery. I longed to let go and moan and cry out at the moment of climax, like mother in fact.

By early summer that year I had the largest breasts and rounded bottom in my class at school. When I played hockey my big tits jiggled and bounced. One of the spinster teachers, disturbed by the number of unemployed men who came to the school field to watch, gave me my first bra. I didn't much care to wear it; didn't think I needed it. If men liked to see bobbing breasts that was all right by me. Besides my titties were beautifully firm and strong, they deserved to be admired.

By June the evenings were warm and although the Firth of Clyde is cold at any time I began taking dips by myself. The chilling sea felt wonderful on my body, almost sexual. I hid a towel and my bathing costume in a cleft in a group of rocks so that on my way home from school I could walk along the deserted beach and have my swim. It was on one of these occasions that I first met Mr Saxon. He was the owner of the quarry and lived in a large stately house with extensive grounds. No one knew much about a Mrs Saxon, although my mother had said there was one somewhere. Through his private acres was the shortest route home for me. He stood watching my approach. I was apprehensive but walked defiantly on.

'You shouldn't be here,' he told me sharply. 'There's a perfectly good road from the beach. Are you from the quarry houses on the hill?' His voice was like a man on the wireless.

I didn't answer and I saw his eyes looking me over closely. My hair was wet from the sea, clinging to my cheeks and neck. As for my dress, it had been Jennifer's and I had grown since inheriting it. I filled it with girlish curves.

'What's your name?' he asked in a kindlier manner.

'Mackenzie, sir,' I said. He did not seem such an ogre.

'One of those. Duncan's girls. Which one are you?'

'Diana.'

'Isn't it rather cold to go swimming?'

'I don't mind. Can I go now?'

'Walk with me,' he said, as if deciding something. 'It's quicker for you if you go through my gardens.'

We walked together without speaking. He wore a smart suit of lovely cloth that fitted perfectly. His large motor car was parked before the ornate steps of his house. He led me around the side, through beds of flowers on paved paths, stone statues of Greek or Roman people, a lily pond and fountains that squirted water. I'd heard at evening parties they could be lit up in various colours. It was then he put his hand on my shoulder and smiled at me, as if knowing I was thinking what it would be like to live in such beautiful surroundings.

'You're impressed. But the cottages have large gardens.'

There was no comparison. 'We grow vegetables,' I answered. Father's potatoes, turnips, leeks were vital items to us.

Mr and Mrs Macpherson were his servants; gardener, chauffeur, cook and housekeeper between them. They lived in the better quarry houses near the town, for which father did not qualify as a labourer. He said the Macphersons had the easiest jobs out as Mr Saxon liked privacy and they hardly ever worked late or weekends. 'Are you peckish after your swim, Diana?' he asked, breaking into my thoughts.

I didn't know what to answer so he asked was I afraid of him? 'Me? No,' I replied. He smiled and his handsome face reminded me of a film actor. Cary Grant, that was it.

Sex and Mrs Saxon

'Not afraid or not hungry?' We both laughed and I decided he was rather nice. About fifty perhaps, but did not look it, unlike worn-looking working men. He stood close enough for me to smell a faint odour of scented soap or shaving lotion. That was nice. I liked smart and clean people.

'We'll go through the house,' he invited, ushering me through a rear door into a magnificent kitchen of steel sinks, cupboards, gleaming cookers with hot plates, even a refrigerator. My mother had worked here as a servant once when guests were staying. Beyond the kitchen was a wide passageway deeply carpeted, hung with gilt-framed paintings, and a wide curved stairway.

'You like this too, I see,' he observed.

Again I said nothing as I stared in wonder. I would live in such a house one day, I decided, even if feminine wiles and my body was all I had to offer. I'd settle for nothing less, I knew, even at my early age. Of course, I had noticed the looks men gave me. It was more than admiration for a pretty and well-developed girl. Even at that moment, I saw Mr Saxon's eyes take in my face and lower to my breasts, going on down to my thighs and legs. His look made a strange feeling stir in my cunt and weakened my knees. He too had a strained expression. We stood face to face alone in the quiet house; expectantly is the only word I can use to describe the sudden atmosphere that had developed.

'Your sister Jennifer used to come here to visit me,' he said with some deliberation. 'Did she never mention that? We were very good friends indeed—'

I was astounded and showed it, my surprise convincing him I had not been aware of their friendship or whatever it was. Jennifer had been a deep one, no wonder she had been so much more worldly with such a secret bottled up. We were close as sisters, I'd thought, but not close enough evidently. That she was more sexually experienced that I, with her knowledgeable talk, I had put down to her courting local boys. My limit was kisses or cuddles and feels with a few lads at school thus far, not allowing more for the fear of pregnancy, which disgrace would have had my mother showing me the door. I'd wondered how Jennifer had risked it. She must have trusted someone. I looked at Mr Saxon.

'I expect you like cake,' he said, taking my elbow and leading me into a room lined with bookshelves. At a wide window with an alcove looking out on a sweep of the beach and sea, with the Island of Arran in the background, was a napkin-covered trolley. He lifted the cloth to reveal a plate of cold ham, with a salad bowl, thin slices of buttered brown bread, and a splendid cherry cake with a wedge already cut. The silver cutlery was wrapped in a smaller napkin and an electric kettle stood ready to be plugged in beside a teapot. There was Ovaltine too, and chocolate biscuits.

'My supper,' he announced. 'I have it here in my library.' He wrapped the generous slice of cake in yet another linen napkin. 'Eat this on your way home. Take a chocolate biscuit too—' When I nodded my thanks, he added, 'Jennifer used to come and make my hot drink some evenings. I hope you and I will be such good friends. Will you visit me? It could be our secret too, like it was with your sister.'

I was highly suspicious of his offer yet strangely intrigued. Had Jennifer done 'that' with him? For all the minimal amount of pocket money we received, she always had some and was generous with it, treating me to the cinema occasionally. And I used to think she was just a good saver! The thought made me giggle and Mr Saxon looked at me sharply.

'What is it?' he demanded.

Sex and Mrs Saxon

'You. You and Jenny—' I burst out.

'You're much prettier than her,' he praised me. 'Better bone structure, fuller figure. You're a lovely girl, do you know that? How old are you, Diana?'

'Sixteen,' I said.

I suddenly felt shy at his flattery as he stood nearer, almost face to face. He kissed my cheek and sat down in the armchair beside the supper trolley, patting his lap. 'Come and sit here. Jennifer used to sit on my knee. She liked that. I think you will too—'

Wary, yet highly intrigued, knowing it was wrong, naughty or leading him on, I nevertheless sat sideways across his lap. 'There,' he soothed. 'That's comfortable and cosy, isn't it?' For several long moments he did not move, then his arm slid around my waist. 'I'll look forward to your visits now we are friends.' I sat stiff and unmoving. 'Relax, Diana,' he added. 'I wouldn't hurt you, you're too nice.'

He pressed a kiss to my now-burning cheek and I wondered what would happen next. I considered jumping off his lap, as any sensible girl should, but remained where I was, excited now, aroused and dying to know his ultimate intention. After all, Jennifer had trod this path before me and come to no harm, or at least seemed none the worse for it. I also wanted to know how I would react faced with . . . what?

'I'm sure you're every bit as trustworthy as Jennifer at keeping a secret,' he said, stroking my hair. 'How very nice you are. So sweet and young. Cuddlesome too.'

His words, muttered into my neck as he nuzzled me, were having the desired effect. Mr Saxon was without doubt a seducer of impressionable girls. There was no doubt either about the effect I was having upon him. Beneath my cushiony bottom, ensconced in his lap, I felt a strange warm hardness grow into an elongated shape that pushed against my inner thigh. He was so gentle with his caresses and soft words that I did not fear him, and the arousal which by now was pulsating through my lower belly made it impossible to not want to carry on, or at least let him continue.

I found myself twisting to face him and we kissed mouth to mouth, gently at first, then he held me closer and our kissing lingered. When his hand moved to cup my breasts in turn I shivered at his touch. He squeezed, fondled and played with them, whispering how nice they were, how he would love to see them, kiss them. Touching them myself excited me; someone else doing it was doubly inflaming. My fingers moved up to the buttons fastening the front of my dress, undoing them from the neck down. I wanted his hand inside to feel the springy flesh of them, to pinch my nipples. His breathing became shorter, and I myself sighed and pressed my lips to his as our kisses grew longer in our passion.

'Sweet girl, darling Diana,' he moaned as our mouths had to part for air. My arms were around his neck by then and I was moving about upon the hard stalk under me which, with my short dress riding up and my instinctively positioning myself, was now directly between my buttock cheeks, rubbing against my throbbing cunt deliciously. I loved it, was even beginning to feel the stirrings of an orgasm, which I had previously only experienced through my own efforts. I wanted him to go on, pushing that rigid thing against me while I rubbed back. Now I was more or less astride his lap, facing him, my mouth open and tongue probing as I had experimented with boys my own age. My thrusting increased on his erection, desperate now to complete the course.

'Push, push! Go on, go on—' I urged him. Between his rampantness and my cunt was a great heat. Then he gasped and shuddered mightily, almost unseating me. For a long moment he held me tighter, then drew his mouth away from mine and ceased his thrusting. I wondered why; he had me so aroused and I wanted him to continue. He moved me away slightly on his lap and I knew he had come, climaxed, sated himself. I was disappointed, angry and annoyed. He had roused me to a pitch and selfishly only cared about his own satisfaction. I rose from his lap and straightened my dress, frustrated and sullen. He did not seem aware. Men!

'You had better go now, Diana,' he said.

'I might as well,' I agreed, my sarcasm wasted on him.

'Your mother might be wondering where you've got to. I'll walk with you to the door.'

When he arose I noticed the large damp patch at the front of his trousers and smiled grimly to myself, *I* had caused that. Suddenly I didn't feel so badly. At the door Mr Saxon pressed a half-crown into my hand along with the cake and chocolate biscuit he had wrapped earlier. This was more money than I had owned in months and was well aware it was payment for sexual services.

'Come and visit tomorrow night,' he said. 'I shall be here by myself and we can have supper together. I'll make sure it's something very special. Trifle and ice-cream—'

I didn't know if I would and therefore didn't answer as I walked away. If he just wanted to use me for his own selfish ends I wasn't keen. Still, I knew I would relive the kissing, fondling and rubbing against him in my bed that night as I brought myself off against the pillow between my legs. It was exciting to think I had aroused an adult male, a supposed gentleman. I knew different. He had not been such a superior being as my parents and his other employees thought when we were kissing and cuddling madly. The same as any other man, I suspected. That's what being a female object of desire could reduce the highest to, and it gave me a warm and superior feeling.

Chapter Three
AFRICA

Despite my worst fears, the affair with my houseboy carries on unabated. We've managed a few whole nights together when Harry is off on business trips. He often takes his secretary with him, a pretty black college graduate, and I'm sure the pair of them make the most of their nights away in Nairobi or Mombasa. I wish he'd tell me about it. I'm neither jealous nor possessive, and I do think a change can be welcome (as I know) and good therapy. In return I'd confess my own affairs, or at least some of them! We might even compare notes on lovers past and present. Harry is no saint. Anyway, while he's away, Cato has filled in for him quite magnificently.

It is strange and nice, stirring in the night to feel his strong young body beside mine; to arouse him from sleep to fuck me again. His skin is smooth and sensuous to touch, of a sheen I've never known in any other man. I go all passionate and lose self-control when he enters me, a lovely and erotic feeling to receive so much inside my eager cunt. I heave to meet his thrusts like a wild woman, crying out with the pure pleasure of it, begging him to continue as I love what he is doing to me, getting me tremendously worked up. I have the wildest thoughts while he is fucking me. Of my mother standing beside the bed and trying to pull me from under him as I convulse and whine and groan. Of Harry joining in to take me at the same time, the two men filling me back and front. The orgasms roll over me. I'm left quite limp and sated, most gloriously fulfilled. Then I sleep as never before.

I've given up worrying about going naked in the house before Cato. He's seen all there is; what's to be prudish about? He soaps me in the bath. I lie back and enjoy the luxury. He dries me in a huge towel and then leads me to the bed, where I'm massaged and oiled, powdered and, of course, made love to. He did much the same for his last employer, the Frenchman, he told me.

I shocked or surprised him by sucking his beautiful prick, I couldn't fight down the desire on our second night sleeping together. Although fellatio is evidently not common among African habits, it's a pleasure he readily enjoyed. He demanded regular repeats. Once when Harry was seated in the garden, I went into the house to refresh his drink. Cato came through from the kitchen and pulled out a stiff and demanding prick, holding it in my direction, his meaning clear.

'Suck,' he commanded, gripping my shoulder. He no doubt liked the idea of me sucking him while Harry was not far away. The thought of my husband waiting for his drink, chatting to several guests, excited me too. I bent and took Cato's rigid shaft between my lips, sucking avidly, apprehensive of discovery. Of course, that added to the illicit thrill of what we were doing. I sucked him in deeply, my mouth full, grasping Cato's stalk and rubbing it at the same time until he writhed, gasped and his pelvis convulsed. His come flooded my throat. No other words were spoken. He buttoned his shorts and returned to his kitchen. I went back out into the garden, taking a mouthful of Harry's gin and tonic to clear Cato's thick emission from my tongue. I felt very wanton as I gloated over the secret happening as I handed over the drink.

One evening, with Harry safely away on business, Cato appeared in the house with his youngest wife, a pretty girl whose skin is jet black. She is called Nandi, a Muganda he had taken as his third wife and the only one not presently pregnant by him. He explained that he wished her to be present to 'help' in the proceedings.

I protested at once. In our situation two's company, but three was an added risk I felt. I was already taking a big enough chance having Cato for a lover. Against any common sense I might have had, strangely game for the experience all the same, the three of us went through to the bedroom and undressed. Nandi eyed my nakedness with interest, no doubt seeing her first white woman in the nude. I was as taken with her body, the dark skin, very pointed pear-shaped breasts with inch-long purplish nipples. Her thighs were smooth and plump and her cunt a hairless split. I could have pressed my nakedness to hers willingly but did not know how she would react. I wanted to kiss her mouth, suck upon those pointed bubs, go down to tongue her tight-lipped cunt. I've been with other women and enjoy such play; I've also been in threesomes, fours, right up to crowded orgies. I knew Cato had it in mind to extend his sexual pleasure, but perhaps only for the gratification of fucking us both.

Therefore I waited to see how he would include his young wife in the proceedings. I desired her. It had been some time since I had enjoyed sex with another female and Nandi's smooth plump body was most appealing. Cato got on the bed and instructed her to pour oil on his genitals and rub him to erection. His prick arose like a tent-pole. The girl stroked away with her tiny hand, a good six inches showing above her grasp. Watching it made arousal surge in my cunt. I found I wanted to squat over him, to impale myself on his great prick in front of his wife.

As I made to get on the bed the girl moved aside obediently, but her husband gripped her wrist and held her near. What he told her I can only guess, but as I positioned myself crouching above him she spread the cheeks of my buttocks wide with both hands as I lowered myself on to his upright prick. I sank down on the taut shaft until its length seemed to go up to my very stomach. That way I rode him in utter and mad abandon, my breasts bouncing over his face as I jerked away to the ultimate convulsion. I turned and pulled Nandi to me in my throes, kissing her mouth with my tongue extended and was rewarded by her grasping me and returning my kisses with passion.

We all slept together in my big marital double bed and before morning Cato had twice injected both of us women with his sperm. Whoever was being fucked he made the other direct his prick into the cunt on the receiving end. I was made to show Nandi how to suck him and she quickly mastered the art. In the morning I awoke to find the young African girl cuddled up to me, rubbing her cunt mound on my hip. I welcomed her by kissing her mouth and breasts, and she held up a nipple for me to take between my lips. I sucked as she pushed herself against me and, by suckling, drew warm milk into my mouth for she was already a nursing mother. Then I eased my thighs apart as behind me Cato awoke and pressed his hardness between my buttock cheeks, seeking my saturated cunt. He entered easily, sliding in deeply. Thus we fucked with his wife in my arms, our pubic mounds grinding together.

In the calmer light of day I had to consider that things had gone too far. Harry never minded me going home to Scotland for shopping and visits to my married daughter and a son in university. I decided to take several months leave of absence, starting right away. When I returned, hopefully Cato would understand the affair was a thing of the past. Much as I had enjoyed his lovemaking, and much as I would have liked to continue making love to his young wife, I felt he was becoming to think of me as one of his wives as well. It was high time to call a halt. Yet one further notable sexual encounter with him was to take place before I flew home a few days later.

It was a lovely evening and I was in the garden with Harry. Hearing cries, I caught Cato beating Nandi in the doorway of their quarters. His other wives did not look at me, squatting over their cooking pots carefully maintaining strict neutrality. My outrage made Matthew, the old gardener, appear from his room, heavy with sleep or drink but very intrigued by my visiting their area.

Nandi ran away howling and Cato stood erect and silent as I told him angrily never to dare allow me to hear he beat his wives. My raised voice brought Harry hurrying across from the verandah where he had been sitting in a basket chair. He still held his newspaper and a glass of whisky. Cato was more perturbed by my husband's arrival than by all my ranting but he need not have worried.

In front of the entire staff and wives, Harry bluntly ordered me to shut up and get back to the house. I saw Cato giving me a vengeful glare as I left, his manly pride no doubt injured. Then on the verandah Harry gave me a telling off for being an interfering bloody woman. What Cato did when off duty was his own business (if only Harry knew!) and to enter into his family affairs was downright unforgivable. If Cato beat his wives they probably deserved it, expected it, and perhaps even enjoyed it. In fact, he ended, shaking out his paper and sitting back down, it was a pity so-called modern husbands ever gave up thrashing their women.

The following morning when Cato appeared with my

tea I saw he was still aggrieved. He didn't close the door when returning for the tray, his usual before getting into bed with me. I kept the sheet covering my breasts as I sat up, for I always sleep nude. Reaching out, he caught hold of the protective sheet, tugging at it.

'Oh no, Cato,' I said firmly. 'Not any more. I'm going away and what we did is over. Remove the tray, please, and then leave—'

He ripped the sheet away and I was left naked. Rolling over quickly, I hoped to escape from the bed and make for the door. Cato was quicker, catching me and holding me face down. One strong hand pinned me firmly by the neck while I struggled to rise. He began to use the other hand to chastise my buttocks, his strong right arm rising and falling vigorously, delivering a flurry of hard sharp blows to my bottom. Smack, smack, smack went his open-handed palm.

I yelped in anger and pain. Stinging, humiliating slap after slap rained down to make me clench my cheeks and draw them in tight, squirming and twisting to alternate each tender part receiving punishment. The blows brought tears to my eyes, making me howl and scream, protesting and cursing him. I had never before been so humiliated yet finally I begged and pleaded for mercy. He ceased the thrashing, leaning over me and panting with exertion.

The sight of my poor pink well-spanked bottom, cheeks parted thankfully again after the strain of clenching and bracing for each expected blow, was too much for him. He reached across to my bedside table and took up a jar of cold cream. I immediately hazarded what he intended. I had insulted him and now he was going to insult me in the most degrading way he knew. He had outraged my bottom by giving it a beating; I wasn't going to allow worse humiliation.

'No!' I screamed. 'Don't you dare, Cato!' at the same time reclenching my arse cheeks.

He overcame the problem of having access by giving me one more tremendous slap on my bum. Then I felt myself being liberally smeared with the cold cream between my cleft cheeks. His finger entered to the knuckle and I implored him to stop. Attempting to rise in desperation, he thrust me flat again, a huge hand squarely between my shoulders and further protests stifled in the pillows. That was how the coupling was made, me face down and rear up as I attempted to scramble away crab fashion. Cato leaned over me, his smooth firm belly curving around my upraised posterior, the added weight ensuring my captive position for his onslaught.

When he entered me, bulbous knob directed with cold deliberation to the tight ring of my anus, the first inch stretched my arsehole round and wide. I moaned, both in humiliation and grudging pleasure. He eased it up a few inches, carefully I must grant him. It felt, despite my shock and anger, more and more pleasant going in. His big prick had never seemed stiffer or longer as it finally penetrated its full length up my back passage. I had to give myself over to enjoying an erotic, expert anal ravishing.

He wasn't the first man there by any means, but it had never seemed more exciting or tormentingly arousing. I've always been a woman who liked her men to be masterful, at times to use and abuse me. There were other times when I enjoyed being the strict mistress. Now I was being used to the limit. Cato had me plugged to the hilt and thrust against me in long slow movements of his groin. I could only reciprocate by grinding my rear back to meet his strokes, making him quicken as his groans grew louder. I felt completely filled with prick as never before, full up to the stomach it seemed with mass and heat, moaning my gratitude.

His urgent thrusts carried me forward until my head met the padded headboard of the bed, my cushiony rear a buffer as he worked against me. His hands reached below and took hold of my breasts for extra leverage. The headboard broke off with a sudden snap and fell to the floor. His balls bounced and thudded against my buttocks. I reached back with both hands to part myself wider, pulling the cheeks open to allow him closer contact. His body gave a great leap and he came deep within me, the hot emission spurting and flooding me, his prick pulsating as he deposited his load high in my back passage. I climaxed myself almost at the exact moment in a series of shudders and jerks that went on and on deliciously.

He had come as I had never known a man to do so before, such was the length of his spasms. But even then he made no attempt to rise from me. His weight held me down and his prick began losing its rigidity, still deep within me and gripped by the tightness of my anus. He made us remain so for several long minutes, talking down to me all the while, his voice taunting and proud.

This was a new Cato as I lay helpless and forced to acknowledge his superiority. He gloated over the buttock-fucking he had given me, revelling in the fact that I had been made to come. Now that I had 'tasted' such, that was how he would have me in future. That was how, he said, his French master had been served by him. I could imagine how the role of master and servant had been exchanged.

When he finally withdrew from me I was left face down, too angry and humiliated to look at him. As a parting gesture he flicked the sheet back over my body as if to show his contempt. I stayed a long time on the

Sex and Mrs Saxon

bed, sore in spirit as well in my abused bottom. Once more in my life I had played with fire and got singed to say the least. Why do I always get into such situations? I always do!

From the passageway I heard the tinkling laughter of his wives as he no doubt proudly boasted to them of his revenge. I decided more than ever that a long leave of absence was the sensible way out of the situation. Let him have his moment of triumph, I considered as I began to cheer up. One day I'd laugh at the humbling he'd given me and even savour the episode, as I did so many others in my past sexually adventurous life. There had been other men before him, and hopefully others to come. All my past lovers worthy of mention had provided sensual experiences I now recall with pleasure. That's going back to an early start with plenty of offers and few refusals. That's how I was made, a woman of pleasure.

Chapter Four
SCOTLAND

I played netball after school the following evening, and then went to the Beach Café with two girlfriends. Both girls' fathers had small businesses in the town. I usually couldn't afford to accompany them, but with Mr Saxon's present I treated us all to fish and chips and ice-cream. Healthy, hungry young creatures we devoured the feast and talked of our favourite subject – boys.

It appeared I was the only virgin of the three, but I did not admit it. I wondered at this; my friends were skinny girls with spotty faces and ratty hair. I had filled out splendidly with breasts and thighs, and my hair was silky and reached down my back, the same dark red as my father's. It shone when I washed and brushed it. My eyes were light brown and my nose straight on an oval face. I suspected my mouth and teeth were a little too big, but my lips were naturally red and my teeth white and perfectly even. If I was still a virgin, I considered, it was because of living out of town with a strict mother who tried to watch my every move. Anyway, my companions had only been with immature boys. I could look back on the previous evening when a grown man had cuddled, kissed and fondled me. Had he continued I'm sure my status as a virgin would have ended.

Sex and Mrs Saxon

One of the girls with me was Anna Geddes, whose father was a local coal-merchant. She was about to go to a private girls' school for which fees would be paid. It would be a waste of time and money for Anna was a dunce at lessons. No doubt her parents hoped it would make a young lady of her and increase the chance of a good marriage. I went with her to her home, furnished in what they considered good taste: fitted carpets, stuffed sofas and a glass display cabinet filled with china. My home had a scrubbed table, linoleum on the floor and one armchair which was reserved for my father. Still I considered it more homely than the Geddes' house. Mrs Geddes, a fat little woman who had once worked on a farm with my mother, obviously didn't approve of me, a mere labourer's child. Old bitch, I walked out of the house to show what I thought of *her*.

It was three miles to my home, but I'd done it thousands of times, walking in rain and snow often. By the gate Mr Geddes was about to put his car in the garage. 'Hello, Diana,' he said cheerily. He was a plump broad man with a thin moustache like the film stars of the time. Fancied himself, he did. 'Been visiting Anna? Hop in, I'll drive you home, lass—'

Knowing this would annoy his wife I got him beside him. It was an old car with stuffing coming out of the seats. He glanced down at my legs, which showed an amount of thigh, my short dress having risen when I sat. 'Good pair of legs on you,' he praised. 'A pretty girl with plenty of boyfriends, I'll bet. What does your ma think of that?'

'She thinks nothing of it,' I said. 'I haven't got a boyfriend.'

'Don't give me that,' he teased, his eyes on my dress, bulging breasts straining the buttons. He put a pudgy hand on my knee even though driving, giving it a squeeze. His hand remained there and I did not try to move my leg. Mr Geddes even! I thought, enjoying wondering what his snobbish wife would think if she knew. Encouraged by my compliance, his hand moved higher, raising my dress until the hem of my knickers showed. He began to smooth my thigh, and then drew off the road into a farm lane and pulled up. There were trees all around us and not a soul near. Enjoying myself, I decided I would allow him a few liberties, even just to get back at his wife.

'Give me a kiss,' he said in a strange voice, hoarse and husky. 'Come on. You won't miss one—'

Whether I had wanted to or not I was pressed in his arms and his wet mouth clamped over mine. A moment later his tongue went into my mouth and his hand went to my breasts. Soon it moved down and sought between my legs, squeezing my cunt roughly. Then I was pushed back along the seat and his hand drew my knickers down while he fumbled with his fly. Looking down over my heaving breasts I saw him draw out his penis, stiff and stumpy, a short fat straining prick. I thought, what is his hurry? Inexperienced as I was, even I knew I should have been coaxed a little, flattered and petted, until I gave in as readily as he wanted me. Geddes was going at it like a bull at a gate. I could smell him too, the odour of sweat and coal, although he had obviously been out on business, washed and shaved and in his best suit. Really, had he used a little subtle cajolery and petted me to arousal I'm sure he'd have had his way. As it was I suspected he was completely out of control and I knew well that was how silly girls got pregnant. I pushed him off me and told him angrily to keep his distance. A deal of my anger was because the stupid man had started something I was hoping to enjoy and ruined it.

He sat back in his seat glaring at me, his fly open and his fat prick sticking out. 'You led me on,' he accused me. 'You're a bloody slut, a cock-teaser.'

'And you put your hands on me first,' I reminded him with some spirit. 'I didn't ask you to touch me—'

He was trembling, furious still at being thwarted. 'You were asking for it,' he swore. 'Cock-teasing bitch.'

'Oh, you would have watched what you were doing? Likely you'd have made a baby the way you were. Who would have had said they was the father then?' I could hardly believe my boldness.

He calmed somewhat, his prick shrinking back as he considered my words. 'Maybe I was a little hasty, lassie,' he admitted. 'I don't often get the chance with a nice thing like you. Mrs Geddes, you know, she's not much on that sort of thing—'

I could have giggled, hearing him say that. He was already eyeing me again with an ardent stare. When he reached for me I allowed a kiss. He took my hand down to his prick and I felt it grow hard again in my grasp. 'You're a nice lass, a sweet lass,' he repeated between kisses, his hand back on my breasts. I felt the usual surge in my loins that was to lead me on whenever a man wanted me. Lord knows I would have been on my back across the seats a moment later but a blaring of a motor-car horn behind us made the pair of us sit up in alarm. Through the back window I saw Mr Saxon's Rolls Royce stopped some twenty yards behind us.

'Bloody hell, it's Mr Saxon,' Geddes said, even in his panic using the 'Mr' in deference. 'What the devil is he doing up a farm lane—?'

I could have told him, of course, but busied myself pulling up my knickers and straightening my hair and dress. 'I'll go now,' I announced. 'Thanks for the lift.'

Geddes was in an awful funk, and was wide-eyed at my calmness. 'He'll see you getting out of my car,' he said in terror. 'What if he speaks to you? Your father works for him. What will you say—?'

'Don't worry,' I assured the frightened coalman. 'I

can get home across the fields from here. I'll say you gave me a lift this far. After all, I was with Anna at your house.'

He nodded in relief, then another thought struck him. 'Here, you'll say nothing of this to her, or anybody. You were as bad as me—'

'Course not,' I said indignantly. 'You are stupid.' Before that day I would never have spoken so to an adult but in my new-found role as a desirable female it came naturally.

Geddes mopped his brow in relief, then fished in his pocket and handed me a shilling piece. 'On you go then and mum's the word. Maybe I could see you another time—?'

'Maybe,' I said and got out of the car. He roared away up the farm track. Clutching the coin in my hand I walked back towards Mr Saxon's Rolls. He sat up behind the wheel with his face a picture of icy displeasure. If he was going to be like that I turned up my nose and made to walk past. Men, whether it was a shilling or a half-crown and cherry cake, they thought they had exclusive rights. All the same, he flew out of the car and confronted me, which pleased me no end. There was no doubt, if not yet a fully fledged one, I was well on my way to being a woman of pleasure, whose objective was to attract men. I was also well on my way, I knew, to being what my mother called a 'bad' girl. I didn't see the harm in taking my fun when it was offered. The men needed no encouragement.

'I waited for you at home,' Mr Saxon said angrily. 'What were you doing with Geddes?'

'I played netball with his daughter,' I retorted haughtily. 'He offered me a lift as far as here on his way to the farm—'

'Are you telling me the truth?' he demanded. 'He's a known womaniser. That man is not to be trusted.'

'And you are?' I cheeked him. 'You can believe what you like. I'm off home—'

He held open the car door, calmer now, but still sullen. I knew he was maddeningly jealous more than concerned about my welfare. He drove along the beach road without speaking until he stopped his car by my bathing area. The first drops of rain spattered the windscreen from a grey sky. Looking between the dunes to the shore I saw the sea was quite rough. Not a soul was to be seen, no ship sailed the Firth of Clyde. Inside the car was warm and snug, only his steady breathing and the ticking of the dashboard clock breaking the silence, but I wished I could run into the sea it looked so inviting. As if reading my thoughts he said I should go in if I wished.

'I've no towel or costume with me,' I said. 'They're at home.'

'Well, there's nobody here to see you. The rain is heavy but you'll get wet swimming. When you come out there's a warm travelling rug on the back seat. Wrap up in that and I'll take you home to dry properly. There's food too.'

It would be fun, I considered. I had never swam naked. With him present it seemed all the more daring.

He opened the door on my side. 'Into the back with you,' he said. 'Take off your things. I'll give you five minutes to have a dip and be back here.' He held up his wrist, showing a gold watch. 'Five minutes. Don't waste them.'

In the roomy back of his car I pulled off my dress, quickly discarding vest, knickers and shoes. Mr Saxon kept his head severely to the front, but his eyes reflected in the driving mirror affixed to the windscreen. I saw him stare at my naked body. I wanted him to see my bared breasts. As I pulled off my socks I lifted each leg in turn, affording him a look between my parted legs. Then I was off, bare as you like, bounding down the beach and into the sea, where the waves rushed to meet me.

The white foam gurgled around my thighs and belly. The next wave slapped my breasts, leaving me breathless. I ducked forward as each roller came in, bobbing up with tits leaping. The feeling of complete freedom was exhilarating. I swam forward again, my buttocks raised, two mounds above the water. Then I rolled over and my breasts floated, the nipples drained of colour and shrivelled tight. I stood and let the next wave break between my parted legs, slapping my cunt. When I turned to face the beach the following wave smacked my bottom like a stinging hand. Certain five minutes had passed I rushed back towards the car, shivering now, my breasts so tight that they barely moved as I ran. The front door of the car was open for me and Mr Saxon watched my approach holding the tartan blanket.

'In here before you freeze, Diana,' he welcomed me.

I was enveloped in the rug and curled up on the seat beside him, my feet dripping a pool on the carpeted floor. He began to rub me dry as my teeth chattered, towelling my neck and shoulders. I began to dry my breasts myself, rubbing hard to bring feeling back to them.

'Let me,' he said, his voice soft and hoarse. I sat back and let him to do as he liked, welcome warmth returning under his hands. The blanket slipped in folds to my waist and he sat staring at my two prominent bubbies, now pulsating with returning feeling. Looking down upon them at the tight clinging valley where they nestled together, I was as ever proud of their size and roundness. I knew he liked them. His hands cupped both of them and he kissed each nipple longingly, making them rise. Then he was sucking me ardently, taking each nipple in turn deep in his mouth. I held his head to me and moaned at the pleasure I found in being suckled. Then his hand drew mine to his lap and I looked down to see his prick rearing upright from the opening of his trousers.

Tufts of hair sprouted near the base and the rigid column was lined with veins as if about to burst. My hand grasped it and began a stroke that had him stretching back in his seat, his hips moving with my rubbing. He moaned deeply and drew the handkerchief from his top pocket, covering his engorged knob with it as he jerked helplessly away in a climax. I watched him relax, the stiffness in my hand subsiding to a wet slug of a thing.

'Thank you, Diana,' he said. 'Thank you. That was a lovely thing you did to me—'

I sat back astounded. 'Don't mention it,' I said testily. Once more it seemed I had been aroused and only his selfish ends had been satisfied. He looked at me curiously.

'What's the matter, girl?' he asked.

'Not a thing,' I said sullenly. 'You'd better take me home after I've dressed.'

He seemed relieved by the suggestion. Of course he would, now that *he* had got what he wanted. 'Is that all you do?' I said bluntly. 'Is that all you did with Jennifer?'

'Isn't it enough?' He paused, adding, 'Jennifer was older.'

In anger I sat up and reached over the back of the seat to retrieve my clothes from the rear of the car. My bottom was almost full in his face and he put out a hand to caress my cheeks.

'The car is hardly the place for much more, is it?' he said, his fondling of my bottom continuing. 'And it is later than I thought. I don't want to get you into trouble with your mother—'

'Let me worry about that,' I snapped. I was still trying to reach my clothes and bent over further. To my utter surprise I felt him press his face to the cleft of my bottom and kiss me there. Then his finger touched my cunt lips and stroked them. I parted my legs as if the most natural thing to do and the finger entered me, probing and going deeper. As he continued I shuddered with the flow of sensuality building rapidly within me. I was moist and two fingers now stroked and smoothed inside.

'Aahh, oohh,' I moaned. 'Don't stop! Keep doing it—' It was both an order and a plea. I thrust myself back on to his hand shamelessly, helpless in the mounting throes of an impending strong climax. My movements were evidently not so wild, however, as instinctively I had positioned myself so that his probing fingers stroked my receptive clitoris. His touch and my own writhings had me gasping and shuddering in ecstasy. My state of arousal did not go unnoticed.

'You baggage!' Mr Saxon exclaimed in delight. 'You delightful little nymph! Why, you *love* it—' I should have burned with shame at his words but was beyond caring. This was the most delightful experience I could imagine. Then he drew me back from over the seat and laid me flat before him, my breasts heaving from my breathlessness. I tried to take his hand and return it between my thighs.

'Look what has happened,' Mr Saxon said proudly, leaning back. His prick rose hard and firm again from his open fly. 'Are you a virgin, Diana?'

I humbly admitted that I was, while his finger squelched within me nicely. 'No lout of a coalman or untutored village youth will have that pleasure,' he said. I saw him lean forward to position himself between my parted legs, holding his prick to direct it at my lubricated opening.

'Put it in,' I heard myself say. 'Do it, do it. I want you to—'

I had always been an athletic girl, taking part in running, jumping and gymnastics. No doubt my maidenhead had ruptured before, probably with my own fingering. I can remember no strain as he eased his prick into me. He went gently at first, then penetrated his full length, fitting tightly but sliding up without pain, only complete pleasure. I found the full feeling in my cunt channel delightful and pulled him closer, my arms about him and one leg curled around the lower part of his bum cheeks. That way I soon discovered I could lever his body to increase his thrusts as he fucked me. I was evidently a quick learner.

Above me Mr Saxon valiantly sighed and groaned away as his exertions grew stronger. Long thrusts had me arching under him to increase his strokes. The rough cloth of his hacking jacket rubbed tormentingly against my bare breasts and stomach, increasing my arousal. I urged him on to shove it up, go faster, until we were a pair see-sawing madly against each other's bodies. I felt my surge and tried to hold back, prolonging the sweet churning and burning in my cunt. I didn't even care if he came within me, being made pregnant with all the shame and scandal such would bring. All I wanted that first glorious time was that his stiff prick remained deep inside me, poking me to convulsions.

There was evidently too much at stake for Mr Saxon to forget himself, even in such an heated coupling. Besides, thinking back, he had already spent himself previously in my hand. When I gave in to the inevitable I came humping and bucking against him. Even as the spasms lessened I wanted it to continue, thrusting away to a second orgasm. As I reached it, bouncing up and down on the leather upholstery below me, he withdrew urgently, sitting up over me, his spurts flying over my belly and reaching my breasts.

He dabbed me dry with his handkerchief, smiling like the cat that had got the cream. 'And did you like that?' he asked quite unnecessarily. 'Was it nice?'

'Oh,' I gasped. 'It was lovely. Heaven. Now I'll want to do it all the time, I expect.'

He looked down at my big breasts, my still throbbing cunt. 'Your body, your nature, everything about you, my dear, was created to give pleasure and be pleasured in return. Will you come and visit me as you promised now?'

'I will, I will,' I said gratefully. 'I want to now.'

So I was a reluctant virgin no more. Taken in the back of a Rolls Royce no less. It's the only way to travel, first class!

Chapter Five
ENGLAND

Children can get one into strange situations, as any parent knows. Son Peter falling out with his latest girlfriend and suddenly deciding to go off on holiday was the direct cause of my next lapse, hot on the heels of fleeing from the clutches of Cato. Peter taking a break to consider his future without his fiancée Chloe Mathison was no excuse for what happened next, you may say. A decent woman should feel shame and remorse. But that too can be like heady wine, making her wanton and glowing in body. Humiliation and its bitter sweet effect can be a very potent aphrodisiac, just as a sound smacking of female buttocks can arouse and inflame when administered at the appropriate moment. For me, to be left feeling marvellously used and abused at times can be a relief from the respectable front we are forced to adopt in conventional life. I suspect more women than admit it, think so too. It can be quite therapeutic.

On arrival at Heathrow I called Peter and got a reply on his answerphone, which always makes me replace the receiver as soon as the recorded voice begins. I therefore called Harry's ex-lover, his so-called Aunt Margaret, whom I'd become good friends with over the passing years. After all, we had something in common. Delighted to hear I was in England, she drove to the airport to pick me up. On the drive back to her Chelsea home I told her the latest on Harry. She in turn said she'd seen Peter around in town and my daughter, Lesley, had dropped in for lunch, when shopping in London, in her last few weeks of pregnancy. On arrival at Margaret's house I phoned her home in Oxford and I got through to her husband, Philip. Lesley, he explained, was out seeing her doctor. She had not been too well that week. I promised to visit them shortly. So I was soon to be a grandmother.

The next day or two I relaxed with Margaret, shopping in the West End, dining in nice restaurants, taking in a show. She also went on her weekly visit to a Turkish bath and sauna to keep away the wrinkles and flab, as she claimed, so I joined her.

It was a discreet establishment with bow windows filled with plants and flowers, nothing to show its type of business catering for an exclusive female clientele. All was spotless paint and tiles inside with cubicles and bathrooms. Soon I was seated in a sweat box, a thick fluffy towel around my neck where my head projected from the opening. The dry heat made rivulets of tickly perspiration run down from my neck, shoulders, breasts and belly, forming a damp pool under my bottom and between my legs. The hair on my mound felt soaked and my cunt itched with the salty downpour. I rubbed myself in the slippery moisture, deciding a nice private come in the warmth of the enclosed sweat box would greatly add to the pleasure. Getting nicely aroused with a finger on my clitoris, I was interrupted by the appearance of Margaret, swathed in a towelling robe, with a blonde middle-aged matronly woman beside her. A few moments more and I would have climaxed.

'This is Helga, my regular masseuse,' said Margaret, introducing the formidable woman, decidedly a large buxom type in a white nylon overall that bulged with her ample curves. 'She's an expert on Swedish massage and gives me relief every week.' I noted Margaret's eyes were bright and her face flushed as a woman's is after an orgasm. 'You'd enjoy her services, Diana, she's so very good. Just put yourself in her hands.'

I was led away into a white tiled room with a massage table and shower cubicle. The towel I was wrapped in was pulled away by the masseuse and I was told to lie face up on the padded table, naked and glistening. 'Your friend's body is in very good condition,' Helga observed to Margaret in a heavy Swedish accent. Margaret had sat down in the armchair provided in the room. 'Yes,' she agreed. 'Diana has always been a beauty. She's retained her looks and figure marvellously.'

'Clean living and a healthy mind,' I said from my supine position, feeling I should get in on the conversation, but the talk went on around me as if I wasn't there.

'See,' pointed out the butch masseuse, squeezing both of my tits in her large hands. 'So very firm they retain their shape when she lies down. Such nipples too, standing up as if aroused. Flat stomach is good. Does she require the special? I think so.'

'Oh, yes,' Margaret agreed, sounding mischievous. 'Diana is here from Africa and missing her husband. I'm sure she'd greatly enjoy your special treatment, Helga.'

I craned my neck. 'Just what is going on between you two?' I demanded. 'Don't I have a say in all this?'

'Just lie back and relax,' Margaret said sweetly. 'You'll thank us for this. Relief is at hand and none better than our Helga to give it—'

I began to sit up but was pushed flat by the Swedish woman. 'You will stay,' she ordered sternly, pouring a dollop of sweet colourless oil between my tits, dripping it from my cleavage down over my stomach, filling my belly button. 'And look,' she pointed out to Margaret. 'Her vagina is quite parted. She was masturbating in the sweat box, I am sure—'

'None of your damned business,' I started to say, but Helga had placed both her broad palms over my breasts and began an energetic circular massage, now and then drawing up her fingers and pulling on my nipples. Whether touched, pinched, fondled or sucked by either male or female they inevitably responded. They grew taut and long; my tits themselves seemed to swell with the treatment. I sighed with pleasure, Helga's hands adding to the heat of arousal already in my loins through my own interrupted manipulation. Shades of Cato, I thought. He had seduced me with massage. Here, with Margaret's connivance, a woman intended the same. As ever, I let it happen gratefully.

With my bosom, belly and thighs anointed and massaged, I was rolled over and the treatment repeated from my neck, shoulders and back down to my legs and ankles. It was both highly relaxing and erotic at the one time. Then my upraised buttocks were given attention; oiled, pummelled, both cheeks kneaded by strong hands and finally given several sharp smacks. The divide of my arse was held apart by Helga and Margaret herself poured oil down the length of the cleft. Helga's hands smoothed me there, over my mound and down to finger the lips. Her finger drew back slowly, going up to press into the serrated ridge of my bottom hole. I moaned with the pleasure of it, pushed myself on to the hand. 'Do, yes,' I mumbled, barely discernably.

I felt her strong hand twist between my buttock cheeks and a hooked finger enter my cunt. I drew in breath sharply as, even as the probing digit flicked over my clitoris, Helga's straightened thumb slid up my bum hole. I was entered both ends and squirmed b 'h pelvis and arse helplessly against the intolerable pleasure. 'She's had it there before,' Helga announced clinically, as if conducting some experiment on a helpless subject in laboratory conditions. 'I can always tell if a woman has been buggered and acquires a taste for it. She has had anal penetration quite frequently, this friend of yours. See how she likes this—'

I couldn't deny that, even while squirming with embarrassment as much as with the effect of a thumb up my bum and the stroking finger tormenting my clitoris. 'Damn you,' I croaked between gritted teeth. 'This is bloody torture. I can't stand it—'

'She has a good grip there,' Helga noted, ignoring my protests. 'Nipping my thumb so strongly. Such an enlarged clitoris too. She responds well, losing control quickly—'

What the hell do you expect? I thought in my haze of arousal so heightened by the unexpected assault on my body. With both orifices entered, stroked and titillated so expertly, I was a mere thing being played to their tune, putty in Helga's sensuous hands. 'Margaret, you bitch,' I grunted as my head jerked to the side and I saw her standing over me with a look of wicked pleasure lighting her eyes. 'You arranged this . . . I've never felt so used. God help me, what you are doing to me—?'

Margaret only laughed at my predicament. 'I wanted you to experience it, Diana. Helga is so good, don't you think? Since my husband died she gives me adequate relief. Let it just sweep over you, dear, the pure pleasure of it. You can't deny it's not heavenly being so manipulated.'

I couldn't deny that by my actions, buttocks thrusting quite wantonly hard against Helga's busy wrist movements. 'I shall come, come,' I moaned. 'You want to witness that, don't you? Oh help, I can feel it—'

'The best is yet to come,' Margaret smiled. 'Helga

doesn't settle for just one orgasm from her clients. She'd be hurt.'

'Fetch the vibrators while I turn her over,' Helga said to Margaret. As I was rolled over on to my back again I saw Margaret at a wall cupboard, bringing out an object with a double stalk. It looked like a pair of white plastic carrot-shaped columns, joined together about an inch apart at their thicker ends, one at least eight inches long and the other shorter but the same thickness. In all my experience I had never seen anything like it before but its purpose was obvious, a vibrating device to penetrate both cunt and bottom hole at the same time. 'A little oil,' Helga advised, and Margaret smeared both stalks with the massage lubricant. I watched with a sort of mesmerised look, helpless to protest as Margaret held open my legs and Helga positioned the double dildo to the fork of my thighs.

The larger shaft and its smaller companion slid up my cunt and my anus together. I felt filled, my stomach tight with the mass inserted within. 'Dirty bitches,' I moaned, 'doing this to me. Bloody sadists, the pair of you—' Helga held the twinned vibrators hard to me, then a click and a buzz followed as the batteries powered the incredible motions inside me, both heads turning, titillating in opposite directions, boring deep into my passages. I began to buck my hips as if electric shocks coursed through my body, my knees coming up to my chest, the spasms wracking my pelvic area. 'I'm coming,' I screamed, not knowing whether in my cunt or arse or both together. The surge continued unabating, making me a twisting turning dervish, past caring how I appeared to my audience in such continuing throes.

'Isn't that the most incredible feeling?' Margaret said. It certainly was, with both my cunt and back passage seemingly on fire and the persistent vibrations pulsing through me inducing waves of sensations rippling up to my heaving belly and back down to both filled entrances mercilessly. I gasped, croaked, brayed, begged for a halt, flopping around so wildly on the table that Margaret and Helga held my shoulders and arms.

'She has multiple orgasms naturally; very easily,' Helga observed. 'I've counted six or seven climaxes so far. We shall let the treatment continue. She could have twenty or more.'

Who was counting? Not I, if I should survive that long. I was on a constant peak of carnal ecstasy, one sapping but glorious spasm following the other. In my delirium, for such it was, I saw Helga loom over me as if through a summer heat-haze. A big double Helga in my wild-eyed state, one overlapping the other. I reached for her, needful of holding on to something, someone, an anchor to hold fast to in my complete loss of control of all senses. My outreached hands grasped her breasts and she opened the white overall coat to reveal two huge hanging orbs. I garbled words, felt an arm behind my neck and a warm weighty breast against my face, a fat nipple pressed to my lips.

I felt the double dildo withdrawn but still the vibrations seemed to continue, my own body fully responding to the pulses tingling both cunt and arse. My senses were unrecovered, my brain wild and woolly. I had been ravaged, plundered, used and abused, reduced to a feeble, washed-out whimpering shell of a woman. I sobbed and clutched at Helga, gratefully sucking upon the nipples held out for me, comforted by her strong arm around me, my face buried in the incredible mounds of her pliant breasts.

'Let her be so for a while,' Helga said quietly, as if warning Margaret not to disturb us. 'She will recover in a little time. Now let her be soothed. Of all the women I have treated, never have I known such arousal and so many climaxes in one session. Your friend is a highly sexual female. There, there,' she went on to quieten me as I gave little sobs into her bosom. 'Helga is here, mama is here. You should not be so greedy when you are being serviced, should you, dear?'

I thought I could hardly be accused of greed when the episode had been sprung on me, but in my gratitude for the pleasant comfort she was giving, I nodded tearfully into her breast. Even after a shower and arriving back at Margaret's house, I had not fully recovered from the act of being so thoroughly dildoed back and front. 'I must have made a fine spectacle of myself, I'll bet,' I said to Margaret. 'And I hope you are pleased with yourself, arranging that orgy. It was almost a rape, the pair of you using me like that.'

'I was quite envious,' Margaret smiled. 'All those lovely comes.'

'And me, a grown woman, being nursed by Helga like a baby,' I recalled, smiling at the indignity. 'She's certainly built for it. I couldn't help myself either. It seemed the right thing to do. What a state I was in—'

'You'd be surprised at the female clients who want to suckle her big breasts while she massages them,' Margaret said. 'She caters for all needs. She'll remember you though, Di. You nearly chewed poor Helga's nipples off, you know. I saw them red and raw while you showered and she was bathing them.'

'Got some of my own back on her then,' I said, but made a mental note I would use her services again before leaving for Africa.

That afternoon I was to visit my pregnant daughter, Lesley, in Oxford, so I bid Margaret farewell. First I called at son Peter's house in Knightsbridge to see if he was at home. I paid off the taxi and pressed the bell to his flat repeatedly until about to give up. The door was finally opened to a common entry hall and I was faced by a youthful-looking male in a very paint-stained shirt and jeans.

'You are no doubt seeking the missing Peter Saxon,' he said cheerfully. 'He's swanned off to the Bahamas for a holiday. Then he'll be in New York if not already there, looking over the art scene. He's a dealer, you know—'

'I did know,' I said. 'Perhaps I could leave a message for his return?'

'Come in,' the young man invited. 'I've the key to his flat and its high time I watered his plants as faithfully promised. Are you a business acquaintance? A friend of his?'

'You could say that. Do you know him well?'

'Very,' he grinned, looking me up and down in a way no man should to a woman old enough to be his mother. 'If you're a girlfriend of his, I must say old Pete's taste has considerably improved.' He ushered me into a first-floor flat. 'He's quite obviously taken my advice—'

'Which is?' I smiled, amused that I should be taken for one of my son's girlfriends.

'That he try a real woman for a change. He usually goes for the skinny model girl type. And I'm Rod. Short for Rodney, believe it or not. My father was a naval officer and hoped I'd follow in the family tradition.'

'Diana,' I introduced myself, offering a gloved hand. 'And you obviously didn't make a sailor—'

'Well, not quite that way,' he grinned archly. 'I paint and try to sell my stuff to Peter.' I wrote a quick note at Peter's desk saying where I would be and he was to phone on his return, sealing the envelope and tilting it against the desk lamp. 'Would you care for a coffee or a drink in my flat?' Rod invited.

'Can I trust you?' I smiled, liking the boy.

'Safe as houses, can't you guess?' he admitted.

'Then why not? I've a train to catch later, but I would like a drink. I've had rather a harrowing morning—'

'Well, lucky old you,' Rod said saucily. 'I still can't believe Peter having the good taste to cultivate you. Your colouring is perfect, you know? I should love to paint you.'

'In the—' I began teasingly.

'In the morning, afternoon, whenever you would pose, but preferably in the nude,' he said seriously. 'You are well aware, no doubt, that you're a beautiful woman. Come up to my studio and see what I do.'

I followed up a stairway to a long room, two knocked into one and in an untidy state from end to end. There was a rough pine table multi-coloured with paint stains, crowded with oil-paint tubes, jars of various sized brushes and oily rags. An unused canvas was set up on an easel under the roof skylight. There was also an unmade bed, a gas cooker, a refrigerator and a wardrobe and kitchen cupboard. 'All you survey,' he grinned, 'is mine. I never thought I'd own so much. See the empty canvas? I was stuck for my next subject and you come along—'

'Not so fast,' I said. 'Remember I've a train to catch.'

'Trains leave every day. Look around, see what I do.'

The walls were lined with unframed canvasses, every one a painting of lovely women posed kneeling, sitting, lounging and standing. The one thing in common, apart from the models all being shapely creatures, was that they were all nude. He was good, no doubt, using a modern subject in an almost renaissance technique. 'What do you think, Diana?' he asked.

'That you like well-endowed naked ladies—'

'Correction. I like to paint well-formed naked ladies. The female form is worthy of adoration, capturing in oils, a beauty on par with any you can name. Besides, they sell well,' he said adding his impish grin. 'What do you really think?'

I walked around his walls again inspecting his work, more impressed as I gave them a closer scrutiny. 'They are brilliant. The colouring quite wonderful, whatever you do to capture the skin tones and such. Your idea of making the backgrounds fade into paler shades, whether water, trees or interior scenes I think works splendidly, for what my opinion's worth, young man. Your draughtsmanship is really excellent—'

'Would you pose for me then?'

'You mean it?' I laughed. 'Don't you think I'm a little past that? Your models are all young girls—'

'The more reason to paint you. The older more mature woman, in her prime, still lovely. All the more for her ripeness.'

'You just want to get my clothes off,' I teased.

'I've never been more serious. Your colouring is what I want to get on this canvas. That auburn chestnut gloss about you, your fine skin, the pale radiance. The marvellous golden speckling—'

'My freckles, you mean. They've plagued me since I was a little girl.'

'And now you are a splendid and lovely woman. It would be a crime not to capture you as you are now.' He walked behind his easel and began to sketch with strokes of a charcoal stick. His strokes were quick and confident, glancing at me quickly before returning to his work. 'What a find,' he exulted. 'What luck!'

'I shall have to go,' I told him.

'Nonsense! Undress,' he ordered. 'I want you on that bed. I shall call it The Awakening, a masterpiece. You are just about to rise after a night of love. I shall make you glow with, well, glow. A woman glowing with after-love, rising from a lover's bed. The satisfied look, fulfilled—' He looked around his canvas as if still surprised to see me standing fully clothed. 'I mean it. You can't not do it—'

Automatically I began to undress as if willed to so do. He did not see me, busy as he was behind his canvas. I placed my coat, dress and underwear over a chair and stood naked on a small square of carpet. When he next glanced across at me he nodded his approval. 'Oh yes, oh bloody yes,' he enthused. 'You are exactly the thing. That figure. You have modelled before.'

'Never,' I said, amused by a thought. Here for once was a man seeing me naked with other than the usual in mind. He came over to me, took my arm, leading me to his bed. He arranged my pose, sitting up with my back to the pillows, the covers thrown right back and one leg out of the bed as if the subject was about to get up. This position allowed a full presentation of my opened thighs, my cunt and pubic bush. He stepped back, considering me. 'One important thing more,' he decided. 'We must make more of your marvellous tits. You have stretched, like after a yawn. Yes, raise those lovely rounded arms. Raise those big breasts for me. You are stretching your arms, yes, behind your head. No, behind your neck, pushing back that glorious hair. Did you have long coppery hair as a girl? Good, even better. I'll give you long hair again, Diana you darling—'

For the next two hours I strived to retain my pose while Rod worked feverishly behind his easel, occasionally shouting his delight at his progress to me. When at last he laid down the brush he was using, he came across the room to me beaming.

'The best yet,' he announced. 'Bloody great, in fact. You have been a real find. I shall pay my usual rate, of course, but you've been so good I should like to take you for a meal. Something special, a little recompense.'

I really stretched and yawned, remembering the train I was to catch had long gone. 'I didn't know posing could be so very tiring. Right now I feel like using this bed to sleep—'

'Then stay,' he said. 'Rest. You deserve it.' He pulled the covers up to my neck and tucked me in nicely, bending to kiss my forehead. 'You've been a sweetie. I shall make some food and when you awake we will dine.'

Astonishingly I did sleep, a combination of tiredness brought about with Helga's session and my posing making me drop off soundly. I awoke to see the paint table cleared and laid with a tablecloth, cutlery set out and even a lighted candle. I arose naked before him and he handed me his dressing gown. 'Sit,' he invited. The meal was a delicious supper of lasagne and salad with a chilled wine. I complimented him and he merely smiled. There was more to Rod than appeared, I thought. The time was almost eleven at night. 'Would you mind if I asked to stay the night?' I said. 'It's rather late to find somewhere at this hour—'

'I have just the one bed,' he warned. 'Why not go down to Peter's flat and use his bed?'

'Because I've been in your bed and it's cosy and warm already. I don't fancy a cold bed in a strange flat. Don't you want me to sleep here? Nothing need happen.' I gave him a long cool look. 'Not unless you want it to,' I challenged.

'I'd like you here first thing in the morning to continue my work. Would you do that, continue posing?'

'Why not? I quite enjoy it.'

'Then I could go down and sleep in Peter's flat.'

'Why should you?' I said. 'I don't snore, and I promise to keep my distance. I rather fancy sleeping with you. Is that so terrible?' I was testing his reaction. He hung his head rather sheepishly.

Sex and Mrs Saxon

'You didn't know I was gay?' he said. 'Homosexual or queer, if you prefer. I'm sorry, that's the way I am—'

'Don't be sorry if that's what you like,' I said.

'It's a long sad story, I'm afraid,' he said sorrowfully. 'I was seduced at school by my housemaster. Since then there's been other lovers. I've tried, really tried, to be a real man, believe me—'

'Have you never made love to a woman?'

'Never,' he admitted, lowering his eyes. 'I wouldn't know how, I suppose. I'd be afraid of not being able, of being a complete failure. That I'd disappoint the lady and be scorned for not being up to it. I couldn't stand that.'

'You wouldn't know unless you tried,' I suggested. Here indeed it seemed a challenge was presenting itself. 'Not all women would be so unsympathetic, especially as she would be your first. It could be a rather special thing to do for you—'

I began stacking the plates in the sink, never being able to face dirty dishes in the morning, but giving Rod time to think over what I'd said. He stood beside me drying as I washed the plates. Then I handed him his dressing gown and got back into bed, lying in wait for him. In all my experience I had never failed to arouse a man to fuck me, in fact I'd never needed to. They had always come on strong without encouragement. To tell the truth the thought of seducing Rod was highly enticing, the more so as I wanted sex for my own satisfaction. When he left the room and returned freshly showered in his dressing gown, I sat up with my bared tits on display and held up the covers in an invitation to join me.

'I've never done this before,' he began. 'Slept with a person of the opposite sex—'

'You might get to like it,' I said, reaching up to push the dressing gown from his shoulders. 'Take that thing off to start with and come in beside me. It's not so terrible.'

He got into the bed, lying beside me without our bodies coming into contact. 'I can't wait until morning,' Rod said eagerly. 'The painting will be my best yet. With such a good subject I can't fail to do it justice.'

'What about the marvellous after-glow of love the woman is supposed to have?' I asked. 'How am I to show that?'

'I'll have to imagine it, I suppose,' he smiled. 'I'm sorry.'

'Don't be,' I answered, rising above him in the bed and taking his hands to cover my tits. I moved his palms against them, then lowered my face to kiss him with a long lingering kiss, my tongue in his mouth. Still mouth to mouth, I brought his right hand down between my legs and held it to my cunt. Then I reached between our bellies and cupped his balls, trailed my fingers over his prick, grasped it gently. He was starting to erect nicely, the warmth and hardness increasing in my hand. I heard him give a distinct whimper and I soothed him, told him all was well, that his manhood felt so good to fondle. 'I want to see it,' I said. 'Want to kiss the sweet thing—'

I peeled back the covers further while Rod lay back as if scared to move. His cock was pale, white and uncircumcised, standing quite erect and a good thick six inches in length. 'I don't know,' he whispered. 'I don't know if we should—'

'I do,' I said firmly. 'I do know, and I shall make you know.' I bent back his stiff cock as if to show him. 'It's such a nice one, Rod, I could just eat it.' From his reclining position he looked down at me uncovering a shining pink helmet as I drew back his foreskin, touching it with the tip of my tongue before covering it with my lips. At first I sucked gently, feeling it tighten and enlarge. His hands came to hold my head and his pelvis gave little jerks.

'Oh Diana,' he moaned. 'Please—'

'Yes,' I said sternly, his prick coming from my lips to stand absolutely rigidly erect. 'We're not wasting *that*.' I straddled him and sank down, guiding his root right into my cunt. It was almost rape, I suppose, but apart from my own desperate need to have his cock up me, I wanted him to know the pleasure a woman can be. I began my up-and-down thrusting and got the desired reaction, his pelvis jerking to match my fucking motions. He reached up to grasp my breasts, stilling their wild bouncing. 'Go on,' I urged him. 'Fuck it up me. Give it all to me. Shove it right up!'

'Bitch, bitch!' I heard him cry. 'You're fucking me!'

Like a duck to water, Rod surprised me by his taking to sex with a female in record time. Twice during the night I felt his hand come over to fondle me, waking me with kisses prior to mounting me. We fucked shortly before he got out of bed to continue his work, bringing me to a climax even as he was shouting out he was coming, our pubic hair mashing and bellies smacking. I've taught him well, I congratulated myself, won him over with my tits and cunt, as his come spurted into me with his last thrusts. He got out of bed looking down at me with the superior smile men have when they know they have brought a woman to a strong undisguised climax. 'That's exactly the look I want, a well-fucked woman,' he said as I sat up to resume my pose.

I stayed three days at his flat, naked almost all of the time while Rod painted, fucked me, then resumed painting. We also made love in his bed several times each night. When completed, the painting was really a work of art, I thought, an image of myself as a satisfied female about to rise after a night of love. Beside me, still sleeping in the bed, was a self-portrait of Rod, or at least his back as he lay turned away on his side. In the background was his studio with his worktable and easel, the battered wardrobe. To see myself in the painting was like a mirror image, my figure, colouring and look captured beautifully.

'I've changed the name for it,' he said proudly when I was at last allowed to view his work. 'I'll now call it what it is, The Artist's Model. I shall never sell it, but keep it as a memento of a wonderful time spent with you.'

I was preparing to leave, gathering my things. 'I don't think you should show it to your neighbour when he returns,' I said. 'Peter may get the wrong idea.' I was forced to giggle. 'Or more likely the right idea.'

'Of course,' Rod agreed. 'I was forgetting you came here to see him first of all. You are a friend of his—'

'More than that,' I admitted. 'His mother.' With that I left to continue my delayed journey to Oxford.

Chapter Six
SCOTLAND

I went home full of wonder at losing my virginity; in its place a slight soreness and pleasant throb. It had been so good, all I imagined and more, that lovely sensation of a rigid prick up my cunt and the convulsive climaxes it produced. My mother was waiting with the usual chores: peeling potatoes for the evening meal, ironing the day's wash; there was school homework too. All these I did with my mind on being fucked by Mr Saxon.

I was too conscious of the experience to sit listening to the wireless with my father or look through the film magazines Anna Geddes had loaned me. I went to bed and took the faithful hard pillow between my thighs, pressing my pulsing cunt against its bulk, fantasising fucking in a car. But fantasies in the heat of masturbating have a will of their own. I was fucking in a car, but not Mr Saxon's immaculate Rolls. It was old-fashioned and had stuffing coming out of the rear seat. The man mounting me was the burly Geddes, uncouth and with massive strength that humped sacks of coal like nothing. He bore down, thrusting me hard against the seat. The wanton thought had me gasping and thrusting to a climax, uncaring that my parents were separated from me by a plasterboard wall.

I rolled over on my back when recovered, hearing

the brass bedstead rattling as mother and father fucked on the other side of the wall. I stifled my giggles at the thought we were all at it together. As for Geddes, wouldn't he have been flattered to know I had climaxed so strongly with the image of him poking me? I could only suppose that I really wanted him to fuck me, and recalled his erect thick prick from the time in his car when Mr Saxon had disturbed us. Would I let him the next time an opportunity arose? It would allow me to compare it with the fuck I'd had with Mr Saxon. Geddes would jump at the chance, and there was the attraction of having one up on his snooty wife.

The next evening after school I had to shop in town for my mother. Geddes came along in his car, peering out as rain fell heavily and his puny windscreen wiper barely swept the window clear. He was crawling at a snail's pace and saw me sheltering in a shop doorway. Drawing in to the kerb, he looked a worried man.

'Get in,' he ordered brusquely. I ran around to the passenger side and sat beside him. As he drove off he made no jocular attempt at conversation, let alone fondle my leg as before. Only a steamed-up bus passed us as we moved out into the countryside. The rain increased, falling in sheets.

'Good job you saw me,' I said sweetly. 'I've got shopping to get home and it's lashing—'

'I wanted to see you,' he growled, but not nicely. 'You didn't mention to anyone about the – you know – last time I gave you a lift?'

'Course not.' I looked him straight in the eye. 'Why should I? That's nobody's business.'

He relaxed visibly. 'I thought not,' he said, giving me an admiring look. 'You're a good lass, Diana. People love to get a bit of scandal—'

'That's because they've nothing else to do,' I replied,

trying to agree with him. 'Chance would be a fine thing.'

'That's true,' he nodded, looking at me as if I'd just said the wisest words imaginable. 'You've a sensible head on your shoulders, as well as a damned pretty one. If a thing like me carrying on got out, even innocently, it could ruin a man. Especially with a business.'

How did one 'carry on' innocently, I wondered. 'You an Elder of the Kirk too,' I said impishly.

He laughed loudly, throwing back his head, his broad beefy shoulders shaking. 'Do you not think I should be an Elder then?'

'Good for your coal round, my mother says.'

He roared again. 'She's right. But I've got to watch myself. There are some hypocrites in the Kirk, I can tell you. Take a wee dram and it's wrong, let alone fancy a lassie. Can't do as we like in this world, can we?'

'Be nice if we could,' I suggested. 'What would you do?'

He glanced at me sideways and there was no doubt, his face leering. I sat demurely with my hands in my lap, effectively seducing the man, who drew into the side of the lane and pulled up at a farm gate overhung by an oak tree. The rain dripped noisily on the roof of his car. 'Want to stop for a while?' he asked suggestively.

'If you like,' I replied. 'What for?'

'For this,' he said hoarsely, curling a strong arm about my shoulders. I was pulled into him and thick wet lips covered mine, his tongue protruding into my mouth. He tasted of tobacco and whisky, a warm sweet combination I did not mind. I returned his kiss, my breasts hugged tight against his broad chest, arousal heightened by the thought of enacting the fantasy I'd used to masturbate by. Mr Saxon had been gentle compared to the fiercely passionate kisses pressed on my mouth. Geddes seemed intent on swallowing me, while fumbling beneath my short dress groping my crotch, his lust beyond control.

I was thrust flat along the seat, my head against the door, legs upended as he pulled down my knickers in his urgency. 'Oh!' I shouted in the surprise and suddenness of his assault, the next moment any further words were stifled as he covered me, his mouth hard against mine, hands tilting up my bared bottom and a knee forcing my legs apart. Of course I had led him on and should have been warned by our previous encounter. I felt the bulbous knob of his prick nudge my cunt, which as ever was receptively parted and well lubricated by my aroused situation. I groaned with a mixture of fear and pleasure as the whole length of his shaft penetrated me. He immediately began fucking me strongly, thrusting and withdrawing, hauling me closer with his huge palms cupped under my buttock cheeks. It was too much, the pleasure too great. I clasped my legs about his waist and thrust back madly; his balls slapped my cleft cheeks. The surge of an impending orgasm made me fuck back even more wantonly as his shuddering and jerking increased. He shot repeated spurts deep inside me. My own climax was no less violent, the strongest yet.

At last he sat up on his knees before me, regaining his breath and looking almighty pleased. Geddes had in effect raped me, although the blame was not entirely his. What concerned me was the flood he had poured into my cunt. I could feel its wetness as traces trickled back out to the seat below.

'Whew!' he muttered, mopping his brow. 'Some fuck! Thought you'd be ready for it, a fine piece like you. Can't remember a better ride—'

'All right for you,' I said bitterly. 'You didn't care.'

His surprise was mixed with indignation. 'Here, don't come that,' he warned. 'You were every bit as all for it as me. I've never known such a hungry cunt. You fucked like a champion. You asked for it—'

'What if I did?' I charged him. 'And what if I'm now in the family way? You did it.'

'I should have told you,' Geddes said ruefully. 'I was that keen to fuck you, lass. You couldn't have a kid, not by me anyway. I can't give babies, that's a fact. Doctors have said so.' It was a struggle for him to admit it, his head bowed.

'What about Anna then?' I challenged.

'Adopted. From a week old. Mrs Geddes and I had tried for years. Don't you ever let that out,' he begged.

All my distrust vanished, seeing such a huge man reduced to admitting his inadequacy. I was also mightily relieved to know I would not be pregnant, having played with fire and got away with it. I determined in future to be more wary. 'No,' I promised. 'I won't ever tell a soul.' I was still laid out before him minus my knickers, knees raised. He was looking down at the arch of my open thighs, my cunt mound and pubic thatch invitingly presented. My loins stirred under his stare despite the good fucking I'd just had.

Instinctively he put his hand out, cupping its eminence with a thick finger idly smoothing a line up and down my still-pouting slit. Settling back on the seat, I felt my cunt respond to the tip of his finger. It was lovely; soothing and provoking further desire to be entered again. That I was fond of it there was no denying, yet my cunt seemed a separate part of me with an appetite that would not be satisfied. Geddes looked down in admiration on it, open for him, pink, glistening and inviting.

'Oh, but that's a beautiful cunt,' he praised it. 'I'll be forced to fuck it again—' His crude talk, I discovered, was just right in my mood; it quickened my arousal and made me talk back in the same manner.

'Fuck it then,' I told him. 'I dreamed last night we were at it in this car. We were in the back—' I didn't admit it was an 'awake' dream, but he showed great delight anyway.

'You did? Come on then, it's roomier back there. Let's see if the real thing is as good—'

Hurriedly, because the rain still lashed down, we jumped out and got in the rear of the car. It was almost dark too, and the interior was cosy in the gloom with the splashing of the downpour outside. He kissed me again and again, fumbling at the buttons at the back of my dress. 'Let's see you, lass,' he said, 'I want to have you bare, stripped off. Let's see them fine big bonny tits that's been tempting me ever since you've been coming to the house with Anna—' I was delighted to comply, taking every stitch off and revelling in his hands roving over my body. 'Such nice young skin,' he said. 'Such lovely big tits. Och, you little cow, you bitch, what you do to me—' His mouth fastened on one of my nipples and his hand sought my cunt, making me raise my hairy mound and rubbing it in his palm to show my eagerness.

'Do it then,' I told him brazenly. 'Put it up my cunt. Go on. Fuck me like you did in my dream. Shove it up!'

He laughed, towering over me, pulling off his jacket and shirt, kicking off his trousers. 'Bare naked's the way to do it,' he chortled. 'By Jeez, I'll fuck you rigid, my girl.'

He flung his discarded clothes into the front of the car, his trousers catching and hanging from the steering wheel. Stretched before him naked, I pondered what a sight we would have made for anyone coming along and peering in the car. But it was still lashing with rain outside and I felt safe enough. Geddes was kneeling before me between my legs, his body pale white in the gloom. Despite our recent fuck his engorged prick rose mightily, erect as a tent pole. It looked thick and massive. I realised my previous view of it had been with half its great length concealed in his trousers.

'It's big,' I said naively. I'd never imagined the like, far in excess of the one Mr Saxon put in me. There was eight inches at least of standing cock. My cunt, being well fingered again, seemed to open as if in anticipation of a treat.

'It all goes in,' Geddes boasted, his confidence returned, 'and didn't you just love it. Guide it in for me—'

I did as bid, grasping his stalk which seemed to grow more rigid, feeling its heat in my hand. It went to my cunt lips and slid up beautifully, the weight of his belly against mine. This time his movements were slower. After our previous hard grinding it was almost a gentle push and thrust that had me squirming under him, uttering sighs of pleasure. I looked up to see him grinning down at me goatishly. 'Keep pushing it up,' I demanded. 'Don't you come yet! Keep it in—'

He threw back his head, laughing at my plea. 'That nice body of yours was made to tempt men,' he said meaningfully, 'and don't you just love doing it! Never fucked a female that enjoyed the prick so much. Pity there's not more like you. Big tits and a juicy cunt, that's what you are, girl. Made for it. Oh, you'll please many a man in your time.'

I could feel the very shape of his monster filling my cunt channel and gloried in it, lifting to meet his thrusts, twisting my hips, now and then relaxing just enough to halt the rush of an impending strong come. I wanted the lovely feeling to continue, and I hovered on the brink of a climax for ecstatic moments until his quickening movements brought us off together with abandoned grunts and cries.

Sex and Mrs Saxon

We lay together naked along the narrow seat, my breasts pressed to his chest, his large belly against mine as we recovered from our exertions. 'Now you can say you've been well and truly fucked,' Geddes informed me proudly, adding boastfully, 'by a master. There's been many a lady customer I've serviced on my coal round. Paid me behind the door, as it were. You'd be surprised if you knew who. Never had any complaints, same as you.'

It was true he had fucked me magnificently, having me out of my mind with the mounting pleasure as he brought me off, but as they say nowadays 'it takes two to tango'. 'How like a man.' I teased him. 'It was all you, was it? All your other women and me had nothing to do with it?'

'What a girl!' he exclaimed in amusement. 'You don't let me get away with anything, do you? And you're right! You are a marvellous fuck, best I ever had. Just a nice sweet girl with a lovely body men can't resist. Built for the job and horny with it. Don't ever let them run you down for loving the prick, girl. You were made that way and never be ashamed of it—' He kissed me fondly, a big hand gently cupping one of my titties as if weighing it. To my surprise a great tenderness welled up in me and I kissed him back with a passion that surprised him.

'What was that for, lass?' he asked.

'Because it was so lovely tonight, what you did. And it's so nice and cosy in here, cuddled up like this.' We kissed again lingeringly and I realised what he had said about me was right. I loved the prick and saw no need to be ashamed of my nature. Reaching down I found his half-erect staff and below, a pair of massive balls that filled my hand. I fondled them, moving up to stroke his prick, feeling the pulse returning under my clasp, growing hot and stiffening under my curled fingers.

'Fuck me again,' I heard myself whisper, as if asking

too much. 'You can do it to me whenever you like. I just love your thing up my cunt. Go on, put it in, please. I swear I will never tell a soul—'

Few men could resist such a plea. Geddes loomed over me, and I parted my thighs and curled my legs around his waist. We kissed, fondled and without the help of guidance I once again felt his prick slide beyond my cunt lips and swell my channel. Now he hardly moved and I did the work below him, thrusting up my hips to take his all. 'Do you fuck your wife as many times as me?' I asked him. 'Is her cunt as nice as mine? Does she like you to suck her tits as much as I do? Fuck it up me, ram it up to my belly—'

Of course such talk in my arousal had exactly the same effect on him. His pace increased, he grunted with each hard thrust as if to pump the air out of me, his big balls thudding into the space below my well-plugged cunt. It was as if he tried to get his balls inside me. I came in convulsions, twice, three times, the best yet for, owing to his previous bouts, his supply must have been near exhaustion. When he climbed off me I lay back sated for once. I could have slept where I was. I must have dozed, then he was shaking me gently, pointing out we had spent over four hours together.

Geddes dropped me as near to my home as he dared. I took my shopping and fled, late as never before. When I walked in my mother screamed at me. Where had I been? She struck out at me and I fled to my bedroom. At once I undressed quickly, the second time that evening, noting my nipples were red and tender-looking from the suckings Geddes had enjoyed, and the hair of my mound stiff as if starched. I pulled on my nightdress just in time for my mother entered the room and would have been certain to have guessed what had detained me. As it was, she was suspicious.

'You've been with a boy,' she accused. 'Any of that

nonsense, my girl, and your father will take his belt to you, coming home at this hour.'

'I never was with a boy,' I maintained, and one could hardly describe Geddes as such. He was as old as my father. Looking at my mother I wondered if she had been one of the coalman's customers who had 'paid behind the door' and taken his splendid prick. Why not? Later I would ask him.

My father then entered the bedroom, anxious for peace. 'Don't get on to her tonight,' he implored my mother. 'Tell her the good news.'

'All right,' my mother agreed, 'but she's getting no supper at this time.' Then her features softened. 'Your father's been promoted,' she said proudly. 'He's been picked to operate the new steam shovel at the quarry. It's more money and we'll be getting one of the brick houses same as the foremen have. Your father's worked hard for years to improve things. It didn't go unnoticed. Believe it or not it was Mr Saxon himself who gave the order—'

I believed it all right. Two meetings with the great man and having him fuck me in his Rolls Royce had gained more for my family than all the years of toil my hard-working father had faithfully put in. The lesson was not wasted upon me.

Chapter Seven
ENGLAND

Telephoning ahead, with no reply from daughter Lesley's home, I boarded the train and on arrival at Oxford took a taxi. Son-in-law Philip's car was parked in the drive and when he finally answered repeated rings of the doorbell he appeared looking somewhat flustered. 'My God, Diana!' he said in alarm. 'Why didn't you call to say you'd be arriving? I didn't expect you—'

'Evidently,' I said, brushing past him and going through to the lounge. Seated on the couch combing long black hair down to her shoulders was a girl I judged to be little more than eighteen at the most. She was what I'd recall as a typical university student of the swinging sixties with beads, loose dress and black stockings. The look she gave me was of pure defiance mixed with resentment.

'This is Diana, Mrs Saxon,' Philip introduced me with obvious embarrassment. 'My mother-in-law actually. This young lady is Annette, one of the students in my biology class. She came for some help with a problem she has—'

'I can guess what,' I said acidly.

'With her studies,' Philip added hastily, looking very sheepish.

'Where is my daughter?'

'Lesley is in the maternity hospital,' Philip said

guiltily. 'Her doctor thought it better she be admitted early.'

'Nothing wrong, is there?' I asked anxiously, feeling guilt myself for the days I had spent with Rod in London.

'Not a thing,' I was assured. 'The baby could come any time now and they thought it better she be on hand, getting proper rest. You know what Lesley's like. I saw her this afternoon and she was fine. Looking forward to seeing you.'

'You obviously miss her,' I said, looking at the girl.

She was listening and watching me without the slightest sign of being perturbed. Bringing a file from her shoulder bag she began calmly and arrogantly filing long silver-painted fingernails which matched the heavy eye-shadow she wore. As she made no attempt to rise and leave, I told her she had better go. 'And take these with you,' I added.

I'd caught sight of an inch or so of pink nylon poking out behind a cushion on the couch. Pulling on it, I drew out a brief pair of flimsy knickers. 'You'll catch cold without these,' I suggested.

'Bitch,' she swore.

'Little whore,' I countered.

Philip was hopping around us from foot to foot, a picture of a worried husband caught out. I quite enjoyed watching him suffer. Men will be men; I didn't hold too much against him for what had been going on before my unexpected arrival. The girl was nothing but a man-hungry little tart, and I should know. 'I think you had better leave now, Annette,' he said nervously, as if fearing us females were about to tear each other's hair out. 'If you would, please—'

'Yes, while the going's good,' I announced, taking her arm as she stood. 'I'll see you to the door, dear.'

She shook off my arm, turning to Philip. 'I'll see you

tonight, presumably,' she said brazenly. 'Don't forget the party at Barney's place. You said you'd be there after visiting your wife.'

'Please, Annette,' said the humbled Philip.

'You've made your point,' I warned her, 'so leave while you think you're ahead. I'm sure you'll want to get home to beautify yourself for Barney's party. That should take hours. Am I invited, by the way?'

She slung the leather-fringed bag over her shoulder, swept back her long hair and regarded me with a look of venom. 'Don't you think you're past your sell-by date for that?' she said mockingly. Her smug patronising little smile got me.

'Depends whether you like real women or skinny girls,' I replied as sweetly. 'Now beat it before you overstay your welcome—'

Her eyes flashed with anger. 'You know what Philip and I were doing when you arrived, of course,' she taunted.

'Fucking. Am I supposed to be shocked?'

'I could have him, take him from your precious daughter if I wished. What do you say to that?'

'That your estimate of your worth to my son-in-law is way out. You're a bit of spare. An available cunt.'

'Charming,' she said, leaving. I felt I'd come off quite well in the duel. I went back to the lounge to find Philip sitting with his head in his hands. 'Buck up,' I told him. 'A fuck is a fuck, not the end of the world. I've never blamed a man for being tempted by an easy piece, and she was a tail if ever I saw one.'

'I don't know what came over me,' he moaned. 'With Lesley in hospital too expecting our child. It's been hard—'

'That is always the trouble,' I smiled. 'I've no intention of mentioning any of this to Lesley, for her sake as well as yours. When did you last have sex with her?'

'Probably two months ago or even more. She hasn't been well in her pregnancy. And I suppose it will be a good month or two before we can when she gets home. I suppose that's why, well, you caught Annette here this afternoon.'

'I'm going to bath and change,' I announced. 'Would you like me to make you a meal before we visit Lesley tonight?'

'No,' he said. 'You've been so decent about this, I'd like to take you out for a meal.'

I had just got out of the bath when I heard the telephone ring and Philip called me. 'It's your Peter, just back in London. Says he got the note you left him and wants to say hello.' I wrapped myself in a towel and took the telephone from Philip, noting him eyeing the swell of my breasts.

Philip stood beside me while I took the phone from him, vainly trying to keep the towel up to a decent level but failing to stop it slipping down to uncover my nipples. 'My God,' I heard Philip mutter almost under his breath before turning away. Then Peter was speaking. 'Got your note, mother,' he said. 'How is Lesley keeping?'

'I'll call you back after Phil and I visit her tonight,' I told him. 'Sorry to have missed you in London. I'll see you before I fly back to Africa, anyway. Your father sends his love—'

'How did you get into my flat to leave the message you were off to Oxford, mum? Did someone let you in?'

'The baby-faced young man from the flat above. He had a key, said he was due to water your plants.'

'That's Rod,' Peter said. 'He's a painter and a very good one. You'd like his work. One day he's going to create a masterpiece—'

'He struck me as being rather feminine,' I said. 'A

nice boy, I'm sure, and very good-looking, but the way he talked I'd say he's very homosexual—'

I heard Peter roar with laughter down the phone. 'He's anything but. Rod tries that ploy on with all his female models. He claims it works very well too. They consider it a challenge to make him change his ways, assert his manhood. He enjoys being seduced—'

I replaced the receiver, thinking back there had been more to young Rod than his skill at painting, smiling that he had thought me worthy of being one of his victims. When I had dressed I found Philip waiting below, smart in a grey suit. I was again struck by his handsome features and figure. He and Lesley had been married four years, and she'd confessed to me his popularity with his female students had not gone unnoticed. Philip, at twenty-eight, loving his wife as no doubt he did, still had a roving eye. Looking at him I could see why girls threw themselves at him, and being who he was found it hard not to take what was on offer, more so with his wife away.

We drove to the hospital and found Lesley sitting up in bed looking very pretty in a lacy matinee jacket. The flowers I'd ordered were in a vase on the bedside cabinet and she was in fine spirits. 'Nothing at all to worry about, mummy,' she said as we exchanged kisses. 'I shall have a lovely baby and make you a proud grandmother, a really glamorous granny. You look so lovely, doesn't she, Phil?'

'She certainly does,' Philip agreed. 'So nice in fact, I'm taking her out this evening to wine and dine her. I've booked a table at the Atherstone.'

'That will be nice,' said Lesley. 'Now I'm sure mummy would like a cup of coffee while she sits here. There's a vending machine in the corridor, Phil. Do please get her a cup.'

Philip left us and I looked at Lesley smiling. 'Why

did you want him out of the way? Something to tell me, dear?'

'Just that I'm glad you are here while I'm laid up,' Lesley said. 'I know Phil. He's a notorious flirt and means nothing by it, but some of his female students are not beyond taking it further. You watch him while I'm in here, mummy—'

'I'll stay in Oxford until you return home,' I promised. 'Don't worry about a thing.'

'I won't now. I don't blame Phil, but there is so much temptation for him with so many girls eager to make a conquest of their tutor. And the poor soul has had a thin time,' she giggled. 'With me being like this he hasn't had any joy for ages. He's so fond of making love too—'

Philip returned at that moment, bearing a plastic cup of coffee, and Lesley quickly changed the subject to ask what state the house was in. 'All will be ready for you to bring home the baby,' I promised. As for my daughter's worry about her husband straying, all men, in my experience, never took much seducing when the chance was offered. 'Don't worry about a single thing,' I told her as we left.

The Atherstone proved a nice old-fashioned hotel and we found a dinner dance in progress when we were shown to our table. The meal was delicious, the wine heady, and my feet tapped to the music of a five-piece orchestra playing my kind of dance music. 'Would it be out of the question for you to dance with your mother-in-law?' I asked Philip. 'I love dancing and it would be a shame to waste the music.'

'I thought you'd never ask,' he grinned. 'I've been looking around. You are the most outstanding woman here, Diana. Am I allowed to say that to you?'

'Flattery will get you everywhere,' I said, using the well-worn rejoinder. At that moment a tall handsome man came over to our table, inclined his head and invited me to dance. He already had me by the hand and I was led out on the dance floor before Philip realised I was gone. As my tall partner took me in his arms, I glanced back to see my son-in-law frowning, pouring more wine into his glass.

'I could not resist asking you to dance,' the man said, holding me very close. 'Are you an actress? Everyone at my table was admiring your beauty.' His accent was American and he was with a party of tourists. He returned for several more dances while Philip drank steadily at our table. When the man approached again, Philip stood up and placed himself between us, looking peeved.

'I'm here with this lady so why don't you piss off,' he said. I was grabbed in his arms and whirled off on to the dance floor. 'I was watching that bastard,' he said darkly. 'Pressing himself into you, getting a cheap thrill. He was hard up against you—'

That certainly the American had been, hard against me, his erection against my underbelly as we danced. I'd quite enjoyed the feeling. As for Philip, for a son-in-law he'd shown the kind of outburst typical of a jealous man. 'Never mind him,' I teased Philip, pleased with myself as any woman is when men show interest. 'You're dancing with me now, I'm all yours. I'm really enjoying myself. Thank you, Phil, for bringing me.'

'My pleasure, for you're a remarkable woman, Diana,' he praised me. 'I mean for overlooking this afternoon's fiasco.'

Suddenly I felt quite wicked, wilful; it was all to do with the wine and the music and being held in the arms of men. 'Shall we finish the night by going to that party at Barney's?' I suggested naughtily. 'You've been invited. I could be your partner—'

'Hell, no,' Philip laughed uncomfortably. 'Don't mention that place, it's a den of whores. I'm liable to be in deep enough trouble with your daughter as it is.'

'Your young friend Annette will be there,' I teased him.

'If you'll excuse the expression, fuck her,' he swore.

'I think you were when I arrived.' I taunted him more. 'Come on, Phil, I feel like a good party. Take me there.'

Barney's house was a rambling red-brick structure with the garden backing on to the river. The front porch was strung with fairy lights and we were admitted by the person who stood nearest the door, I imagine, for no one queried whether we had an invitation or not. The passageway was filled with young people drinking and laughing, as was the stairway. Each room was well packed. We had drinks put into our hands and became integrated into the throng. I saw Annette with her arms around the neck of a burly young man, still with a glass in one hand and a cigarette in the other as they kissed lingeringly. In a pause when their mouths parted she spotted me across the room. I raised my own glass to her and inclined my head like royalty. She made a face and stuck out her tongue.

Barney I was to meet soon after when he saw Philip and gave us an official welcome. 'Come on through to the lounge,' he invited us. 'Wouldn't you know it, Annette is going to do her party piece, taking off her clothes. She fancies herself as a striptease artiste—'

'I think we'll miss out on that performance,' Philip said. 'We're quite settled in here with our drinks.'

'This I want to see,' I insisted, pulling his sleeve. In the larger room Annette was swaying to music, circled by watching men and girls. She had already discarded her dress and was flouncing about in a barely-filled bra and the same pink briefs I had recovered from under a cushion that afternoon. The bra was unhooked and she threw it up into the air. She shimmied, shaking a pair of tits at us hardly worthy of a twelve-year-old. The young man I had seen her smooching with earlier was standing beside Philip and myself.

'What a girl,' he announced. 'Annette's a game bird, isn't she? She'd make a professional stripper.'

'Make a professional stripper laugh,' I told him. Using an old Scottish phrase, I added, 'I've seen more beef on a herring. Are they supposed to be tits she's shaking?'

The young man looked at me with astonishment. 'Well, at least she gives a show. Starts the ball rolling—'

'You want to see the real thing, son?' I found myself saying. 'I'll show you how it should be done—' Don't ask me why I had the urge to show myself off. Maybe it was because I had stripped to music before at parties and knew I had the body to make this crowd's eyes bug. Mostly I think it was to have one up on the scrawny Annette. As I made to move into the circle created by the spectators, Philip grabbed my arm.

'God no, Diana,' he pleaded. 'Let's get out of here.'

I prised his arm away and began to sway about before the surprised watchers. The music continued so I shed my dress seductively, drew off my slip and whirled about slowly in my bra, briefs, suspender belt and stockings. I noted a deathly hush had fallen on the room. Annette stood beside me with her pink knickers in her hand, showing thin thighs and a wispy bush of cunt hair. Even she was struck dumb. Then I unhooked my bra and hung it over the head of Barney, giving my breasts a good wobble before his face. To discard my briefs I faced away from him, lowering them just enough to show the cleave of my rounded bottom, then stepped out of them and whirled them about a raised finger. Suddenly a huge cheer went up, loud applause as the men at least clapped my performance. Then Philip had me by the arm, my clothes gathered in his other hand, leading me off right outside and bundling me into his car.

I sat beside him holding my dress over myself while he put his head to the steering wheel. 'God almighty,' he said, as if to himself. 'What a woman. I'd never seen the like—'

'Was it that bad?' I said. 'It was a spur of the moment thing.'

'It was bloody marvellous,' Philip choked. 'Jesus, it stopped that crowd cold. Poor bloody Annette will never dare strip again after that. You've ruined her big party piece.' He shook his head, chuckling. 'You know what Barney said when I was dragging you away? You can bring her here anytime, he said. I didn't know whether to laugh or cry.' He glanced across at me. 'If all women could be like you—'

He suddenly put his arm around my shoulder and drew me to him, kissing my cheek fondly. 'Just as well they are not,' I said. 'Be like me, I mean.'

'Life would be a lot more fun,' he said, his face close. He kissed me again, moving his mouth around to meet mine, hugging me tighter. For a brief moment I allowed it, kissing him in return, feeling his tongue slip between my teeth. His hand went to find a breast, pulled away the dress I held up, cupped the pliant mound. My resolve weakened, I kissed him back fiercely, rolling my mouth against his lips. He took my hand down to his lap and I felt the bulge of his erection. It pulsed under my fingers, long, hard and hot, very much bigger than the average prick.

'No, not with you, Philip,' I begged, short of breath and drawing away from him. 'You'd better take me home.'

He drove off silently, speaking only when we stopped

at a traffic light showing red. 'I should apologise, but I won't,' he said. 'Kissing you was marvellous; I wanted to continue. Being celibate has been bloody hard for me.'

'What about you and Annette?' I asked.

'That was the first. I'm bloody sorry it happened. I don't want her. I just needed a fuck, any fuck.'

'That's why I said nothing about it,' I agreed.

We sat silent until we arrived back at his house. I went indoors and upstairs even while he was garaging the car, my mind in a turmoil, pondering the unusual situation; sorry for him in his arousal for me, sorry for myself for having the lewd thoughts that I had. I badly wanted a fucking myself and there was an eager and attractive young man in the same house. Any other young man but Philip, I decided, my daughter's husband whom I'd been charged to see was not tempted by other women. I slipped on my bathrobe and went along the landing to the bathroom. On my return to my room I met Philip coming upstairs after locking up. He stood directly in my path.

'Goodnight,' I wished him. 'Do let me pass, please, Phil—'

'Annette was just another fuck,' he said meaningfully. 'With you it would be different—'

'But not right,' I said feebly. 'I'm thinking of Lesley.'

'She would never know. I want you so badly, Diana. At least I wouldn't be going with other women, would I? I mean keeping it in the family—' He looked at me hopefully.

'Like I was providing a service?' I said weakening.

'Precisely. Keeping me out of harm's way.'

'I suppose it would,' I agreed, both of us searching for an excuse to have each other. 'Put that way it makes sense. I mean if we sleep together you wouldn't want anyone else—'

Sex and Mrs Saxon

He came to me face to face, eyes meeting, mouths meeting as he took me into his grasp. The next moment I was being led through to his bedroom unresisting, the bed he shared with my daughter almost lying in wait. 'I want to see you again,' he mumbled, pushing off my bathrobe. 'See that glorious body and big tits you showed off tonight at Barney's.' He stood back admiring my nakedness, kissed my nipples, ran his firm hands over my hips, thighs and buttocks, muttering his delight and full approval. 'Oh yes,' he repeated. 'I've wanted you for a long time, Diana, mother of Lesley. From the first time I saw you I wanted you. I wanted both mother and daughter.'

'Have me then,' I told him eagerly. 'Fuck the mother too!'

'Oh, I will,' he promised lewdly, 'and properly. I've had dreams about this moment too long for it to be just a quick poke. We'll fuck ourselves to exhaustion front, back and sideways.'

'Yes,' I agreed fiercely, conscience thrown to the wind. 'Show me how good you are. Front, back and sideways, any way you like—' With trembling urgent fingers I began to pull at his clothes, helping as he threw them aside. He stood before me naked, with his magnificent cock rearing hard to his belly. I could not help myself, tempted by such a mouth-watering huge erection. My knees sank down to the bedside rug, I took it in both hands, admiring it at eye level, cupping the tight sac of his balls, gripping the shaft.

'Eat it,' Philip said, almost a command.

'Oh, I will. I want to, I can't resist it—' I looked up to where he towered above me, unable to stop myself seeking further lewd arousal. 'Does – does my daughter do this for you? Go on her knees and suck this lovely prick?' I pressed little kisses to the glistening pink circumcised helmet, licked down the shaft and nibbled at his balls. 'You should make her—'

'She sucks,' Philip gloated, confident now he would have his way with an eager and willing partner. 'Lesley's a greedy bitch with a prick in her mouth, going at it until she's drained your balls. A horny little cocksucker, your daughter—'

He was already in my mouth and I sucked avidly on the thick shaft, feeling it jerking against the back of my throat. 'No!' he decided suddenly, drawing me up and then laying me back across the bed. 'It's too easy that way. Later when we've done other things, yes. Now I want to look at you—' He stood back, his prick upright and wet with my saliva, staring down at where I lay with breasts splayed and thighs parted.

'What do you see?' I asked him.

'A fine woman made to fuck,' he said.

'Then come and fuck me,' I urged. Philip was obviously savouring the moment, anticipating the pleasure. Keeping me waiting and heightening my need. To tempt him I raised my knees, legs widened, presenting my cunt as an offering.

'Play with yourself,' he ordered. 'Masturbate.'

'What?' I said, surprised. All the same my hand went between my legs and I began to stroke myself. 'Is this a game?'

'Just a bit of pleasant foreplay your daughter and I enjoy before we make love. Lesley lies across the bed just as you are now and does as I say. It arouses her tremendously—'

'I think I'm aroused enough already. If I play with myself any longer I shan't be able to stop myself coming.'

'Lesley does too. I like to see it. Bring yourself off, Diana. Let me watch you.'

'Kinky devil,' I called him, but the effect of him watching me and my own fingering now going strongly and bringing on my surge had me jerking helplessly before him.

'Go on, let it go. Moan and groan, don't hold back,' he encouraged. 'Give yourself a lovely come, Diana. Let it all come out—' His eyes were wide with beaming delight as I at last gave up, fingering furiously, crying out as I flopped about and squirmed in my self-induced climax. 'Great,' he said, nodding down at me. 'It's a lovely thing to see a woman bring herself off. You orgasmed superbly.'

'I could have done that in my own room by myself,' I began.

'I'm sure. But it's twice as naughty and nice while being watched, isn't it? Admit it gave you a kick to do it.'

'I was hoping for more than doing it myself,' I complained. 'Nice as it was, with a big hard cock facing me I could think of a better way.'

Philip laughed, sitting down beside me and fondling both of my tits. 'The night is young. That was just a little entertainment.' He took my hand and placed my fingers around his huge root. 'Ask nicely and you can have this,' he teased.

'I thought you were desperate to have me?' I reminded him.

'Correction. Desperate to *know* if I could have you. Now I know it's on, well, half the fun is enjoying the games two can play. What about a little bottom-smacking now?'

I had to laugh at him. Truly it takes all sorts. 'Does my daughter go along with all this nonsense?' I asked. 'I always thought Lesley was such a goody-goody type of girl.'

'It was she who started all this stuff,' Philip said.

'You don't know your own daughter. Not that I'm complaining about her sexual preferences—'

'Tell me more,' I insisted, squeezing his prick gently.

'She likes a bit of bondage. I tie her to this bed and make love to her. She pretends she's helpless in my clutches sort of thing. It's harmless make-believe and gives her great climaxes. She begs me not to ravage her while I'm in her. I like it myself—'

He looked so appealing I kissed him. 'I'm glad you both have such a fine fulfilling sex life,' I said. 'I can see why you've missed having your fun while she's been pregnant and unable to do all the pair of you usually do. Is it this bed you tie her to?' The thought intrigued me.

'Yes, to the head and the feet.' He began to kiss my neck, muzzling into me, his hand grasping at my breasts, as if much more interested in my being beside him stark naked. 'I'm sorry I started with those damned silly sex games. I should have done what we both wanted, got down to a bit of straight fucking. It was just that Lesley likes that sort of thing so much I thought you might appreciate some of it yourself—'

'I appreciate that,' I agreed, 'and I'm always willing to try a new experience.' I smiled wickedly at him and added, 'Like being tied to a bed, for instance. I've never had that.' I gave the stiff shaft in my hand several jiggles. 'What do you use to tie Lesley to the bed with?' I inquired.

'Just soft cords, the kind you tie back curtains with. I say,' Philip suddenly realised, 'are you suggesting I tie you down? Shall I fetch the cords?'

He went to a chest of drawers and came back with lengths of gold-coloured silken cords about the thickness of a thumb. 'How do you want me?' I asked. 'Face up or down? What's usual?'

'We do it both ways, usually face up to start with. Our

games can go on for hours.' Philip looked down upon me and admired what he saw. 'God, but you're lovely laid out there stark naked. Let's not waste any more time. I want to fuck you now—' His hand touched my cunt, smoothed my hairy mound.

Maybe it was the effect of the wine I'd had that evening or that I was finding the situation so intriguing. The fact I'd just brought myself off so strongly also helped to curb any impatience I had to be penetrated by my son-in-law. Anyway, I held up my wrists to him. 'Go on,' I urged him. 'You started all this. I want to know what you and Lesley find such good fun. Have your wicked way with me.'

Philip wrapped one of the cords around a wrist. 'If you insist,' he grinned, 'I must admit it's a great turn-on.' My wrists and ankles were quite tightly bound and the cords pulled taut and secured with Philip on his knees tying knots to the castors at the four corners of the bed. I was in effect spreadeagled on the bed with my bound arms and legs making the shape of an X, like a St Andrew's cross. I tested the strength of the bonds and found, although the soft cords in no way cut into my wrists and ankles, I was quite unable to move except for a wriggle of my hips or a lift of my bottom from the bed. It was so well accomplished that he'd obviously had much experience of binding Lesley to the bed.

'What next?' I asked, giggling a little tipsily with the combination of the wine I'd drank and the amorality of the whole thing. Me, tied helpless to a bed and my son-in-law leering his pleasure over me, naked and with a massive erection. 'I want you to do everything,' I heard myself saying as his hand stroked so teasingly over my cunt, displayed so lewdly by the wide parting of my bound legs. 'Everything you've ever done to my daughter—'

'All in good time,' he promised. 'First we usually do the wine ritual. Lie there and think about it while I fetch a bottle.' He left the room to return with an opened bottle and one glass which he filled. 'It always helped Lesley enjoy herself more with a drink or two—'

He leaned over me, his stiff prick pressed against my thigh as he tilted my head and made me drink the whole glassful. 'More?' he asked, and I shook my head, already being in that happy tipsy state that makes all final inhibitions fly away. 'Well, it's not just for your benefit anyway,' he added. I craned my neck and saw him carefully tilt the bottle over my breasts, stomach and raised cunt, dripping wine as he went. I guessed he meant to lick it off me and I shuddered delightfully. My cunt, already hot and ready, parted with anticipation of pleasures to come, stung with the wine as he pushed an inch of the bottle neck into me and poured in an amount. He kept the bottle there while I squirmed my thighs.

'Lap it up,' I begged him. 'Lick me clean—'

'Ask me nicely then,' he teased.

'Please lick me clean, pretty please. And then fuck me—'

'Fuck me, dear son-in-law,' he insisted grinning.

'Yes, yes, dear son-in-law,' I repeated, 'but I want it now!'

He withdrew the bottle neck and wine ran from me, into the cleft of my arse, and then his face was against me, hard between my thighs. His tongue worked rapidly, reeming me inside while his mouth sucked. The come I had was a glorious and seemingly continuous one. Then his lips worked their way up over my belly and on to each breast, each nipple, and he was positioned in the fork of my thighs, his hard prick nudging my cunt and sliding up to the very hilt. Thus he fucked me long and hard, both of us grunting out words of lust, and then we slept, Philip across me. When I awoke it was almost dawn, the light still on and myself still bound to the the bed.

In the days that followed, between visiting Lesley, keeping house and cooking meals, Philip's lust for me, or mine for him, manifested itself in our fucking in almost every spare moment. He could not pass me without running his hands over my breasts or bottom. On his return from tutoring at his college, before anything else he'd take me with the vigour of a virile and randy young man. I was taken on the couch, over the sink while peeling potatoes, he'd join me in the bath, and each night we slept in each other's arms between frequent bouts of coupling in every varied position. Once while tied again to the bed, helpless to stop him, he brought nail scissors and a battery-operated shaver and I was shorn of my pubic hair amid my shrieks of protest and the reddish chestnut thatch around my cunt lips was vanquished. Often while in the throes, urging him to give me more with his big stout prick embedded up me, he'd taunt, 'Like mother, like daughter. I've had the two randiest bitches on the earth to satisfy.' Well satisfy me did he, making my stay in Oxford a highly pleasant and memorable experience, and he certainly did not wander or crave after other women while I was there.

Lesley too was delighted to find the house spick and span and her husband looking so well and well looked after on her return from hospital with a baby daughter. 'I can't thank you enough, mummy,' she told me, sitting nursing the baby while Philip sat nearby full of pride. 'We've decided to call her Diana after you. Philip says you've been an absolute treasure while I was away. He's never been so well looked after. I'm sure he's going to miss you—'

I heard Philip give a little cough and mumble his agreement. When my taxi arrived for me to leave, he pressed a small package in my hand. 'A little something for all your kindness and the services provided, Diana.'

Only when arrived back at Margaret's Chelsea house and unpacking in my bedroom did I open the wrapping paper. Inside were four lengths of silken cord similar to the ones he'd used to bind me in our games. 'A reminder of a binding agreement we had,' said a written note enclosed in Philip's hand. 'Thanks for the memory, you were marvellous.'

For myself, looking back on the adventures or misadventures that had befallen me in the weeks I had spent back in England, it was time to think of a return to Africa and my husband before further involvements, that always seemed to lay in wait, tempted me.

Chapter Eight
SCOTLAND

Well on into that summer I visited the big house on many occasions. Mr Saxon was fifty-one. We fucked on his splendid four-poster bed at least twice a week; that with me meeting Geddes as often for sessions in his car in some country lane. So I was regularly supplied, but always in the same position – on my back with my legs apart. I truly thought it was the only position. My lovers were obviously as ignorant as I about the finer points.

Saturday afternoon was always a special visit to fulfil Mr Saxon's needs. There was more time and I enjoyed the quiet and freedom of the lovely house with its many fine rooms and corridors. We would make love as soon as I arrived, naked together on the eiderdown, then Mr Saxon would slip under the covers to sleep for a while. Sleep was impossible for me, a young lithe spirit. I enjoyed the feeling of being bare and free to explore. Often I would take a plate of the food prepared and sit in his library, fascinated by the large books with reproductions of famous and beautiful paintings. I couldn't remember my seven-times table after years of schooling, but I knew of Goya and Rembrandt, Titian, Botticelli and Velázquez. It was mainly a summer of low clouds and rain; pleasant inside on an afternoon with showers washing the windows and grey sea scurrying in the distance.

Often I went to the rooms his wife had used before going off to the South of France, finding Scotland as unattractive as the Romans had. I tried on her hats before the long mirror in her dressing room, picturing myself as the lady of such a stately house. They were huge and dusty, but I liked looking at myself naked with just a hat on. My breasts seemed even more rounded, the nipples more prominent, my thighs and buttocks shapely and curved since losing my virginity. I didn't keep count but there had been many times I had made love since. To that was the gifts of money Mr Saxon gave me. Hidden at home were over ten pounds. Geddes never paid, but I couldn't resist his size.

The two men were oceans apart except for their love of fucking me. Geddes was crude, using words that aroused me in our trysts; Mr Saxon was ever the gentleman, warning me of the pitfalls of life while indulging in his satisfaction with a teenage girl. He was easily shocked even after what we got up to, such as me using Geddes' technique of dirty talk while fucking and being told it was 'not nice' for a young girl to use such language. I came back to his bed once after roaming the house and fondled his prick to erection. 'Fuck me,' I said naughtily and was lectured on propriety. For all that I liked him and he was kind, even generous. I was sorry when, in the height of summer, he told me guests were arriving and my visits should stop for a while.

I swam more frequently, and I met the mysterious Mrs Saxon a few days later when crossing the estate to the beach. I was halted in my tracks by a piping voice. 'Little girl, little girl,' it called.

Costume and towel under my arm, I was deciding whether to bolt but curiosity made me stand my ground. She was a thin, pale woman with bobbed hair. She wore a linen suit and one of the wide hats I'd often tried on. With her was a handsome woman of forty and a tall good-looking boy of nineteen who had the looks of Mr Saxon about him.

'You are on private land,' the woman quavered. 'Trespassers can be prosecuted, you know, girl.'

I didn't answer, looking her boldly in the eye. If she but knew it I had been fulfilling her marital duties.

'Insolence,' said Mrs Saxon.

'I haven't said a word,' I said.

'For God's sake, mother,' said the young man. 'Let her go on her way. What harm is she doing?'

'Who is your headmaster or headmistress, cheeky girl?' Mrs Saxon demanded. 'I intend to report your disrespect. Have no doubt about it—'

'Bloody nonsense,' exploded her son. I liked him.

'You'd go to my school to report me?' I said, amazed that anyone could go to the bother. I have learned in life since that such is no bother if you like that sort of thing.

'What does it matter if she's trod our sacred ground,' the young man butted in. 'On your way,' he smiled at me.

'Don't upset your mother, Horace,' the beautiful forty-year-old woman with them said. At the sound of his name I giggled. He winked at me, grinning broadly.

'Awful name, isn't it? Actually I call myself Harry, and I wish everyone else would do the same. You know that, Aunt Margaret. Never mind what mother thinks.'

'Cheerio,' he called as I walked off. Most boys would have remained silent with such an overbearing mother. He seemed entirely at ease, even enjoying the scene.

When I came out from my swim he was sitting in the sand, dressed now in tennis whites. I had bought myself a new swimming costume with some of the money his father had given me, a yellow one that I filled nicely. I saw him eyeing me up with open admiration. 'Never seen a girl before?' I challenged him. 'Don't tell me this is your beach?'

'Never you mind my old lady,' he said. 'I suppose you know you're a jolly splendid girl?'

He meant of course he liked my full breasts and rounded bottom, but the compliment pleased me. 'You're Horace Saxon, I suppose?' I teased him.

'Harry,' he corrected me. 'My friends call me Harry. Are you my friend? I did stick up for you back there.'

I sat beside him on my towel, noting his eyes take in the plunging valley of my bosom. 'Friend,' I said, holding out my hand. He held on to it, squeezing my palm suggestively.

'I could come here for a swim with you tomorrow,' he said. 'Would you mind that? I'd like to very much. How about it?'

'It's a free country,' I said, secretly pleased.

'Right. About this time. May I ask your name?'

Diana, I told him. 'Who was that nice woman with you?' I asked. 'The one you called Aunt Margaret.'

'A family friend,' Harry said. 'She's not really my aunt. I call her that when my mother's there, because she expects me to. You liked the look of her, did you?'

'She was lovely,' I said. 'Like I would want to be at her age. I suppose she's got a rich husband?'

'Which is what you'd like when you marry?' he guessed, laughing at me. 'And why not? A pretty thing like you. I'd marry you myself, if we were older.'

They say many a true word is said in a jest. But at that moment we were disturbed by the urgent tooting of a car horn. On the road sat Mr Saxon's Rolls Royce and he was getting out of his car looking none too pleased.

'My father,' Harry said cheerfully. 'I get the feeling he's not very pleased with a houseful of guests. Likes to be on his own, like a hermit. Can you blame him, with my mother the way she is? He needs a good woman, I reckon.'

'Perhaps he's got one,' I suggested slyly.

'Not a chance,' Harry laughed. 'He's too old for a start.'

Mr Saxon came towards us with a face like thunder. 'What are you doing here?' he demanded of his son. He glanced at me in annoyance and I quickly poked my tongue out at him. 'The tennis tournament is starting and we're waiting for you.'

'With you right now,' Harry said, rising and brushing sand off his white trousers. 'Goodbye,' he said to me, grinning. 'Don't do anything I wouldn't do.'

'Is that the way to speak to a young girl?' his father said angrily. 'Is that how they teach you to behave at college?'

'Nuts,' said Harry, leaving with his father but turning to give me a conspiratorial wink. I liked the look of him even more, but it was his cheerful spirit of defiance that made me love him from that moment. It was a new experience for me and I already longed to see him again. But as I dressed to go home I considered his life and mine. Better to get such nonsense out of my head. He would go back to college and there was my own future to consider. Soon I would leave school and aspired to more than a typist's job in a local office. An exciting world awaited beyond the confines of my corner of Scotland. I intended to go out and see what it offered, not knowing then it would be very much sooner than I imagined.

That evening I met Anna Geddes in the café, hearing her go on about her latest boyfriend, a pimply youth who had felt her up and sucked her little tits in a beach shelter the previous evening. She would let him go all the way the next time, she said, and offered to find me a boy for a foursome. I could have told her a few things: I had two men lovers, one of them her own very well-endowed father! Walking home the beach way, it was darkening by the time I reached Mr Saxon's estate and took the short-cut route. Through the trees I heard the sound of dance music and the fountains before the house were lit in gorgeous colours. I ventured closer, looking upon another world. Beyond the windows men and women were dancing in the big hall. One day, I promised myself, I would be at such a party, in a low-cut evening gown outshining all the other ladies, the handsome Harry Saxon jealously fending off all other admirers. It was at the moment Harry came out on to the balcony by himself, dressed in bow-tie and evening suit. He came down the steps and walked towards me, as if knowing I was concealed among the trees. There he waited and I could have called to him softly, and was about to, when another figure in an evening gown came down the stone steps and joined him.

It was the handsome woman he had called Aunt Margaret, the family friend. No doubt they had come out for fresh air. I was no more than a few yards away and drew back into the shadows. To my utter astonishment she went immediately into his open arms and they kissed long and sensuously, their bodies pressed hard together. Why, he was just a boy, I thought indignantly, and she a mature woman! I was madly jealous, never for one moment thinking my own lovers were older men. The dirty bitch, I said silently to myself, why doesn't she pick on someone her own age?

Nevertheless I was fascinated, watching them kissing so passionately. When they parted I heard her laugh softly, putting her hand down to the front of his trousers. 'How hard it is, poor boy,' I heard her say teasingly.

'Have you been saving it for me? We must do something about it, musn't we, darling?'

'It's been over a week,' I heard Harry complain, as his lovely companion drew out his prick. I saw it plainly in her small hand, rearing above her grasp. They went together, lips meeting in another clinging kiss while she fondled his standing cock. 'Damn my mother always wanting your company. I can never get you alone.' His hands drew up the folds of her dress, clutching her bottom, twin cheeks that glowed pale in the darkness. I could see no sign of her wearing knickers – the horny cow had obviously left them off in anticipation. Harry had the dress well above her waist.

'It's been as bad for me,' she soothed him. 'My poor cunt has been missing that lovely stiff young prick of yours too, dear boy. I think of you fucking me constantly.' Her randy talk and the movement of her hand on his erection made Harry groan in ecstasy.

'Let me put it in then,' Harry said urgently, guiding her back to a tree. I could see her long shapely limbs part as he pressed against her positioning himself between her thighs as her hand guided his shaft to her cunt. 'Aaah,' I heard her gasp, her arms about his shoulders, kissing his mouth lewdly while his bottom thrust back and forth as he fucked her. The sight was so arousing to me that I pressed myself harder into the tree I sheltered behind. By moving against it my mound was pulsating as if it were the pillow I used to masturbate. I was actually working up to a climax viewing the pair fucking before me. Then I heard Harry gasp loudly and Margaret cried out as he shot his load into her with much jerking and final convulsions. They sank down to the soft grass, Margaret with her back to the tree, dress still around her waist showing her open thighs and a cunt dark with hair. Harry lay prone, trousers wide and almost down to his knees.

I rested my cheek against the tree trunk secluding

me, hardly daring to breathe, recovering from the strong orgasm I had experienced. 'Dear Harry, that was lovely,' the woman said gratefully. 'You're such a good fucker for me. Young as you are my husband isn't nearly so good at satisfying me—'

Harry, reclining before her, looking directly at her cunt, laughed shortly. 'I've had a good teacher,' he praised her. 'It's three years now since you came to tuck me in bed that night, in this very house too.'

'Is it that long since I seduced you?' Margaret said. 'I couldn't resist it. You were sweet sixteen and a virgin. Was I a terrible woman to do that?'

'I'd fancied you before that,' Harry admitted. 'Since I was about fourteen actually. I longed to see your big tits.'

Such candid talk was highly entertaining to my eavesdropping ears. 'Yes,' Margaret laughed softly. 'I'd noticed the way you looked at them. You like them big, don't you? I saw you eyeing that young girl we met earlier today. She was very pretty, I thought, quite charming—' Hearing such praise unsolicited about myself made me revise my opinion of the woman. She was obviously sweet and kind. If she liked a handsome and strong young boy to fuck her, why not?

'I'm seeing her at the beach tomorrow,' Harry said. 'I'd like it if you would keep my mother busy in the afternoon.'

'Of course,' Margaret said. 'You were a quick worker, making a date so soon. She's extremely shapely. I've no doubt you hope to fuck her. If you do, you must tell me all about it; every detail, mind.'

'So I will,' Harry promised. My face flushed at such a thought, but I could only surmise sophisticated people had no use for conventions and modesty. It was highly exciting to hear. Then Harry crawled forward on his knees and to my further astonishment plunged his face into the forest of dark hair between her thighs, kissing and tonguing her cunt while she moaned softly and held his head against her. My own cunt stirred at the thought of it and I wished madly that Harry's face was between my legs.

The way her head fell back and her sighs of pleasure told me how much she loved it. Her hands left his head to push the wide neck of her gown from her shoulders, revealing two large firm breasts. A strange feeling came over me. I wanted to leave my hiding place and join them, to add to her pleasure by kissing and sucking on her magnificent tits, a feeling new to me. Then she was fondling them herself, squeezing them tightly as if the pain added to her ecstasy of the moment. 'Lie back, Harry my darling,' I heard her command, and Harry fell back to stretch out on the grass. She bent over him, pushing her breasts into his face, feeding the stiff nipples to his mouth, then with an almost anguished sob took his revived prick in her hand and began kissing the knob almost in a frenzy.

Again I was rooted to the spot in fascination. As I watched she took his whole prick into her mouth and sucked avidly. Harry squirmed below her, thrusting up his hips as if to fuck her sweet mouth. Then she was over him with legs straddling his waist, her dress pulled high to reveal her rounded buttock cheeks as she lowered herself over his rampant shaft. She enveloped his prick as if impaling herself upon it, then rode him with her breasts over his face. When they fell apart, gasping from their wild exertions, she still had strength and desire enough to get back over him, her knees either side of his face, cunt directly above his mouth. 'Now my dear Harry darling,' she told him, 'suck me off again. Lick me clean.'

She left after adjusting her hair and dress, telling Harry to follow at a decent interval to allay suspicion.

He waved from his prone position, relaxing on the soft grass without bothering to pull up his trousers. The wave was in my direction and I cowered further behind my tree. 'Come on out,' he called. 'I know you're there, Diana. I saw you hiding when I first came out. Did you enjoy the show? Were you shocked?'

To show him I was not I walked boldly out. 'Why should I be shocked?' I asked. 'I'm not a child. I know what a man and a woman can do.'

'Well, good for you,' he said. 'And do you do the same?'

I didn't answer and he patted the grass beside him. I sat down and he drew my hand across to his prick. It was already half-erect. I held it, feeling it grow as he kissed me with his mouth and tongue. 'I would have sooner had you,' he said. 'Margaret's all right, but you are young and sweet—'

'I didn't hear you complaining,' I giggled. His mouth covered mine and a hand reached to clutch one of my breasts. I knew that within moments I would let him do anything he wanted; hoped he would do the things he had done to Margaret. Then we were rudely interrupted by a torch shining full on us. Standing there was Mr Saxon's servant Macpherson, his expression one of vast disapproval.

'What the hell, Macpherson,' Harry complained. 'Put out that damned light.'

'Your father sent me out to find you,' the man said. 'He must have thought you'd be up to no good. Not with this young trollop, however. Wait till I tell your father about this little scene, Master Harry.'

'Do what the devil you like,' Harry said. 'I'll come in when I care to. Shove off.'

'You'd better go in,' I suggested. 'I'm off anyway.' The way Macpherson looked at me it was obvious how he and his wife would relish spreading the news. They would go to my parents as well, and I could imagine how my mother would react. So I went home with my mind decided.

I slept the night there and rose early, packing a small case, counting my savings, leaving a note to say I would be in touch, and then crept out of the house. Two hours later I was on a train for London and a new way of life.

Chapter Nine
AFRICA

Returning from England I was much relieved to learn Cato had moved on with his wives, taking with them as many of my possessions as they could carry. It was well worth it to have him out of my life. Husband Harry was none the wiser that his wife and the houseboy had been so intimate, so once more I had got away with a risky infidelity that might have taken some explaining. Harry said he had come home from a business trip to find Cato decamped and two of his suits missing, plus most of the contents of my wardrobe such as dresses, shoes and blouses. As I had been enjoying shopping in London and returned with more of the same, what I'd lost was a small price to pay to get a very real threat to my marriage out of my hair.

Other changes had occurred in my time away. Cato's replacement was a very shapely and pretty young Muganda house servant named Ndegi. Harry explained she had come recommended by the local church mission who sought to place girls in such positions of employment after training them in domestic duties. As Harry had needed someone to cook, wash and housekeep for him, he'd taken her on. I bet he jumped at the chance, Ndegi being a most attractive young thing, amply fleshed and with the firm swollen tits and plump behind of the local native girls. From the studied casual way he introduced her to me, and the way she lowered her big wide eyes guiltily, I suspected he'd had her in our bed for company during my absence.

To tell the truth I would sooner he had, rather than fuck any of the European women in our small white community, who would therefore feel superior over me for having had my husband. Anyway, the girl was clean and attractive and I couldn't blame Harry for fancying her. The house was spotless and all in order for my return, and whether he'd fucked her or not, Harry was delighted to see me again. At least he was by his actions, having me across the bed almost as soon as I got home from the airport. We threw off our clothes and I was supine before him, legs apart, admiring as ever the big erect prick he had attained during undressing each other with fondling and fumbling. It was then he paused, looking down between my thighs to the thrust-out cunt I was offering to him. It was still bare of hair from Philip's trimming.

'What's this, a shaven haven?' Harry grinned. 'All that lovely chestnut cunt hair gone. That's not like you, Di.'

'Give it a kiss, darling,' I put in quickly, before any explanation was necessary. 'I shaved it especially for you. I thought you would like a change—'

Harry pressed his lips to my cunt, pecked kisses on the outer lips, tried a tongue tip inside me. 'Nice, but let it grow again,' he said. 'I've never licked out or fucked a hairless quim. It looks so defenceless—'

'Don't be fooled,' I told him. 'It's the same hungry cunt you know and love.' I had hold of his shaft, guiding it to me, feeling it slide within me as he thrust his flanks. 'Oh, how lovely to have that in me again,' I sighed. 'Fuck it up me, balls and all, Harry love. I've been dying for it.'

'No one else been there in the meantime?' he

inquired, getting in a nice thrusting rhythm as I curled my legs about his waist. I told him, of course not. Neither did I ask the same of him. Later perhaps, during lovemaking, to further arouse ourselves we might allow something to be confessed. At that moment we became too engrossed with being together again, doing what we do so well, naked and fucking without a thought for anyone or anything else. So we went at it lovingly, gently and fiercely in turn during my first night back.

Harry had already left for his office when I awoke in the morning, lying with a single sheet over my naked body, coming to and glad to be back in East Africa. I relaxed with the familiar bed under me, looked about the room where Cato had brought me my breakfast and then fucked me every morning. Already at seven the bright sunlit day beyond had lightened the curtains. Tropical birds twittered and chattered outside. It was good to be back indeed and I stretched luxuriously, sated in body and mind. There was no doubt of my love for Harry, despite my indiscretions. They were mere adventures. My relationship with my husband was the most important thing in my life. Two of a kind, we really got on so well together as partners. He knew well what pleased me. His prick and his tongue never failed to give me great climaxes.

While thinking of this I heard talk and laughter outside my window, followed by two distinct splashes. I arose and peeked through a divide in the curtains. Across the garden a man and woman, both absolutely naked and dripping wet, climbed out of our swimming pool and poised themselves to dive back in. The moment or two was enough to assess both complete strangers. The male was tall, very well-built and blond, a man in his late thirties, I judged. His female partner's golden hair was coiled in plaits around her head, a handsome woman whose athletic physique matched the man's. Large weighty breasts hung free from her chest, attractively full yet pendulous by their size and mass, the nipples long and thick. Her thighs were strong and a pouchy cunt cleft was shaven bare like mine.

She faced away to make her dive and I saw her fully fleshed rounded buttocks, each moon nestled tightly together. The male turned to pick her up, both of them laughing as she struggled against being thrown into the pool. As he threw her his prick swung with the movement, a good thick eight flaccid inches curving over a heavy pair of balls. I was more than interested at once. Who were these splendid specimens frolicking naked in my pool so early in the morning? I certainly intended to find out. Apart from their liberal use of my garden and my pool, they looked very much my kind of free spirits. I fancied joining them for a swim, as bare as they were.

Thus I stood peering through a parting in the curtains when a knock sounded at my bedroom door and Ndegi entered, wide-eyed to see me turn toward her naked. She was no more than sixteen or seventeen. Her eyes took in the size of my breasts and the plump shaven mound of my cunt with much the same interest that Cato had shown on seeing a white woman revealing all. 'What would memsa'ab like for breakfast?' she asked. I was famished, feeling so fit and well after a good fucking and a deep sleep. 'Bacon, egg, toast, marmalade and tea,' I told her, 'with a grapefruit to start. And who are those people using the pool?'

Ndegi's mission school English was very good. I learned my unusual visitors were both doctors from Germany, living in the next bungalow to ours. Mr Saxon had given them permission to use the pool and they did so every morning early, without their clothes. The black girl giggled as she told me.

I slipped on a cotton housecoat and went out into

the garden to introduce myself. They stood before me at the poolside naked and unashamed, two very extremely handsome people. I told them I was Harry's wife, Diana. They in turn smiled and shook my hand, announcing they were Doctors Gunther and Lotte Pohl, members of a United Nations team on a six-month voluntary aid medical tour in East Africa. I found it hard while conversing with them to draw my eyes away from Gunther's huge penis and his wife's beautiful big tits and her plump cunt mound, so cleanly shaved with the outer lips looking so very prominent and large.

'We are your family doctors while here,' the man Gunther said, his accent pronounced. 'Your husband came to us for a medical check last week and he is a very fit man—'

'I could have told you that, after my return last night,' I said wickedly, testing their sense of humour. They both smiled broadly.

'Of course, he would be glad to see you again,' agreed Lotte, beaming. 'He would miss such a fine wife. Is that word right? Fine?'

'Beautiful,' her husband said. 'We looked forward to meeting you, Diana. Harry spoke a great deal about you.'

'Well, I'm back to look after all his needs now,' I said.

'Yes, but you must look after yourself in this climate too,' Gunther announced solemnly. 'I see from my notes that it is well over a year since you had a proper medical check-up, Diana.'

'I don't think it necessary. I always keep so well.'

'Are your vaccinations and injections up to date?'

'Yes,' I said. 'I had them all done in England before I returned here.'

'You do look fit,' Gunther admitted, 'but it is wise to have a regular check, more so while living in the tropics.

Your husband was pleased to know all was well. You should do the same.'

'I never even get a headache,' I laughed.

'It would do no harm to have a complete medical examination, just the same,' Gunther insisted. 'Can you come to the Grade A hospital this afternoon?'

'I suppose I could,' I relented. 'I intended to lie here by the pool in the sun.'

'Much better to be safe than sorry,' Lotte chipped in. 'My husband specialises in preventive medicine. In Germany he attends members of the government. Let Gunther examine you. I am sure you would welcome a clean bill of health, Diana.'

I had a strange feeling that they were working in concert in a scheme to get me undressed by Gunther or both of them perhaps. The idea amused me. 'Will you be present?' I asked Lotte.

'If I can get back from Kampala in time. I have some morning surgery appointments in Mulago Hospital, but I should be back—'

'Three o'clock this afternoon then,' Gunther stated as if the matter were settled. So saying, the pair of them shook my hand again and dived back into the pool to resume their swim. I refrained from slipping off my housecoat and joining them just then, determined to find out just what they had planned for me that afternoon. Perhaps because Harry allowed them use of the pool they were repaying a kindness. On the other hand I had a strong feeling Gunther and Lotte were intent on drawing me into something very different. I'd go along, as ever I did when the unusual presented itself. Doctors were the last people I ever wanted to see with my robust Scottish health, but I was more than intrigued. The pair were obviously a very uninhibited couple, at least regarding going naked before me completely unconcerned. So

Sex and Mrs Saxon

I had been back less than a day and a new adventure beckoned.

I was ushered into Doctor Pohl's consulting room that afternoon, a typical practitioner's office with desk, couch, glass-fronted cabinets with rows of bottles, and a weighing machine. Gunther dismissed the African nurse after welcoming me. I sat while he inspected my eyes, ears and throat most professionally. He took my blood pressure, nodding and saying all was well so far. Then it came, Gunther standing and toying with the stethoscope around his neck as he regarded me.

'Strip,' he said, as if he was used to being obeyed. 'We shall require a complete examination—'

'All of me?' I asked amused.

'How else can I examine you?'

'Bit by bit?'

'Ach, I am a doctor,' Gunther swore. 'I have no time for false modesty. I cannot examine you with your clothes on.'

I stood before him undressing without using the screen I saw in a corner of the room. Gunther sat on the edge of the desk watching me with what I considered more than professional interest. I folded my clothes carefully on a chair and turned to him completely naked, hands at my sides and smiling at him. Perhaps I shouldn't have given him any sort of encouragement in the circumstances, although I was sure he'd set his mind on whatever was to happen. So let's see how you operatate, doc, I said to myself. He was nodding at what he saw.

'You are a most attractive woman,' he observed. 'Good firm figure and high breasts. Most attractive indeed.'

'Do doctors notice such things when examining a patient?' I asked innocently.

'Of course,' he said positively. 'We are human and

Sex and Mrs Saxon

you are a lovely woman, very lovely. Now sit up on the couch, if you please, Mrs Saxon.'

'You called me Diana this morning,' I reminded him, complying with his order and sitting down. He drew up a chair and sat close before me, our knees touching. 'After all, we have little to be formal with each other. I've seen you and your wife both completely starkers. Now I'm in the same situation.'

'Starkers,' Gunther pondered. 'An English expression for being naked, I suppose. You don't seem to object being naked before me—'

'You or anyone else,' I told him.

'Very good. Stupid modesty, convention and inhibition cause more stress and ill-health than can be measured. I have always considered such as diseases. Now I am going to examine your breasts.'

As his splayed hands advanced on me I became acutely aware of my tits, looking down my nose at the curved mounds of rounded firm flesh and the tight nestling cleavage. As if in anticipation of being handled they seemed to swell, their nipples sticking out like thick thumb tips, erected and engorged even before being touched. As if to present my breasts for inspection I pulled back my shoulders and thrust out each teat, feeling them lift and tremble. Gunther stilled them with cupped palms under the rounds, hefting each one as if assessing their weight. I shivered with the coolness of his touch, the pleasure of his grasp, the gentle yet insistent squeezing of pliant flesh.

'That is nice?' Gunther inquired.

'You know very well it is, doctor. You're enjoying it too.' His thumbs and fingers stroked my nipples, gripped them, pulled on them.

'Your breasts are very beautiful, firm and shapely,' he said as if giving a medical opinion while fondling each tit most seductively. 'Nothing wrong with them, in fact they are delightful. So uplifted for their size and weight—'

I could plainly see the huge bulge thrusting out under the white medical coat he wore. The monster prick I had eyed by the swimming pool was responding naturally to his examination, or perhaps more truthfully his fondling, of my tits. I was not unaffected myself with his treatment, feeling the urge arousing my cunt to moisten and throb. My hips squirmed and I expelled a little sigh. It was seduction plain and simple.

'Lie back,' Gunther ordered. His cool hands went to my stomach, pressing various points, nodding his satisfaction. He continued on down to my mound with its missing thatch of hair, giving it a friendly stroke. 'You have shaved,' he said, pleased. 'So much more hygienic in a hot climate. It is very good. I also always think it improves the beauty of a cunt. I take you for no prude, Diana. You do not mind me using the English term?'

'That's what it is, a cunt,' I moaned as his hand covered it and a finger was inserted in me. It went in easily, my hair-trigger lubrication making the entrance slippery. He praised me for that attribute, his finger squelching as he stroked expertly, knowing all the right spots, no doubt.

'Lie back, relax,' he advised as my shoulders lifted and I gave a series of little convulsions. How could I with him touching up my clitoris so nicely? I could only moan my intense pleasure and squirm before him on the couch. 'I think you seek relief,' he said. 'You wish to orgasm?'

He was a cool one right enough, acting as if all was very professional and proper while masturbating me as expertly as one could wish. 'Damn it,' I ground out in my agony. 'Whether I wish it or not, I shall have to—'

The door of his office opened and in some alarm I

made to sit up, only for Gunther to ease me on my back again and carry on titillating my cunt. His wife came up beside him, beaming down at the sight of me, nodding her pleasure no doubt at my helpless writhing. 'She is indeed quite beautiful,' said Lotte. 'She responds very well, Gunther. Such breasts, so firm and youthful for her age. Her nipples are so erect.'

'No bloody wonder, with what your husband is doing to me,' I managed to respond, my voice thick with arousal. Lotte took hold of my breasts and squeezed them hard as if testing their resiliency. 'And that's not helping either,' I groaned as she twisted my nipples in strong fingers. 'You two are just having your way with me—'

'But such excellent therapy,' Lotte soothed. 'It is so good for a woman to let herself be completely in the hands of others, to release all tension this way. In Germany, Gunther and I have many such women patients. Do you ever have difficulty in attaining orgasms, Diana? Gunther is very experienced in teaching female sufferers to climax.'

'I'll bet he is,' I said, my voice now almost a hoarse croak. 'I can vouch for that. Don't stop now, I'm too far gone. Please finish it—'

'Perhaps then you would prefer penetration?' Lotte suggested. 'Gunther would not object to having intercourse with you, would you, my dear?'

Of course he wouldn't, I knew. If I was well worked up into high arousal, Gunther's bulge at his trouser front and his face flushed with lust told of his desire for having me. All the same he paused to consider the matter. 'Does the patient require it?' he asked in his best medical voice.

'I'm sure she would welcome it,' Lotte said on my behalf. 'Note all the signs of her being very aroused. The high colour of her face and facial expression; the breasts and nipples very pronounced; her writhing at your internal examination. It would be unkind not to provide full satisfaction. I strongly recommend it—'

You are enjoying this, you pair of lecherous bastards, I thought, looking up at the two of them playing out their little routine. I grabbed Gunther's wrist and worked his hand hard against my crotch, seeking final relief. 'Do not worry, *liebling*,' Lotte assured me. 'Gunther will give relief. Do not suffer the frustration in you. Let him service you.'

'Do something then,' I urged. 'Tell him to fuck me—'

'*Wunderbar*!' Lotte exclaimed. 'Do not keep her waiting then, dearest.' Gunther needed no urging, crossing to lock the surgery door even while throwing off his white medical coat. He was kicking off his trousers as he returned to us, coming upon me naked and strong in body, his prick rearing up from balls as tight as could be. Obviously no mere unzipping of his flies for the job in hand for him. Also as fast as he had left me, withdrawing his finger from my cunt, his wife had taken over, slipping two of her fingers in my sopping channel and directly finding my clitoris. Her touch was gentle and tormenting; as always a woman's touch so different from a man's. I could only moan and mutter in the deepfelt pleasure, arching my back.

It was seduction accomplished by a highly skilled pair of experts working in concert. Of course, it may be said I was an easy subject for their operation, but that does not detract from the expertise shown. I'm sure many a less highly sexed woman than myself had succumbed to their wiles. As it was they had me begging for satisfaction of any kind, Lotte's fingers or her husband's big prick. 'Give it to me,' I howled. 'Get on with it, please. Oh do, I want it now. I want to come—'

'Not long now,' Lotte sympathised. 'It will be all the sweeter and stronger for the waiting.' Her fingers explored deeper, causing me to thrust my cunt against her hand. 'Is it not sweet torment though? You know, my *liebling*, we did the same for your husband, your Harry. With you gone away from him he needed relief too, poor man. He came to us—'

Even in my arousal I was able to show surprise. 'You mean he fucked you?' I gasped.

'Gunther advised it. My husband was present of course when it happened. Your Harry was very good at fucking me.'

'I've no doubt,' I said acidly, thinking how he would enjoy all that pliant Teutonic flesh under him; but then too I could not blame him if this pair of devils had given him the treatment they were giving me. 'Did he tongue you, lick your cunt?'

'Of course. It is encouraged in the therapy. Advisable for the man to do to the woman to further arouse her in the preliminary stages of lovemaking. Does it not excite you to think of your husband licking and fucking me? I know it does—'

I was thinking more of Harry telling me he had never licked out or fucked a shaven cunt, and no one's was more bare than Lotte's. But while pondering this, Gunther lowered himself between my thighs and was poised over me with his huge red-topped weapon looking menacingly enticing. I swear I could see the veins throb in its iron rigidity. My hand went out to clasp it wonderingly, hardly able to span its great girth.

'There, isn't it a splendid one, Diana?' Lotte smirked in my ear. 'See how it rears up for you. Do you not wish to suck such a lovely thing a little before you take it up your cunt? To wet its dear helmet for easier penetration, to make it even bigger and stiffer for your enjoyment—'

I could only nod dumbly, wanting that glorious shaft in my mouth, to suck upon it like a child with a lollipop. Sitting up, I turned my head and Gunther fed it to my lips. I gobbled at it like a glutton, my mind spinning with the depravity of what the three of us were engaged in. Once I had the warmth and taste of it over my tongue and between my cheeks, my greed increased, gripping it and sucking avidly as if my life depended upon taking it all down my throat. With my free hand I cupped his big balls, squeezed them, milked them, wanted to drain every drop of their gruelly contents into my eager mouth. It was with mounting lust and excitement that I would settle for making him come and swallowing his load while his wife continued to finger my cunt. I was giving full suction to the cock in my mouth and working my hips against Lotte's expert fingering when her next words stopped me once again. She leaned forward close to my face, whispering conspiratorally.

'It is a nice one to suck, *ja*? As big and nice as Cato's?'

'What?' In my surprise Gunther's prick slipped from my mouth. 'What did you say?'

'Go on sucking me,' Gunther ordered as his tool left my lips with a plopping sound and reared free, the rosy crown glistening with my saliva. 'Such a sweet mouth she has. She sucks well—' His knees were shaking, I noted, his face flushed.

It was his wife who gripped the big moist stalk and directed it back to my mouth. 'There,' she said sweetly. 'Comfort yourself sucking on that, Diana *liebling*. All I said was did you find Gunther's penis as big and nice as Cato's?'

Again I let Gunther's prick slip from my mouth. 'Don't say that,' I begged anxiously. 'I don't want it known—'

'What are you two on about?' Gunther demanded,

prick in hand and obviously keen to put it back in my mouth. 'What were you saying to her, Lotte?'

'That her houseboy Cato was fucking her very often before she left for England,' the German woman said with almost malicious pleasure. 'Is it not true, Diana? He fucked you very good, eh? Very often—'

'Please,' I said, my voice strained. 'That has to remain a secret—'

Gunther meanwhile was showing great interest. 'The black boy fucked her?' he asked, both pleased and amused at the thought. 'The one who was her servant? Does her husband share this information?'

'No, he doesn't,' I spat at them. 'It's not true anyway.'

'It is,' Lotte said definitely, speaking to her husband. 'She lies. I was told by Cato's youngest wife. Before they left I treated her baby and gave her medicine to take with them. We became very friendly. She told me that her husband went to Diana's bedroom every morning to pleasure her; also that she herself and the memsa'ab had made love while in bed with Cato—'

'Oh no,' I moaned at such indiscretion becoming known.

'Oh yes,' Lotte beamed at me. 'We are not judging you, Diana. I think Cato and his young wife would be very good lovers. Now Gunther wants you. Let him fuck you too.'

In truth their revelations had drained all the desire I'd had for being brought to a climax by the pair of them, my arousal gone. I also felt very much in their power. 'You won't let all this get out,' I begged. 'My friends would have a field day. I don't know how my husband would take it—

'Your secret is safe with us,' Lotte assured me sweetly. 'Are we not doctors who have taken an oath of a patient's confidentiality?' Her fingers stroked at my clitoris but for once I was too concerned to regain some semblance of arousal. 'Now,' she added. 'Relax and part your legs again, *liebling*. Gunther is waiting.'

He was nodding eagerly. 'One never knows,' he chuckled almost wickedly. 'We have such a good subject here, haven't we? A wife who not only takes her native servant to bed, but has the boy's wife too. A classic case of uninhibited sexuality among expatriate women. Worthy of a medical report, I'd say. I shall write it up, publish a paper. The patient would remain anonymous, of course—'

'Just get on with what you intend to do,' I snapped, wishing now to get out of their clutches. I was certain Lotte was behind getting me to agree to their so-called medical examination, and with the knowledge of my affair with Cato to aid her would get me to do as they wished. She was obviously a voyeur who got great pleasure from seeing her well-hung husband fuck the wives of friends. They had had my husband Harry, now I had fallen into their circle of lechery. Lotte actually put on a pair of spectacles for better viewing, bending over close as her husband's thick tool penetrated me. If I let out a groan it was not with relief or pleasure, but at the great size of it stretching me, mixed with my feeling of remorse.

The whole length was engulfed inside me, Gunther's big balls bouncing against my bottom as he began his thrusts. I decided I would get it over with, for once in my life not finding a thick and lengthy shaft up my cunt bringing an instant response. To encourage him, however, I sighed, took my legs up and around the small of his back, gripped at his buttocks for leverage as I lifted my cunt to his movements.

Gunther, I will admit, was no slouch at making love. He shifted his angle of penetration to nudge me from different directions, he withdrew to the end of his knob to tease before thrusting deep again, his pace quickened and slowed in turn. Did I feel the first flutters of a response in my cunt? Perhaps so, but it was Lotte's contribution that got me going.

She bent over my face, whispering to me like a conspirator as her husband manfully fucked me. 'Was Cato's prick so good? Did his big black penis fill you as much? Tell me, *liebling*. I want to know—'

'Please, Lotte,' I squirmed in embarrassment. 'That's in the past. I want to forget it.'

'But why should you?' Lotte insisted. 'I'm sure it was so nice for you. He was so young and strong. You would love it, love his black prick filling your cunt. Was it a nice big one? Did you suck it for him as well?'

Her whispered lewd insinuations plus her husband's plugging me so expertly was having its effect, as no doubt she expected.

'No one must ever know,' I moaned, arousal now churning my stomach, my thighs lifting eagerly to accept Gunther's deep thrusting. 'But it was so good, so good when he fucked me—'

'And you couldn't refuse him?' Lotte beamed.

'No, I wanted him, wanted him to fuck me. It was so good, he fucked me so good,' I admitted. 'I loved his big prick.'

'And your Harry was fucking you too all this time?'

'Yes, I had two men fucking me. Harry at night and Cato came to me every day—'

'How nice for you. So you were taking both their pricks. In the mouth too?'

'Yes, yes. Oh Lord, I'm going to come, come—' My hips were bucking like a wanton. I raised myself to get all I could. 'Your husband's fucking me, he's making me come!' I grunted. The strength of the spasms that wracked me made me hardly aware of what I was doing or saying. 'Fuck it up!' I screamed.

'Continue, Gunther,' Lotte said to her husband. 'She is coming strongly and will no doubt have several orgasms. Diana is indeed a fine subject, highly sexed and a weak woman when tempted. I'm sure she has had many lovers—'

She was right there, and right about my having a series of climaxes before her husband gave a strangled cry and worked his pelvis ever faster until shooting a long come into me with shudders and spurts that brought me off in a final orgasm. I lolled back somewhat shattered by my exertions, recovering to find Lotte sitting beside me with a glass of water. Gunther was dressing himself, looking very pleased, as I thought he ought to. I gulped down some water, gasping my thanks.

'That was quite an afternoon,' I told Lotte. 'Some medical examination, I'd say. Do you do this sort of thing with all your patients?'

'Those we think attractive enough and likely subjects. We have had no complaints. Sometimes we even treat husbands and wives together. We could do so for you and your husband.'

'I don't think so,' I rejected her offer. 'You've had us both so let's leave it at that. I shall say nothing to him about his fucking you. As for the business with Cato, I trust that remains between us.'

'Of course,' Lotte promised. I was suddenly reminded that I was still very naked and vulnerable as her hand came over to fondle my breasts. 'But such a pity,' she said. 'We could have made such a delightful foursome—'

'I've no doubt,' I said, removing her hand and rising to dress. My fear was that in such an arrangement, which could have been interesting to say the least, with Lotte's love of sexy talk during the couplings she may well give my secret away. I dressed and drove back to my bungalow, my cunt still squishy with Gunther's sperm and pulsating from the shafting of his outsize prick. I showered and was in my housecoat when Harry returned from his work.

'What have you been up to today, love?' he asked.

I returned his kiss and told him nothing very exciting, just more or less relaxing after the flight back and our previous night's lovemaking. 'It's so good to be back, darling,' I told him. 'Being away makes it all the nicer when I come home to you.'

'I couldn't wait to have you here again,' he said. 'Though I may have to take a trip myself in the near future. Business in New York. I'd make it quick though, just a day or two if I can get it over with.'

'I see we've got new neighbours,' I ventured to say. 'I saw them using our pool this morning and went out to see who they were.'

'Yes, an odd-bod couple of Jerry medicos,' Harry said easily. 'Both into naturism or nudism, whatever they call it. Handy having a couple of doctors next door, I suppose.'

Too handy perhaps was the thought that came to my mind. I had a dire feeling that my liaison with Lotte and Gunther would not be the end of it for us. Not from what I had seen of them or the way they manipulated people for their own special sexual deviations and entertainment.

Chapter Ten
ENGLAND

Whatever the bright lights of London might offer, on my arrival I had to put such thoughts aside. Less than eight pounds remained of my savings after paying my fare. I walked the streets near the station in light rain, feeling rather lost and lonely. All around people hurried past under their umbrellas, having places to go. I reminded myself this was the big adventure of my life so far. Something exciting would happen. I had a face and a figure men found attractive and I would use my assets to gain any advantage. First things first, however, I had to find a base, a place to stay.

Cards in a corner shop window advertised rooms to let and one requiring a cook/cleaner. 'All housekeeping duties' the neatly printed notice stated. I inquired within how to find the address given and was soon knocking on a door in a quiet side street. The woman who answered was fortyish, short and plump, her voluptuous figure shown to full advantage in a smart grey wool jersey dress. Her black hair was combed severely back from a centre parting and she looked me over like a severe schoolmistress.

'What is it you want?' she asked sharpish.

'I'd like to apply for the job. Cook and cleaner.'

She glanced down at my shabby little suitcase. 'Just arrived, have you? Left home?'

'I'm applying for the work advertised,' I repeated, not intending to tell her my business.

'You look a bit young to me. Scottish obviously. Have you ran away, girl?'

Old bitch, I thought, turning to leave and not giving her the satisfaction of cross-examining me, but she stepped back into a carpeted passageway. 'Bring your case and come in,' she ordered. 'Can you cook and clean?'

'Of course.'

'Of course nothing,' she snapped. 'I've had women here who couldn't boil a kettle.'

'I can do more than that,' I said. 'My mother made sure I could.' The woman appeared to smile faintly, leading me through to a comfortable living room with chintzy armchairs and fresh flowers. She had good taste. From a silver box she took a cigarette and fitted it into a holder. Her fingernails were painted bright red, matching the full lips of her sensuous mouth. I could not but notice, too, her breasts were huge, thrusting out forward and sideways, globes of firm rounded flesh moulding the front of her dress, jiggling with every slight movement. I saw her regard me as if reading my thoughts, considering.

'I'll give you a week's trial,' she decided. 'There's a spare room, so you'll have bed, board and ten shillings a week if suitable. My name is Roberta Cole. *Miss* Cole, that is. Who are you?'

'Diana Mackenzie, miss.'

'Wherever did you get that dress, Mackenzie?'

I looked down at myself. The dress, as ever, was one of sister Jennifer's hand-me-downs and I was considerably more well-developed. My bulging breasts strained the buttons, while the cloth was tight across my hips and bottom, revealing every curve.

So I started work for Miss Cole, headmistress of a

private school for young ladies. That day I cooked lamb with roast potatoes and three vegetables, followed by an apple sponge. I ate in the kitchen and went through later to clear Miss Cole's table. She was taking coffee and smoking a cigarette in the long ivory holder.

'I think we may suit each other,' she conceded, 'but we can't have you bursting out of your clothes. When you go to your room you'll find I've laid out one or two of my dresses on your bed. They may need some alteration. Can you sew?'

My room was neat and cosy with a dressing table, cupboard space, wash-basin and a comfortable bed in which I masturbated on my first night to celebrate my good fortune. Miss Cole was not the easiest person to work for but was fair, if aloof at times. I did not consider being her maid my career but I lived well and free, and could add to my savings. Then I would go my own way and discover what London had to offer. In my day off in the first week I took the underground to the West End, seeing beautiful women being escorted into smart hotels and restaurants. The men with them eyed me up with interest as they alighted from limousines and taxis. My day would come.

There were frequent visitors to the house, all of them women in their thirties or older. I had retired to my room one evening, hearing music and talk from below as Miss Cole gave a party. Coming from the bathroom I glanced down from the landing, seeing two women sitting at the foot of the stairs. Their arms were about each other and they gazed face to face like lovers. To my utter amazement they kissed, long and passionately, parting mouths to sigh and mutter before kissing again. I could not believe my eyes yet was strangely aroused by the scene. Naive as I was, men went with women and women went with men, a perfect arrangement so far as I was concerned, but the two women fondling and kissing proved so highly erotic I found my hand going between the fold of my dressing gown and touching the slit of my cunt. I drew back as Miss Cole came into my sight.

'Come on, you two lovebirds,' she chided them. 'Time for all that later—' At that moment she glanced up and saw my face. Burning with embarrassment I fled to my room. Nothing was said about it when I served breakfast next morning, yet I suspected there was more than met the eye about Miss Cole and her female friends. Why not, I considered, if they like that sort of thing? Thinking about it and what I'd witnessed was highly arousing, but what could two women *do*, apart from kiss and cuddle? That day when Miss Cole was out on school business I tidied her bedroom. Her dressing table was a trove of beauty compounds, scents, creams and oils. Her jewellery box was unlocked and I admired her necklaces and rings. Among them was a key and I tried it in several drawers before it turned.

What I uncovered sent a thrilling shock to my senses. There were several canes, a leather strap, a short whip with tails, and a soft cord used, even I could guess, for tying up wrists and ankles. They were not for school use, I knew. Beside this array were several false pricks, moulded in rubber, some of them doubled in the shape of a 'V' and with elastic body straps that were adjustable. I knew well what a real prick was. There was no doubt these were perfect replicas, ranging in girth and length up to ten inches. Some even had veins and the plum head of the real thing, as well as balls. Handling them was not exactly like the real thing I'd had experience of. They felt the same in size but the warmth and *throb* I loved in my hand was missing. Still, I knew, one of them up my cunt would be the next best thing. Eager to try, I chose one and anointed the stalk with a little oil. After a few experimental strokes against the lips of my cunt, it slid in beautifully. I fell back from my sitting position on Miss Cole's bed and fucked myself, gripping the monster with both hands. I thrust deeply and came off.

I washed and dried it carefully, returning it to the drawer and locking securely, amused Miss Cole had such 'toys'. It was, after all, only a more sophisticated method than the pillow I used. It proved she had needs to be satisfied. That evening after dinner I was taking the bath she insisted I had every day, stepping out on to the bath mat glowing pink and nude, when she entered the bathroom. At first I was tempted to cover myself. She eyed me like a lustful male, staring hard at my breasts and thighs. Why I suddenly felt coy, embarrassed, I did not know. I had been naked before men. So I let the towel drop to my feet. If she wanted to admire my body, as I was certain she did, I had nothing to hide and everything worth showing. I felt a stirring in my cunt as her eyes roved my body.

'I'm going out tonight,' she said. 'Don't expect me until the morning.' There was a definite tremor in her voice. 'I won't need breakfast. You may have a lie-in, Mackenzie.'

'Thank you, miss,' I smiled, pushing out my breasts.

She turned to leave, reluctantly I felt. 'You are quite a beauty, young madam,' she praised me, her voice soft and meaningful. 'You must watch out that men don't take advantage of you.'

'I will that, miss,' I promised like a good girl. She went to her room before leaving. When she had gone I took the key and inspected her secret drawer. Several of the dummy pricks were missing, as were the straps and cords. She was off to a party with her female friends, I guessed, and I would have loved to have been going with her, if only to satisfy my great curiosity about what went on. Why she had aroused me so by looking at my body I could not surmise, but the fact was its effect on me was as dramatic as being ogled by a man. To relieve my heightened state I 'borrowed' one of the rubber pricks and satisfied myself with it, picturing Miss Cole administering it while I laid before her naked.

When I awoke in the dawn light it was still in place up my cunt. Before withdrawing the instrument I idly toyed with it until I was stroking myself with the prick well penetrated and climaxing with loud groans. I fell asleep again quite exhausted by the several strong orgasms produced, awakened in broad daylight by the sound of a taxi at the door. I hid the dildo, as I learned it was called, under my pillow.

I went to the foot of the stairs, still tying the dressing gown Miss Cole had given me. Underneath I was completely nude. She came in looking not her usual painted and immaculate self, wishing me good morning. 'Run me a bath, my dear,' she ordered, something she had never asked me to do before, or call me her 'dear'. When it was ready, steamy and sudsy, she came into the bathroom in a black silk robe. I was about to excuse myself and leave, hoping to return her dummy prick to the drawer before she missed it.

'Don't go. I want to talk to you, Diana,' she said, using my first name instead of the usual curt 'Mackenzie'. Before my astonished eyes she let the robe slide to the floor, standing completely naked. Her great breasts were truly amazing, heavy with their own weight yet thrusting out as if defying gravity, creamy white, rounded and surmounted by red erect nipples as big as thimbles which I would have sworn had been well sucked recently. Between plump smooth thighs bulged the most prominent cunt-mound imaginable, thickly forested with strong black hair yet allowing a glimpse of the peeping split-butterfly lips of her quim. I had a strong impulse to reach out and hold her tits, to cup and kiss them, handle their lovely weight and mass.

Her nipples were especially inviting, tilted and begging a mouth to suckle.

Miss Cole's cunt pouted as if expecting a finger or prick, pink showing through the dark thatch of her bush. She gave me her usual secret smile, enjoying my wonderment, stepping into the warm bath and lolling back among the scented bubbles. Both breasts floated high and her hairy cunt mound peeped above the surface. I had never seen my mother or any other female naked. The splendidly curvaceous one before me was again proving I could be aroused, even lustfully wanton, by a woman as readily as by a man. And, of course, I knew her ploy was deliberate: the use of my first name, having me attend her in the bathroom, dropping her robe so effectively, all were calculated moves in the art of seduction.

'I'm having my friends visit tonight,' she announced. 'A few special guests. I'd like you to serve us, just drinks and snacks during the evening.'

'Yes, miss,' I said.

Miss Cole nodded. 'Good. I shall give you a list of the things we'll need. You can shop this morning. Then tonight when you serve my friends you can pretty yourself up. Wear one of the dresses I gave you. Let them see what a nice young maid I have.'

When the guests arrived, all women as usual, I took their coats and handbags, showing them into the lounge. One, a tall and handsome woman with pure white hair and expensive evening gown, smiled expressively at me. 'Bobby has been keeping you a dark secret, the sly thing,' she said. We were stood in the passageway on her arrival and she squeezed my hand suggestively.

'Who is Bobby?' I asked mystified. 'I know no Bobby.'

'Why, your dear mistress, Miss Roberta Cole,' she

laughed teasingly. 'What do you call her, sweet young thing that you are?'

'I call her Miss Cole,' I said. 'I work here.'

'And very nice work if you can get it,' the woman said. 'You may call me Cynthia. And I do hope you will call me. I must give you my phone number—'

We were still holding hands, or rather she was stroking mine, when Miss Cole appeared from the lounge. 'Cynthia,' she cooed, but I saw her glance disapprovingly at our joined hands. 'Take Lady Bellinger's coat and handbag, Diana. Then you may serve the canapes.' With that she ushered her guest into the lounge. I went to the kitchen to collect my tray. A few minutes later Cynthia Bellinger came through to join me, eyeing me like a delectable sweet.

'I can offer you more than you'll ever get here,' she came straight to the point. Her slender hand smoothed the line of my shoulder, going down over the short sleeve to caress my bare arm and squeeze my hand again. 'Oh, I could do so much for a young beauty like you. So sweet, so fresh and sweet,' she praised me. 'May I steal a kiss? One little kiss?'

Before I could express my surprise the woman swept me into her arms and glued her painted mouth to mine, lips open and tongue probing. Her breath was sweet, tasting of wine, and the kiss went on lingeringly and passionately while she pressed her well-upholstered body to mine, moving her pelvis against my thighs. When she broke loose it was to kiss me once more, a tender peck on the forehead.

'Beautiful, lovely creature,' she said. 'Such gorgeous auburn hair, such a firm young body. We must meet again, but I shall have to go now, before Bobby comes through in a jealous rage. I told her to excuse me while I used her toilet but she suspected me, of course. No wonder! Oh, I could ravage you, sweetie. Don't let that fat cow have you—'

I went through to the lounge with my tray. The guests, a dozen or so, paid little heed to my arrival. They were all female, ranging from the late thirties to forties. One or two sat on the laps of other woman. Some danced in the centre of the room, a gramophone playing the latest foxtrot. One or two of the dancers kissed gently, barely moving in the confined space, breast to breast. Cynthia Bellinger gave me a warm smile, touching my hand as I offered her the tray. Miss Cole was busy serving drinks. I took empty glasses to the kitchen and washed them, returned them, made up the fire, all the while the women were holding hands, stealing sly kisses, dancing. What would happen after that I was not allowed to wait around and see. Miss Cole thanked me gravely, said I would not be needed any more that evening and could go to my room.

I felt irked, cheated. This would be the time, I reckoned, when the rubber pricks and the leather straps would be brought out and used. Did the women get naked, I wondered, as I did with men? Well, Mr Saxon and Geddes the coalman liked me stripped off completely. The only way to do it, I reckoned. I went to tidy the kitchen before going upstairs, reluctant to go, when Cynthia Bellinger appeared beside me. She came behind my back, put an arm around me and squeezed one of my breasts. 'What I could to do you, my dear,' she threatened. 'I could teach you so much, so much pleasure. Has Bobby had you? Do you sleep in her bed with her?'

'Of course not,' I said, turning. I took her hands from fondling my breasts in fear of being discovered by Miss Cole. 'Nothing like that goes on. I have my own room—'

'Don't you believe it, sweetie. There's a seduction

planned, have no doubt. You wouldn't like that creature slobbering all over you, would you? Give me another kiss, do please. Quick now, in case that old bitch seeks us out—'

I was in her arms, our mouths clinging, before I knew it. But her perfume was so heady, her kiss so passionate, that I let her continue. She muttered how sweet I was, so lovely, her hands roving over my tits, getting me quite aroused. I never would have believed it, being so taken with a woman kissing me. My arms went about her neck of their own accord. She said, 'That's right, dearest, let yourself go. It's so nice, isn't it? Your lips are so delicious—' and I was backed against the kitchen sink where she began to thrust her pelvis into me, cunt against cunt. 'Oh,' I said sighing. 'Oh, you've made me feel all funny.' Actually it was the same feeling of high arousal I got with my men lovers. Her hands kneaded my tits and I wanted to take them out of my dress for her. Thus we were when Miss Cole came into the kitchen and let out a scream.

I was packed off upstairs to bed, hearing the yelling and angry raised voices of arguments continuing for some time. The front door slammed. Then there was quiet. I got into my nightdress and sat on my bed, sure Miss Cole would come up and give me a row for what she had seen Cynthia doing with me. When she did come upstairs she went to her room first. I thought she had decided to say nothing about it. Then she pushed my door open and stood before me in the same black dressing gown, obviously with nothing underneath for her breasts, nipples and all the contours of her body were moulded by the silk.

'What I caught you and Cynthia Bellinger doing tonight was unforgivable,' she said. 'I take you into my house and this is how you repay me. My party was ruined. How could you?'

'Please, miss,' I said. 'She started it. Honestly. She surprised me—' If it wasn't for needing a place to stay, well—

'It looked very much to me like you were encouraging her.'

—but for a roof over my head I'd have given her what for. As it was I had to humour her. 'It wasn't like that,' I said. 'She started everything.'

'Suppose I take your word for that,' she said, 'and we forget this incident. Don't you think you should be punished for spoiling my party? So that we can make a fresh start, make you sorry this all happened tonight under my roof?'

'If you say so,' I said petulantly.

'I do say so.' She left the room and returned carrying one of her whippy little straps. 'I won't be too hard on you, my girl. No more than your parents would do, I'm sure. Pull up your nightdress and bend over the bed—'

I did as was bid, legs together, hands clutching the nightie around my waist, revealing my bared bottom. My head touched the counterpane and I waited, determined she could do her worst but not a sound would I utter to give her satisfaction. When nothing happened for a moment or two, hearing the rustle of silk, I turned my head and saw her standing behind me nude. How her big breasts hung!

'Open your legs to balance yourself better,' she said, and I did, showing my cunt and my bumhole to her. The strap whistled down and made me flinch. 'Do cry out if you want to,' she said, so with each stroke I howled and flinched. My bum cheeks went very warm. The glow spread to my cunt quite pleasantly.

I found I had not minded the beating at all, if anything I had enjoyed it. I was certainly aroused. Looking at the woman as I stood, I hoped she would start something.

Little did I realise that Cynthia Bellinger's kisses and fondling had aroused me greatly.

'Oh, miss,' I blubbered, 'I'm sorry for what I did. I won't do it again,' and I went into her arms, mine about her neck. Her breasts pressed to mine. When I raised my head we kissed. I put my tongue in her mouth and she clung to me. It was pure seduction on my part. She put me into bed, got in beside me, and I cuddled up, feeding on her big nipples, cupping her tits, enjoying her hand which sought my cunt and toyed there, slipping a finger in and touching me in exactly the right place, as well a woman knows about another of her sex. She brought me to orgasm, petted me, then slid down in the bed to kiss my cunt, tongue it. I held her head, bucked against her face, coming once again. Then I slept.

It was morning and Miss Cole was gone. She came into the room fully dressed a little later, saying she had made her own breakfast and was leaving for school. She kissed me goodbye on the cheek, patted my hand, and left.

I rose and bathed, using a liberal amount of her bubble bath. When she came home in the evening I wondered if she would want to love me again. Whatever, I had better get the housework done, the evening meal prepared. Then the phone rang and when I answered, Cynthia Bellinger was on the line. 'I waited until I was sure she'd left for her school,' she said. 'Did she give you a hard time, the bitch? Of course she was madly jealous.'

'She beat me with a strap,' I was wicked enough to say.

Cynthia Bellinger did not seemed surprised or perturbed. 'And did you enjoy that, you little minx?' she laughed. 'I knew right away from our meeting last night that you were a true spirit. Come on, own up that you enjoyed it.'

'Well, I think I did,' I admitted. 'I thought about you when she was whacking me. My bare bum all warmed.'

'That I would have loved to have seen,' said Cynthia quite lecherously. 'Do you know why I've called? I need a little companion like you. A ward if you like. Want the job? If you do, stop your work now and I'll have my chauffeur over to pick you up within half-an-hour. Don't bring any clothes with you, my dear. I shall enjoy rigging you out completely. Then we soon leave for the South of France, you know. Monte and the season. Would you like that?'

'Yes. But who is Monty?'

'Monte Carlo, you goose. Be ready now for when Atherton comes with the car. Look out for him. Will you leave a note for you-know-who?'

'Yes. I'll tell her I've gone back home to mother.'

'Bright girl,' laughed Cynthia again. 'You come to me and let me mother you.'

My mother was never like Cynthia, but her offer was an exciting one. I did pack my clothes, leaving the dresses Miss Cole had given me. One thing I did take as a souvenir of the time spent there was the dildo I had secreted under my pillow. Not that I thought I'd have much need to resort to that in the Bellinger household. I was more than right.

Chapter Eleven
AFRICA

I quickly settled back into the pleasant routine of an ex-patriate wife in East Africa, a life so different from that in England. My lapse with our neighbours, the Pohls, was temporarily out of my mind as they had gone off on safari to Tanzania. I was happy to see them out of harm's way. There was so much else to keep me occupied – parties, golf, swimming and barbecues. On occasion, too, there were government and business functions to attend as the wife of Harry. For these I'd dress in my evening-wear finery, do up my hair and face to look beautiful and impress on important people what a fine wife he had.

I always found myself an object of flirtation by the male guests; I was propositioned for secret meetings and had my bottom pinched by everyone from an ambassador to ministers of state. They were all at it, men being men whatever their position in life. In fact, the richer and more powerful they were the more they sought affairs or expected no refusal when the offer of a one-night stand was issued. It became almost an art to put them off nicely and without causing offence. It was for the sake of Harry's reputation that I played hard to get.

His pet project on my return was his plan for an ambitious irrigation scheme for the northern territory which would enable the local tribes to increase crop yields and grow grass on sparse land to feed their large cattle herds. As a consultant engineer he was excited by the project, trying hard to gain support and the necessary aid money to finance his scheme. I knew little of his plan but had been on a visit to the area with him and seen how poor the soil was; it was practically desert. Consequently the small farmers and herdsmen scratched a bare living for themselves and their families, hardly existing above the starvation level.

When the Ugandan Government's Minister of Agriculture, who could approve Harry's scheme to make it official policy and help him apply for financial aid, invited Harry and I to be guests at one of his many sons' weddings, it was politic to give an expensive present, attend the ceremony and show our white faces at the reception which followed. Okot Kidepo, being also a tribal chief of the Mutoro as well as the minister of agriculture, was really more interested in providing resources for his own particular region and not the northern Acholi people. All the more reason to flatter and butter him up, Harry reasoned, if the irrigation scheme was to be made an official government project and become a reality with financial backing.

Before the wedding day dawned, however, even without the official go-ahead, Harry took the bull by the horns and set off for America to seek a promise of financial aid for his project from United Nations' funds. His appointment in New York coincided with the wedding date and he chose to be where he felt his presence was the more vital. 'Can't be helped, my love,' he announced in our bedroom as I packed his suitcase. 'If I come back with a firm promise of aid money, even President Obote himself can hardly turn my scheme down, much as he likes spending everything on himself and his army. I know there's water up there. With bore holes and wells we can revive a whole large arid area, even into southern Sudan. There could be decent-sized lakes to stock with fish, pasture land, farms that could produce even in long droughts.'

I knew how excited he was about his brain-child, too engrossed to pay any attention to me despite my doing his packing dressed merely in an open housecoat, hopefully revealing my naked goodies to tempt his eyes. 'You've more than an hour before your flight, Harry,' I suggested.

'Must shower and change,' he said, ignoring my hint. I don't give up so easily, slipping off the housecoat and lolling back on the bed, my legs parted and over the edge.

'Give it a goodbye kiss at least,' I said, raising my cunt to him. 'It's going to miss you, you know—'

'You really are the horniest creature,' Harry laughed. 'Didn't you get enough last night? I really must get ready—'

To tempt him further I played with my cunt, one hand parting the outer lips to show him the moist inner pink, the other one dipping in and stroking my clitoris. The self-induced pleasure, increased by doing it before an interested spectator, mounted in me rapidly. I groaned and Harry stood over me, looking down on my fingering myself with a shake of his head and a grin. 'I might have known you'd try something,' he said. 'Is this a game two can play?'

'If you're quick about it,' I could only moan, for I'd been so quick at exciting myself. 'It's so good I'm going to have to come. I don't want you to go without fucking me. Hurry up and put it in—'

'Not yet,' my husband teased, loosening his dressing gown. 'You're doing such a grand job yourself, my dear, and I love to watch you masturbate. You really bring yourself off so strongly. Years of practice, no doubt.'

'Damn you, Harry,' I blurted out. 'Put it in me or I'm going to come!' I saw that his prick was spectacularly erect and was in his hand being stroked.

'Yes, yes,' he encouraged me. 'Come! Let me watch you come. I'm coming too—'

Well into the final throes, my lower body bucking and my hand working furiously, I craned my neck the better to see him. Harry's knees seemed to buckle as he wanked himself off ever faster. Then we were both crying out lewd oaths as the spasms shook us in our climaxes. 'We are such beasts,' I called, coming strongly even as the silvery arcs of his spurts splattered on my tits. His last jerks weaker, the rich goo fell over my shaven mound, sparkling the returning wisps of hair with pearls of come. 'Now here's another fine mess you've got me into,' I said, going into peals of laughter. 'I'll join you in the shower you were about to take.'

Under the lukewarm spray we soaped each other, using the lathering to feel and fondle, our bodies clinging as we kissed. The water poured on to my neck and shoulders as I knelt to suck Harry, enjoying the stiffening and lengthening of his prick in my mouth as he regained an erection. 'Stand up and turn around,' he ordered suddenly, fiercely. 'Hold on to the shower pipes and stick out your bum—'

I obeyed, turning to the tiled wall as I taunted him over my shoulder. 'Don't tell me, you're a sodomist as well as a wanker. You, sir, are not nice to know.' The suds ran down my back, infiltrating into the crease of my arse. I felt the fat knob of his shaft against my anus, pushing into the puckered ring, penetrating an inch or so. As ever I expelled breath and relaxed my bottom, gripping the shower fittings as I dipped my back and tilted my rear for him. Harry's wet flanks slapped against my buttocks, he rose on tip-toe to gain more depth. I felt full, pleasantly plugged. Behind me

I heard his delighted mumblings and groans. His hands grasped my hips and he rotated against me.

'Beast, bugger,' I told him as he reamed me so determinedly. 'You like this best, up my poor bum. Arse bandit—'

'And who tails you better and who taught me?' Harry reminded me. 'Remember?'

I did remember as he pumped his length in, withdrew and went into me up to the hilt again. It had first happened a night long ago, in the early years of our marriage. Harry was starting out his career as an engineer. For a young couple putting a home together with money tight and two young children to raise, what better and cheaper entertainment and pleasure is there than a mutual enjoyment of making love? We had decided to limit our family to the two we had, so in our fucking precautions had to be taken at the time. But often in our urgency, the act of my rolling the condom on to Harry's erection didn't get priority. I would be mounted and he'd fuck me, leaping off at the crucial moment just before coming.

One evening in those early days we had put young Peter and Lesley to bed, tucked them in with a bedtime story, and on returning to the living room had our usual cuddle and kiss that invariably led to having sex. Wind and rain rattled the window and it was a perfect night to settle before the fire. Harry caressed me, kissed me slowly and lewdly with his tongue deep in my mouth. His hands cupped my bum cheeks and I felt his erection as he drew me to him. In turn I dragged my cunt mound over the bulge in his trousers. Of one mind we undressed on the rug before the hearth until naked, fondling eagerly as young lovers do.

'Throw some cushions down in front of the fire, Di,' Harry said. 'I'll get a rubber from the drawer—'

I'd taken the chance to say something I had wanted to

say since we had married. 'We don't need to use a sheath all the time, Harry,' I said shyly. 'There is another way, you know—'

My young husband's face had shown interest and amusement at the same time. 'Tell me more,' he grinned, his prick standing hard against my stomach and his hands around me cupping my bum cheeks. 'What's this other way?'

'You must surely know,' I said.

'Your mouth?' he teased. 'Between your tits? Under your arms?' He was laughing at me. 'We've tried all those, so where else?'

'Well, guess, you idiot,' I said, more embarrassed.

'I wouldn't dare, not what I'm thinking. You tell me.'

'Up the bottom, you fool,' I blurted out. 'Would you—'

His delight was apparent. 'I've always wanted to and didn't like to ask. Are you sure, Di?'

'Never mind the condom just bring the Vaseline,' I'd said, committing myself. I smeared his prick thickly from knob to base, then bent over to present the moons of my behind. 'Use your finger to grease me now,' I instructed him, grasping the arms of the chair to steady myself. The greased finger entered and I squirmed with the nice feeling it gave me. 'Try it now, try it now,' I urged him. 'Easy and gentle at first, but it will go in all right, I'm sure, dear. Go on—'

'You're dead keen for me to do this, aren't you?' Harry accused. 'Game for anything, my wife—'

The finger up my bottom hole was producing delightful feelings, making me want more up there. 'Are you complaining?' I gritted out in my squirming. 'Get on with it for God's sake. I want it, I want it—'

'Then take it, my love,' Harry said, replacing his finger with his cock, the lubricated shaft forcing a passage and corking me tightly. I groaned my appreciation as his hands pulled my cheeks apart and he curled his body over me, well embedded. My bottom, seemingly afire, pierced to my stomach, now rotated against his belly, changed its motion to thrust back hard into him. 'Oh lovely arse,' he cried out. 'Tight as a clam. Why haven't I fucked you before?'

There is always an added lewdness in being penetrated up the behind. It had its effect on Harry too. He lifted his head and crowed like a cockerel, went on tip-toe to get extra depth, had a hand around me grasping my tits and the other at my cunt nipping and pulling on my clitty. 'So good, so good,' I joined in his cries. 'Come up me, Harry. Squirt a load in my arse. Do it, do it!'

I was keening and whining, jerking like a puppet at the shunting in and out of his prick, coming strongly. Then Harry was grunting and I felt his hot jism spurt into my insides. It was the first of many such encounters. 'You've done that before,' he accused me impishly as we disengaged and slumped to the carpet.

And now he had been in my bottom again before departing for the airport, leaving me to represent him at the wedding of the agriculture minister's son. This was a pity, as Harry would have been proud of his wife. I wore a wide-brimmed picture hat with a lilac ribbon to match the new silk dress I wore for the occasion. With the importance of the father of the groom, nothing less than the cathedral at Kampala was good enough for the occasion. The Archbishop conducted the service and I was in high company with the President himself and members of his cabinet. Having shown my face and chatted to the people who counted on Harry's behalf, I decided to skip the reception, being an unaccompanied woman.

It was then I was approached by a man I knew slightly

in our small white community, a French professor of medicine who tutored in Kampala University. A snappy dresser in a blue-and-white spotted bow-tie and a white linen suit, with his beard and short stature I only knew him as Toulouse Lautrec, the name used behind his back at the local club. He came up to me and swept off his Panama hat, even bowing slightly.

'Mrs Saxon,' he began before introducing himself. 'I have noted you in Entebbe Club on occasion, of course. I could hardly fail not to appreciate such a beautiful woman. You have always reminded me of the actress Elizabeth Taylor with your looks and figure. Forgive me, I am Professor Leconte. Marcel Leconte. I have met your husband, Harry Saxon. I do not see him here with you, madam.'

I told the little man Harry was in New York. 'Would you be so kind as to drive me to the reception at Kjansi?' he asked. 'I have no car at present, you know. It was stolen just yesterday.'

That was not unusual in Uganda. 'Hop in,' I invited him. 'I'm not going to the reception but I pass the place and will gladly drop you off.'

We followed a procession of motors from the cathedral, a long line of expensive machines including Rolls and Mercedes. The convoy threw up red dust from the murram track as it reached the approaches to Kjansi township, its residents standing at the roadside fringed with banana plantations as the magnificent ones drove past. Ragged peasants and potentates separated by a few yards and a million miles. Professor Leconte obviously had the same thought as myself.

'What do those people think, you suppose?' he asked in his strongly French-accented English. 'Are they pleased to see their own so rich and powerful? The splendid uniforms of the army, the government ministers and their women so richly dressed. The people are so poor—'

'They wanted independence, they got it,' I said sharply. 'Let them get on with it.'

'Not a very humanitarian view, my dear,' Leconte chided me. I agreed it was churlish of me, blaming my ill-humour on the fact I was missing Harry. The township we had arrived at was a crowded collection of shacks, clapboard hotels and bars, even some thatched circular mud huts one saw in villages far out in the bush. But here and there were some splendid brick-built modern ranch-style bungalows with hard-standing for several cars in their forecourts. These were the homes of the elite, Presidential favourites and senior military officers. I drew my car up before a fine structure with a smart red-tiled roof. On the wide patio before it large umbrellas had been set up over tables and chairs, with a host of servants providing food and drink to early guests. It seemed an entirely African affair, army uniforms and the gaily coloured local native garbs predominating.

'It would seem that you and I will be representing the entire white race today,' Leconte observed. I was about to inform him I wasn't attending the reception when Okot Kidepo himself came up to my car. He was a giant of a man, very black and dressed for the occasion of his son's wedding in a long white kanzu gown that came down to his sandels. On his head he wore a flat multi-beaded Muslim cap and completed his regality with a long elaborately carved tribal staff.

'Dear Mrs Saxon and Professor Leconte,' he greeted us. 'Welcome to my home. Do come and eat and drink with my guests.'

There was no chance off refusing and offending him. He led the way through rooms packed with a mass of humanity eating and drinking as fast as they were served. In the throng I lost my French companion and, as is usual at such events, Kidepo took me to a room reserved for the senior women. His four wives were resplendent in brightly coloured silk *busutis*, the flowing dress which had become the national costume for women. They gathered around me to touch and discuss my deep chestnut hair, lifting my hat and chattering excitedly in their Luganda language. They had obviously been drinking and were in high spirits. Kidepo handed me a glass and they giggled and made signs that I drink it down.

It was a native beverage called *waragi*, a type of gin distilled from bananas. I'd tried it before but this brew hit me like a blow in the stomach. I was given more and found my eyes difficult to focus. One woman had brought a *busuti* costume from a wardrobe and held it up against me. They obviously wanted me to wear it and the excited women started to undress me. In the spirit of things I let them continue, even helped as they surrounded me. Off came my dress, bra and briefs, my difference to them causing delighted comments as they pointed out my white breasts and the reddish hairs sprouting back on my cunt mound. As the *busuti* was lifted to put over my head screams and great giggles went up when it was discovered that Kidepo was still in the room. He was immediately pushed out with gales of laughter but not, I noted, before he had studied my nakedness with great interest.

It was indeed a time for comparison. Several of the women brought out fat tits to show their ebony colour and the dark purple of their nipples against my pale tits and the pink tips of my nipples. Tipsy as we were, there became a general show of cunts and bottoms before the *busuti* was finally slipped over my head and I was dressed as they were. Kidepo was then allowed back into the room and stood regarding me with narrowed eyes. Everyone in the room especially myself had a good idea what was in his mind.

'The *busuti* suits you, you look beautiful in our native dress. Would you care to allow me to show you over my house?' he said. Those women around who could understand English all went into giggles again, covering their mouths.

'I think I had better find Professor Leconte,' I thought it safer to say. 'I promised I'd accompany him—'

Kidepo did not look pleased. 'Of course, your husband has gone to New York,' he said meaningfully. 'You know, his project has not yet been authorised by my ministry and this trip of his is quite unofficial.' He took my hand, smiling at me with strong white teeth. 'We should discuss the matter, I believe. With a little encouragement I'm sure I could be persuaded to advise my President to make it an official government project.'

I'll just bet you could, I thought, making my escape and finding Professor Leconte at a table and joining him. I was glad to sit, feeling curiously unsteady on my feet, my head swimming and the heat of the room doing nothing to alleviate what seemed a very sudden drunk feeling. I fanned myself with his straw hat feeling very odd.

'I think we had better leave,' Leconte advised. 'These African celebrations are liable to get hectic and go on for days. The native costume is very becoming on you. Do you intend to return home that way?'

'I think I can manage to change into my clothes,' I said. 'Then I think you had better drive me back—' I tottered my way to find the room where I'd been dressed in the *busuti*. Tribal chants, singing, ululating and drumming assaulted my head and in the room itself I found my clothes laid out over a chair. The women had gone and there was no door to close for complete privacy as I made to change, only strings of glass beads hanging down to the floor in the doorway. I found it too much of a struggle to pull the *busuti* over my head, so intended to step out of it. The costume was down to my waist, my breasts bare, when Okot Kidepo came back into the room.

'Professor Leconte says you are leaving,' he said, his eyes ogling me. The *busuti* fell to my ankles in my stupor, revealing all. 'You know, I have had more thoughts on your husband's irrigation project. I am sure I could get it approved—'

'He would be most grateful,' I said, awaiting his move. 'If you could—'

'I shall give it priority,' Kidepo promised, his hands gliding up my thighs. 'Yes indeed. One good turn deserves another, you agree?'

In my somewhat inebriated or drugged state I was in no position to disagree, already being lowered back on to the bed. I'm about to be raped, I considered, and this fact became more apparent as he drew his *kanzu* robe over his head and threw it aside. Focusing my eyes to look up at him hovering over me I saw a massive black figure with a large belly. Rearing between the fork of his legs was a straining circumcised prick with a huge plum head and a thick stalk of exceptional length. Kidepo climbed on me, his great weight flattening me, positioning himself with animal-like grunts and thrusting his big rigid root up my cunt with the finesse of a bull elephant. I squealed and felt the whole length driven in as he heaved his flanks and fucked me. This one was for him, I decided, for I was getting little pleasure out of his selfish ramming. For him and Harry, too, I consoled myself, if the irrigation project got the go-ahead out of it.

Therefore to show I had some heart for it, and to encourage him to get it over the sooner, I moaned and curled my legs over his broad back. 'That is good,' he growled. 'Good for you too, eh? You make good fuck for a *mazungu* woman, Mrs Saxon. You like African prick, yes—?'

'Oh, yes,' I moaned, more than a little sincerely too, for the prick up me was beginning to have an effect, as the stirring in my cunt showed. My head was over his shoulder as he bore down upon me and I saw two very young and engrossed black faces looking in at our fucking from between the beaded string screen at the doorway. 'We are being seen,' I gasped. 'Two boys are watching—'

'My nephews,' Kidepo ground out in mid-stroke. 'They will see we are not disturbed. I told them to keep all others away while on guard. Do not worry, Mrs Saxon.'

Why should I? I thought, seeing as how I'm being used and abused without a say-so and two very interested boys are getting an eyeful of their uncle fucking me. But as my response grew and the fire in my cunt demanded satisfaction, Kidepo called out loudly some obscure words and his hips gave mighty heaves as he emptied his balls into me. I was left in limbo as it were, on the verge of a climax, but he was off me and pulling his robe back on. When he departed I was slumped on the bed, dazed and as if in a dream.

I closed my eyes and seemed to drift for a moment or two, helpless to rise. A hand came on my breasts, feeling each one tentatively. Another unknown hand was between my legs, touching me as if exploring. Then I felt a body on top of me, a stiff prick entering me. It seemed all part of the dream, my mind so woolly I concentrated to regain some semblance of what was happening. The prick in me seemed real enough, rigid and poking strenuously. The weight above me was so much lighter than Kidepo's bulk. I risked opening my eyes and saw a young face directly over me and another beside it watching closely. Kidepo's nephews had continued where uncle had left off. As the boy fucked me I felt my interrupted arousal returning strongly. I lifted my hips and returned the thrusts.

Well, if they wanted it and I needed to be satisfied, why not? I reasoned. When the boy above me became frenzied in his movements I tried to slow him, my climax building but not yet at the unstoppable stage, when he cried out and jerked his come into me. His brother immediately took his place and, as if in an uninterrupted coupling, I continued my undulations. The small hard prick in me brought me orgasms and the boy jerked away in his own spasms. In a daze still I was vaguely aware of little old Leconte in the room ordering the pair of young rascals to go. He got me to my feet and somehow drew the *busuti* over my head as the easiest garment to get on me. Then I was being walked with his hand supporting my arm out to my car, everything and everyone around me a blur.

The car journey was a complete blank as I slumped back in the seat, unaware it was to Professor Leconte's house I'd been taken. To me, everything I tried to focus my eyes on seemed as if viewed through a rain-washed window. I remember being gratefully laid out on a bed, desperate to close my eyes as the *busuti* was pulled off me. In a state of absolute weariness through drink and copulation, I drifted off to a dozy kind of semi-consciousness as I felt a mouth cover my cunt. You too, Prof, I could not but think wryly, even in my stupor. I sighed as if in sleep and parted my legs. Why not drop off with a gently lapping tongue soothing me?

Leconte, with his very tickly Van Dyke moustache and beard pressed to my crotch, began licking me clean. Then the blessed sleep I sought overwhelmed me. When I came to it was with bright sunlight dappling the curtains in the strange room. The professor peeped in, saw me awake, and returned with a tray. 'How are you this morning, Mrs Saxon?' he inquired solicitously. 'I have black coffee and some aspirin for you to take. Are you feeling better?'

Better than I ought to feel, I considered ruefully. I drank off the coffee and refused his pills, sitting up with the sheet up to my neck. 'Thank you for rescuing me from that party,' I said. 'I'm sure I'd have never made it home last evening.'

'No harm done,' Leconte smiled. 'I brought you here because I'm not sure where your house is.'

'I'm not a drinker,' I said. 'God knows what was in those couple of drinks they gave me—'

'Some drug undoubtedly. It's quite a usual thing at such celebrations. I should have warned you—'

'Did I make such a spectacle of myself?' I dared ask. 'Most of what happened seems like a dream now, with me just floating through it letting it happen.'

At the foot of the bed was the silk *busuti* I'd worn. He lifted it and smiled. 'At least you have a souvenir of the occasion. Your other clothes are in your car outside. Do you wish breakfast or to take a bath before you leave?'

I thanked him but was soon on my way wearing the native costume for ease of dressing, arriving home to find Ndegi waiting for me and all eyes at the sight of the splendid *busuti*. 'A present for you,' I told her as she ran my bath and I slipped out of the dress. After relaxing in the warm sudsy water I was hungry, wonderfully headache-free and fit after the debacle of the wedding reception. It was then after a good breakfast that the phone rang and it was Harry calling from New York. He sounded delighted.

'Had a call last evening from Okot Kidepo,' he said very excitedly. 'Said he'd had a talk with the President at the wedding reception and my scheme will be approved. I've had talks with representatives of an Arab state that might well be good enough to give financial aid. They think my scheme would be beneficial in their country too—'

'Well, congratulations, darling,' I said. 'You deserve success.'

'Kidepo said he'd seen you at the wedding reception. He sounded quite impressed. Did you talk with him?'

'Yes,' I said. 'We had quite a tête-à-tête. He impressed me too,' I added, remembering Kidepo's great weight on me.

'How did the reception go?'

'They served firewater. I got out while the going was good, I think. You'd better hurry home. I'm missing you, Harry.'

'Me too, my love,' my husband assured me. 'Just a few more days or so and I'll bring you back a nice present for being such a good girl.'

'When have I ever been anything else?' I asked him, signing off with a kiss blown down the telephone. Who knows? I considered, it could well be that water for live-giving irrigation could flow in the arid northern region all because the government minister concerned had fucked the wife of the project engineer. As for his nephews getting in on the act, it couldn't have hurt to spread the bribes around the family. Besides that was the sort of thing that invariably seemed to happen to me without trying. Par for my course.

Chapter Twelve
ENGLAND

My little suitcase packed with all my worldly possessions, I went to the front bedroom window and saw a silver Rolls Royce parked before the house. Leaning against it nonchalantly was the chauffeur Atherton, all six foot six inches of him filling the tailored grey uniform magnificently. He drew on a cigarette and looked about with a studied casualness, no man's lackey. When I emerged from the front door he took me in from top to toe, nodding as if quite satisfied. 'You're prettier and better filled out than the last one,' he observed, giving me a sly wink. 'Best yet, in fact. Lady Cynthia picks 'em right enough. Young and manageable—'

'Don't be so familiar,' I told him haughtily as he took my case. He only laughed, his tremendously broad shoulders shaking. Under the peaked driver's cap his face was handsomely rugged, a boxer's face. I wondered who the last one he had compared me with had been, and where she was now. But the die was cast. I was heading off to a more exciting way of life, I was sure. As if reading my thoughts, he reassured me.

'You're moving up in the world, miss,' he smiled. 'The Bellinger residences all knock this little two-up two-down into a cocked hat. Pretty poor neighbourhood, I'd say—'

I thought Miss Cole's house the very ideal, in a

tree-lined avenue with railings and tidy front gardens before every semi-detached dwelling. 'I've been in a bigger house before,' I felt bound to say, remembering Mr Saxon's lovely home. 'With a beautiful view of the sea too.'

'Lady Cynthia has places with views of the sea in at least three countries,' Atherton replied. 'You've seen nothing yet, girlie. Wait until you get a load of where I'm taking you now, her house in Park Lane. Mind you, I must say you'll add to the look of the place. I suppose you do know what you're in for, taking up with her?'

'What's that to do with you,' I said sharply. 'Of course I know what I'm doing—'

But I didn't. I was going to a strange house on the invitation of a person I hardly knew. All I remembered were her hands fondling me, her long wet passionate kisses and sweet words. I supposed she wanted more of the same, but then she'd seemed kindly and I had enjoyed her arousing me so. I would see what befell and the whole idea was a big adventure. Atherton was studying my face as if reading my thoughts again.

'Had a bit of hanky-panky with you, has she? Sucked on your nice tits and kissed your sweet little cunt? I'll bet she has.'

'None of your business,' I snapped, my face reddening. 'Are you here to drive me or act like my mother?'

'Bit of a tartar, was she?' Atherton laughed. 'Don't get mad at me. Just putting you into the picture a little. As for sucking your tits or kissing your cunt, I don't blame anyone for that. I'd do it myself quick enough given the chance—'

'Chance would be a fine thing,' I retorted smartly.

'You never know in the Bellinger establishment,' the forward chauffeur said cockily. 'We're all one big happy family there. I reckon you'll fit in sooner than later. Lady Cyn has her way of life and who's to say it's wrong? No one's forced to stay and they pay bloody well for all services. I was lucky when I came out of the Grenadiers and was taken on. Get in the car, miss. Do you want to sit beside me? I don't suppose you've ever ridden in a Rolls—?'

I could have told him *I'd* been ridden in a Rolls. 'I shall ride in the rear,' I told him. 'Drive on, Atherton.'

He was laughing as we glided off. 'Oh, I like the sound and look of you,' he said. 'A right handful in more ways than one, eh? Milady collects beautiful things and she's certainly got a young beauty in you. She'll doll you up, mark my words; have her guests with their tongues out when they see what she's come up with. Wouldn't surprise me if old Lord Bellinger takes a fancy to you. Make a change from his young men—'

'Young men?' I said mystified. I had quickly learned that females could lust for each other, kiss and fondle and more. Miss Cole, when we were naked together in bed, had given a low heartfelt moan as if unable to resist and then slid down to kiss and tongue my cunt after fingering it. She had heightened my arousal so nicely and expertly that it was obvious she'd done that before with other women. The way her tongue had lapped and licked, probed and flicked at my clit, sending me into convulsions, had been marvellous. It had been lovely, a woman's face hard to my cunt, tongue delving deep, its stiff pointed tip at my pink pearl, her mutterings as she sucked at my vitals. I just had to thrust up, grasping her hair, coming so strongly right against her open mouth. It had been my first but I'd taken to it as a discovered delight. Hopefully there would be other women. Lady Bellinger perhaps? But men with men?

'Yes, men,' Atherton laughed. 'So you're not so worldly wise as you make out, young Scottie. The old boy is getting on, but Lord Lionel likes a bit of vice-versa, recapturing his youth as it were. Comes from his service in India, I reckon, where bumtailing and pig-sticking ranked along with polo as good sport. He's not much of a reader, despite having one of the finest libraries in England, but he loves getting to the bottom of a page. Have you never been properly corked yet, girl? That's a pleasure you've got to come, and can get well accustomed to in time. Seems you've a lot to learn, and you've come to the right place. Where have you been kept away from the facts of life?'

I pondered all this new information as we drove into Park Lane, stopping before a large three-storey house fronted by fluted columns. The double front door was opened as if awaiting our arrival by an elderly butler, who eyed me with more than mere interest. As I walked up the marble steps I would have said his look was of pure lust. He stood stiff as an aloof ramrod but his eyes gloated. He must have been almost seventy, a plump man with a face reddened from good port, I imagined, mutton-chop whiskers and dignified in a dark morning suit, his hands in white cotton gloves.

Atherton, coming behind with my case, saw the look too. 'Here's a young beauty if ever there was, Porlock, my old mate. I can see you drooling, you old lecher—'

Porlock's solemn features went sour. He drew up his short fat frame, stretching his neck out of a stiffly starched collar. 'You will address me as Mr Porlock, Atherton, and I am certainly not and never will be your old mate. Take the young lady's case up to her room while I show her to the morning room.'

'Where's the footman? It's his job—'

'Robert is cleaning the silver. You do it.'

Atherton gave me a broad wink and proceeded up an ornate and curved stairway with my case. The house was obviously grand, the entrance hall I stood in spacious. Chandeliers hung above, marble statues graced the alcoves. My room had been mentioned; I was sure it would be a chintzy, well-furnished and airy place. Porlock bowed his head slightly and led me off, opening a tall white double door and ushering me in. Lady Cynthia Bellinger was directing the hanging of a painting above the fireplace, two men in blue overalls doing the work while a man in a pin-striped suit stood by nodding at Lady Cynthia's words. Porlock gave a slight cough.

'Ahem. The young lady is here, milady.'

Cynthia was in a grey silk dress that showed off her full figure splendidly. Three rows of pearls adorned her neck. When she turned it was with a look of delight at seeing me. I went into the room fascinated by the painting in the gilt frame. There had been a reproduction of it in the art books I'd studied in Mr Saxon's house while he'd rested after fucking me.

'Renoir,' I said. 'The Boating Party.'

'Yes,' Cynthia said, obviously pleased. 'Isn't it quite delightful? And how lovely to see you again, Diana. I'm busy now but Porlock will show you to your room. Then we'll have coffee later. I'm sure you'll be happy here, my dear.'

How could I not be? I thought, surrounded by luxury and beautiful things. As I turned to leave with Porlock, the hulking chauffeur stuck his head around the door. 'I must see you, milady,' he said. 'A matter of importance – has come up—'

'What, right now, Atherton?' said Cynthia as if annoyed.

'It is most urgent,' he insisted. 'As Lord Bellinger instructed I carry out—'

'Oh, very well,' Cynthia conceded with a sigh. 'But I'm very busy. If you can't wait, you'll have to make it quick.'

'It will be, milady,' Atherton assured her.

I saw Porlock shake his head and raise his eyes.

I found my room as neat and feminine as I could have wished, with adjoining bathroom and lots of cupboard space, a dressing table or vanity unit with a silver brush-and-comb set, bottles of lovely perfume and all kinds of make-up. My window overlooked a rose garden. After investigating I sat on the bed, growing impatient as the minutes went by before deciding to look around the surroundings. The landing was curved, with several doors, and the stairs led up to another floor. I walked along the big thick carpet, so deep in pile my steps were silent. One door was slightly ajar and I heard voices, Lady Cynthia's and Atherton's.

'This is very bothersome, Atherton,' I heard her say in complaint. 'Surely you could have contained yourself? I have the art-gallery people to see to—'

'Balls to them, they can wait, I can't,' Atherton rejoined. To speak so to his mistress surprised me enough to make me put my eye to the jamb of the door to see her reaction. She looked more flustered than angry at his insubordination, flushed in the face as if aroused. 'Only doing what his Lordship told me. Keep you supplied while he's away—'

'You know very well you do that while he is here as well. It excites him to think about you and me—'

'Fucking,' Atherton put in grinning. 'As for why right now, it was bringing that young girl here that done it. What lovely big firm tits and round arse for a kid. She's bloody lovely. Got me hard just looking at her.'

'She is a delightful creature, crudely as you describe her. I forbid you to touch her. Seeing her has aroused the beast in you but I warn you now she is mine—'

'Greedy,' Atherton chided her. 'There's enough to go around.'

'You will leave her alone,' Cynthia threatened, 'or it will be the worse for you, beast—'

'Keeping her to yourself, milady? I think not. You'll be showing her off to your special friends, I'll bet. They'll be having her at those parties you like to arrange. So what's up if I want my share, eh? Look what bringing her here for you has done to me.' Atherton unbuttoned his breeches trousers, lowering them with his underpants to the tops of his laced-up knee boots. When he scooped up his uniform jacket and shirt his great erect prick stood out, rearing with a red angry head. 'It's more'n ready, you want it?' he said, 'because you're going to get it. Get the knickers off, Cyn—'

'You will *not* call me by that name, Atherton,' Cynthia remonstrated, but began hitching up her dress to draw down her knickers. 'This has become too much of a good thing. I'm considering giving you notice to leave. With Diana here, yes.'

'You'd miss this too much,' Atherton growled, waggling his monster prick at her. 'And I'll be putting it up your Diana before too long, you bet. Be a good lady now and bend over that chair while I fuck you—'

All this talk about who was having me, the sight of Atherton's remarkable prick, so stiff and long, and now Lady Cynthia, his mistress, taking up a stance bent over an armchair, head to the seat, plump arse raised and poised, had its effect on me. I felt the arousal rising in my loins, lubricating and pouting my cunt. Cynthia presented a fine full-mooned bottom. With her legs apart I could see the neat serrated ring of her arsehole in the deep cleft of her buttocks, and just an inch or so below the hanging bulge of a crinkle-mouthed quim curled with hair. Atherton felt up both orifices while Cynthia groaned and writhed somewhat.

'That's a well-fucked cunt and bum hole,' he told her.

'For all you seem to prefer young girls and having it off with them, you can't resist a stiff prick up you, can you? Say it! Go on, admit you do—'

'Never,' swore Cynthia. 'Fuck me if you are going to, but I will not say your dirty filthy words. You swine, you beast, I won't say them!' It was like a game of words between them.

'You will, because here comes the belt,' Atherton promised.

'Not the belt! I forbid it. Don't you dare—'

'You can forbid fuck-all when you're here like this – your arse turned up for my use.' He reached down to his knees, drawing the leather belt from the hoops of his lowered breeches. 'Like his Lordship said, "Atherton, give her arse a good belting if she needs it", like right now,' he reminded her.

Cynthia turned her head as if in defiance just as Atherton cracked down the belt across both her tilted bum cheeks, making her arse jerk and flinch. She cried out a protest. Four, five, six hard strokes followed, her bottom reddening. 'Say it,' he repeated. 'What I told you.'

'Please, please!' Cynthia cried out. 'Yes, yes, I love your big prick up my cunt. I adore it, just don't thrash me—'

'You'll let me fuck Diana?'

'Not that, no! I don't want you to. Not yet—'

The belt came down across her bared bottom harder than ever. Although Cynthia yelled, threatened, squirmed about, clenched her plump arse cheeks, she did not move from her set position or attempt to get away. It made me think she was getting pleasure from the humiliation of her servant whacking her, the sweet painful submission. Miss Cole strapping me like a naughty girl had had much the same effect.

'Say I can fuck young Diana then,' he repeated

harshly, the belt cracking on her cushiony bum like a thunderclap.

'You'd do such beastly things to her,' howled Cynthia. 'I know what you are—' Several more sharp blows striped her poised backside. 'Enough, enough,' she cried at last. 'Swine, you can fuck her. Just stop, please please—'

Her chauffeur dropped the belt, edging up to her and presenting his prick to her cleft, an already parted furrow. I clearly saw the plum head edge in and she gasped, thrusting back her arse to his belly while he began to thrust in and out of her. She took a firm grip on the arms of the chair, dipped her back and arched herself to receive him better, accepting each forward heave as he fucked her from behind.

Watching the pair of them go at it like wantons, I was reminded of a dog with a bitch on heat below him the way the big chauffeur's arse pistoned away as he fucked his mistress. Between her groans and drawing in of breath, despite her crying out protests, it was plainly clear that milady was loving the servant shafting her.

'Dirty beast,' I heard her cry out. 'Making me do this – using me – fucking your mistress! I shall fire you, Atherton. How dare you fuck me!' He replied by telling her she loved it, in the crudest terms, loved his big prick up her hungry cunt, all the while the both of them gasping out the words in their exertions. The scene was the more exciting to me as I was spying on them by chance, privileged to see two real experts enjoying their sex games uninhibited and unaware they were being observed.

The effect upon me was an arousal such as I'd never known. Viewing couples fucking was so erotically fantastic; something I have since that day greatly enjoyed. I was rubbing my thighs together, not able to tear myself away from the show but eager to get to the privacy of my room and masturbate to relieve the itch in my cunt. What a house I'd come to, I thought, revelling in the idea. As for Atherton fucking me like he'd threatened he would, his thick and rigid prick was indeed a tempting thing. I was watching him using it, in and out, long withdrawals then a mighty plunge back into Cynthia's cunt, the lips of which gripped the stout shaft like an elastic band. I wished it were me on the end of it. My hand was about to reach under my skirt to frig myself when a cough behind me made me leap back from my spyhole. Porlock stood there, giving another of his polite warning coughs, but for how long I did not know.

'Perhaps Miss Diana would care for a bath after her journey,' he intoned, as if I'd travelled from miles away. 'It is the duty of Patience, the upstairs maid, to run it for you. As she is otherwise engaged shopping for cook, I shall do so.' He gave me a knowing look and went to my room.

I stared for the last time into the room occupied by Cynthia and Atherton. Her buttocks were thrusting back into her fucker's belly, with the odd twist and squirm to alter the angle of entry, her moans now a mumble that rose to announce she was coming, coming, oh lord she was coming, coming! Both she and Atherton thrashed together in their final frenzy before slowing like a train reaching the station and stopping with a hiss and release of steam. Cynthia stood, tidying her hair, stepping back into her knickers and straightening her dress while Atherton adjusted his uniform.

'I shall want the car this afternoon at two sharp, Atherton,' she ordered, as if nothing untoward had gone on between her and the chauffeur.

One of Porlock's coughs made me turn away again. I was informed my bath was ready.

In the tiled bathroom I lay back and luxuriated in the

deep sweet-scented water, my breasts floating and asking for their nipples to be admired, pinched and pulled before my wet fingers went down to my pulsing quim. It felt soft, pulpy, pouting and parted after the wonder of watching Cynthia and Atherton. I remembered the way he had summoned her from the morning room, talked to her so roughly and treated her like a common woman in a way she seemed to have reluctantly liked. I wanted a cock up me, desperately, and remembered the dildo I had taken from Miss Cole's collection. I arose from the bath to fetch it and was opening my shabby little case when Porlock tapped on the door and entered. His eyes lit up to see me standing naked. Over his arm he carried two large fluffy pink towels.

'I thought you might need these, Miss Diana,' he said, his stare taking in my two thrusting tits before going down to ogle my cunt mount with its auburn thatch. Aroused as I was, I did not mind giving the old man an eyeful. He advanced on me, to unfold the towels and rub me dry from the shoulders down. He took his time drying my breasts, using a circular movement that I aided by steadying myself and arching my back. Then he towelled between my legs, warming up my already warm cunt even more. He dropped to his knees, drying my feet, his ruby face level with my bared nest.

'Lovely girl,' he said hoarsely. 'Let me lick you—'

In reply I did not use words, lolling back on to the bed cover, legs apart and hanging over the edge, showing my cunt, even tilting it up for him. In a moment he was there, his face between my thighs, two palms slipped under me and cupping up my bum cheeks, his tongue lapping, licking at me, tickling at my clitoris. When I sighed my pleasure and reached for his head, lifting myself into him, he muttered into my cunt, 'That's right, young miss, let yourself enjoy. It's a honeypot, your sweet cunt. Do let me lick it out often please, missey.' I craned my neck to look down at his grey head of hair, his mutton-chop whiskers tickling the insides of my thighs. 'You dirty old thing,' I told him, deep in the throes of being brought off, my pent-up climax mere seconds away. My whole body rose from the bed and I cried out helplessly, shuddering with the pleasure. I lay back before him, tits lolling on my chest, legs apart. I'm sure my cunt was palpitating like a heart beat.

When he stood before me I saw his cock was out of his trousers, stout and stiff, what looked like a good nine inches. He took it in his hand and began to stroke it fondly. 'They were fucking in that room, weren't they?' he said. Still recovering from the glorious come he'd given me with his tongue, I nodded, all I could manage. 'This is a bigger one than his,' old Porlock said proudly. 'When I was a footman and young Lady Cynthia Glaister as she was then came home from her boarding school, she loved to dandle and suck upon this. She would come to the pantry for it.'

'It is a big one,' I felt bound to say.

'Later I fucked her with it often,' he reminisced, 'for she took me with her when she married Lord Bellinger.' He continued rubbing up his cock while talking, poised over me. 'Now, of course, that lout Atherton fucks her. His Lordship always liked the male members of his staff to give her a good rogering. Kept her pleasant, he always claimed, though he liked to think about her getting fucked by the downstairs staff. He'd asked me to tell him what it was like, how she took it. Liked to hear all that, he did—'

His prick had seemed to thicken and stretch alarmingly as he stroked it. Then it jerked in his hand. I saw the split tip open and spurt its liquid pearls over me, my tits taking the most as if a point of aim. Three, four jets flew to land on me, seeping into my cleavage cloyingly, dripping from both nipples.

It was quite an emission, enough for a young man to produce.

'I beg your pardon, miss,' Porlock apologised, sedately as if he'd spilled tea in my saucer. 'Couldn't help it, like. Those splendid tits make such a tempting target—'

I was unable to resist a smile. I had wanted satisfying and I had been given a lovely helpless come, so what if the pompous old lecher wanted to finish what he'd started? He used a towel to dry my tits, mop up his come while I sat up and let him proceed. Then he left and I lay back on the bed, revelling in the afterglow of being brought off so well. I was relaxing so when Cynthia looked into the room.

'Sweet girl, you do look a picture naked. I've neglected you, but I've been so busy—'

'Something came up?' I said innocently.

'Yes. But it's almost lunchtime and this afternoon I'm taking you shopping for nice things. What have you been doing?'

'I've just had a lovely – bath.'

'You are a young beauty,' Cynthia praised me. 'Lying there all warm and pink and naked. There's a glow upon you. I find I can't resist you, can't resist kissing those perfect breasts. Do let me—'

I held them up in my hands for her and she lowered her head to kiss each nipple then suck upon them in turn, the very nipples Porlock had just dabbed his gruelly come from. She stopped only to go down between my knees and give my cunt a light kiss.

'Shall I?' she said. 'Yes, of course, I shall. Your poor dear sweet little cunt seems very receptive already, parted and pouting as if sitting up to beg for it. I must eat it, yes I must. It's just too tempting—' Her long tongue went lap, lap, lick, flicking at my clitoris, bringing me to the boil again.

'Oh, you'll make me come, make me come,' I

warned her, as if that was so terrible. 'Yes, do that, do that—' and again my body stiffened, my toes curled and I grasped at her head, pulling her to me and bucking against her mouth. Looking down I saw her hand between her legs, moving rapidly from the wrist. She too went into spasms at about the same time as myself.

'What a pair we are,' Cynthia said on recovering, kissing me over my lips and face, her hand fondling my tits. 'We shall have many an amusement together, and perhaps if you wish, with other nice people. Now let us have a good lunch and then go out to spends lots of money on you, darling girl.'

I had no quarrel with that, suddenly feeling ravenously hungry and deciding that I had definitely landed lucky.

Chapter Thirteen
AFRICA

I wondered, as well I might, just what would ensue with such lustful sexual deviates as the German doctors Lotte and Gunther Pohl so handily placed in the next bungalow to ours. I had had more than my fair share of intimate encounters in my time but had tried on the whole, not always successfully, to play away from home. This latest situation was one I'd never quite envisaged even in my varied experience, the temptations to be faced on our very own doorstep. We had all fucked with each other already and the Pohls, with their outlook on free love and nudism, were evidently not the sort to leave it at that. They were self-confessed tireless libertines.

I hadn't mentioned to Harry that I knew he'd been seduced by the formidable Lotte as I'd undergone similar treatment in their skilled hands. Now I envisaged regular romps taking place between the four of us, starting with early morning naked dips in our pool followed by partner swapping, wife watching and orgies non-stop. Probably with outsiders brought in to add spice and variety. I have nothing at all against any of these activities at the proper time and place, but some sense of propriety had to be maintained. My husband held a responsible senior post with an overseas aid organisation. I had to protect him from the like of the

Pohls. Scandal was the last thing he, or his wife, could afford to be involved in.

Gossip was the very life-blood of the tight white ex-pat community. Hardly anything we did escaped notice with the servants we employed, who provided a valuable network of information, reliably passed on to eager ears. I had plenty to hide but so far had been fortunate enough to get away with my own escapades. With the Pohls I felt I would be no longer in command of the situation, fearing dire consequences if we became involved in their free-living and loving lifestyle. Fortunately the problem became halved when, on the day the lecherous German couple returned from their safari, Harry had to fly off to the Gulf and meet people interested in putting up the aid money for his desert irrigation schemes. I drove him to Entebbe airport and was relieved for once to see him leave. The Pohls I could now handle, I thought. The best-laid plans, however, oft go for nothing, to paraphrase the words of the poet Robert Burns.

I arrived back home after midnight, noting the lights were still burning in the Pohls' domain. My house was silent as the grave and I did not like being on my own at night. I mixed myself a strong gin, downed it and drank another, was on my third when the telephone rang and made me leap at the sound. It was my neighbour Lotte. 'We're having a little party,' she said, 'and we thought of you all by yourself tonight. Do come and join us.'

It was weak of me, I know, and my resolution to keep the Pohls at more than arms' distance went by the board in my lonely state. At least, I told myself, I'd allow no hanky-panky, but when Gunther answered my ring at his verandah stark naked and clasped me in a bear hug of welcome, I at once regretted my decision to join them. Inside in their comfortable lounge, Lotte sat as nude as her husband, big pointy-tipped tits sticking out as she chatted, with a drink in her hand, to two guests still dressed incongruously in evening suits. I knew them by sight as men in government departments that Harry did business with, both big and black and eager.

I accepted a drink but determined I was going to keep my clothes on come what may. Lotte then sat down on the long settee beside Gunther, joining him and immediately allowing her tits to be cupped and fondled. Within moments Gunther had her below him, penetrating her uptilted cunt as she raised her knees for his access. There followed a skilful display of fucking in various positions without Gunther even uncunting, as they say, as the pair rolled about. It was all very arousing viewing, whatever one's ideas on such outrageous flaunting of their sexual partiality. It was meant to be.

The pair were the most blatant exhibitionists I'd ever met, enjoying each other greatly and even more so undoubtedly with an audience present. The two African guests and myself stood entirely fascinated by the show with drinks in our hands, looking down on the energetic coupling from right above them. I felt the familiar ever-lurking twitch of arousal in my lower belly, the moistening of a cunt so ready to lubricate in anticipation. I was being eyed by the men beside me as a candidate to relieve the erections visible in their trouser fronts. It was time to take my leave, I decided, knowing full well I would be expected to join in a general melee.

However, in the prevailing atmosphere of sex and drink, I really did not want to retire from the field. My decision to leave brought protests all around. In my own house I consoled myself with another drink and prepared myself for a lonely bed. The Pohls were dangerous people to know, bringing in outsiders who would undoubtedly boast of the night's orgy. Much as it would have been an experience to have participated, discretion had won the day. I felt well pleased with myself, proud of my willpower. As for the strong arousal I still felt, I would settle for relieving the urge by masturbating. I was about to get into bed when a knock sounded at my window.

Lotte had her face pressed to it when I parted the curtain to look out. She signalled for me to open the door. I put on my dressing gown and went to let her in, determined I had no intention of returning to her house and would say so. She stood on my verandah in a long woollen dressing gown, smiling as I let her in.

'Those two men know my husband,' I told her. 'Don't ever inveigle me in anything like that again. You and Gunther can fuck whom you like but include me out. Who do you think I am?'

'A very sexual woman,' Lotte said calmly. 'We had such a nice time planned—'

'You had better get back to your party then,' I said. 'They'll miss you. Those guests of yours looked ready to rape me. No wonder, with what you and Gunther were doing—'

Lotte nodded. 'They were disappointed you did not stay, Diana. Now they have all left to show Gunther the night clubs of Kampala. I told them they would not need me there. You need me—'

'You what?' I asked. 'Why should I need you?'

'A woman left alone, a woman aroused. I could see by your face, *liebling*. You were brought on watching Gunther and I making fuck, but you rushed away.'

My amusement showed at her brazenness. 'It was quite a show,' I admitted. 'You and that husband of yours do go at it so well. I was about to relieve myself, if you want to know. As a doctor, sexologist, whatever fancy name you give as a therapist, you'll understand that.'

'I knew, I knew,' Lotte said triumphantly. 'That is why I came. You would need me, I know.' She took me in her arms, before I was aware of her intention, kissing me passionately. Her wet thick lips rolled over mine and her tongue slipped into my mouth. Her kiss was long, sweet and as passionate as any man's. Weakly, I could only return it, my body hard against ample and yielding flesh. We stood mouth to mouth, breasts to breasts, belly to belly, straining at each other. I felt something different, a rigid protuberance, an outgrowth, pressing into the fork of my thighs. Lotte made little jerks with her hips, fucking movements against my mound.

'What is it?' I asked. 'What's there?'

I stood back while she slipped the dressing gown from her shoulders. An extra had been added. She was all there, naked and pale white as blonde types are, large tits and uptilted thick nipples, the slight belly and strapping thighs of a buxom woman, plus a huge upright and realistic dummy prick protruding from the split of her cunt, the visible half of a vee-shaped double dildo. How much of it was inserted inside herself I could only guess. The portion rearing up before her looked a good thick foot in length with its ovoid head big as a large egg. The whole was strapped firmly about her.

'My God,' I said, surprised. 'You've come to fuck me—'

'Yes. Have you been dildoed before? By another woman?'

'Not,' I giggled shyly, 'by such as that. It's so big. I couldn't take it—'

'Nonsense,' Lotte said sharply. 'You can and you will, Diana *liebchen*. Other women have said that and then came to love it, its length and the fullness it gives.' Her hand had extended and her fingers were almost idly stroking my cunt lips. 'See, you are already receptive, quite wet down there. It can satisfy as much as any man.

Even more, for it remains the same until you beg it to stop. Go on, touch it, grasp it. Does it not feel nice, like the real thing—?'

The combination of drink, the excitement of the evening and Lotte's expert titillation of my cunt had me fully aroused and willing. I took the upright object in my hand, was at once intrigued by its warmth and natural feel. 'It feels hot,' I said.

'Squeeze the scrotum,' Lotte instructed. 'See what happens.'

My hand slid down the long shaft to the big balls attached below. With the little pressure I applied, an arc of thick greyish liquid shot out from the dildo's split dome. 'It comes!' I giggled again.

'A little mixture of hot water and condensed milk,' Lotte explained. 'I filled it before I came here. It adds greatly to the act. You come and receive an emission, exactly like the real thing. Come now—'

I was led through to my bed, my dressing gown pulled from my shoulders and laid out naked before her. She kissed me slowly, lingeringly from my eyes, mouth, neck and gave special attention to my tits, nipples and cunt. Lotte was so expert she could put a man to shame with her unhurried foreplay. It had me keening and moaning, reaching for her as she drew back, begging for her lewd caresses and kisses, pleading to hold her lovely breasts and suckle on the thick nipples so temptingly kept from me. My hand sought between her legs to draw the big false prick to me. I wanted it penetrating its length inside me, filling my burning cunt. 'Now, now!' I urged her. 'Give it to me now. Fuck me with it—'

'Learn patience,' Lotte said sharply. As I sat up to pull her on to me, she took a step back and raised an arm, bringing down her hand to smack me smartly across my breasts. They stung and I howled. Next she gave me a push back and slapped her palm quite viciously several times over my buttocks. I lay still like a good little girl awaiting her pleasure. She gave me a lengthy tongue-fucking with her large face pressed hard between my opened thighs, making me writhe and clutch at her hair and throw my hips up wildly. When she stood up over me again her hair trailed down over her face and her eyes had a wild lustful look. 'Oh, my beauty,' she said hoarsely. 'You are mine, all mine. To do with as I wish—'

It was with a gasp of utmost relief mixed with gratitude that I took the dildo as she relented and mounted me. The thing slid in, filling me, touching the sides, enlarging my lubricated channel, a monster almost of the proportions of a good-sized cucumber. I reached down and found inches of it still to enter me. Clasped together, with Lotte in the man-superior position as if to the manner born, she grasped my ankles and brought my legs up over her shoulders. My knees were each side of my face and I was bent double, my cunt upthrust for her deeper penetration. Our mouths sucked each other's tongues, our tits mashed and flattened together, bellies now wet with perspiration slapped loudly as we thrust and churned together.

We cried out in our lust, Lotte's shouts sounding cruel and triumphant as she subdued me. Penetrated to the whole length, the false balls thudding against my bottom as she fucked me, I climaxed in a series of spasms and felt the warm liquid jetting into me, pints of it it seemed, until at last, as predicted, I begged her 'No more!'

When Lotte arose from me, the dildo sliding out slowly, my cunt leaked with the concoction she had used. As it ran out of me she lowered her face between my thighs and lapped up the juices. Then she came into bed beside me and nursed me soothingly, cupping each breast to my lips in turn as I fell into weary sleep in her strong arms.

Sex and Mrs Saxon

We were in bed together still when Ndegi the housegirl came through in the morning with my breakfast tray. Without a change of expression she left the tray on my bedside table, returning with a second one for my guest. I wondered if she had seen Harry in that same bed with Lotte during my absence, or been in it herself with him. So what? I thought, sitting up to gratefully drink my orange juice. I was hardly the one to complain. If my husband had fucked them both, I was not the kind who equated an occasional bout with a different partner as cause for breaking up a good marriage. The bed had seen so much action with me I could have carved notches on it. The list was varied. Harry, Cato and his youngest wife, a very attractive Swedish airline pilot met at a party while my husband was away, and now Lotte had dildoed me most successfully. Not wishing to encourage her, I hopped out of bed to shower before she worked her wiles on me again.

I did not see her for the next day or so, avoiding her until she called in with a handsome youth beside her, whom she proudly announced was her son, Viggo. He had joined his parents in East Africa during his school vacation. Like them he was well-built and blonde. How well-built I was soon to find out, for like his father and mother he was a naturist, nudist, whatever it is called when people discard their clothes for reasons other than sex. He swam in our swimming pool naked that day, while his parents were at their surgery, and I swam in my bikini. For his age he was beautifully well-hung, endowed with the same thick penis of considerable length as his father. I noted him looking at me with more than casual interest, deciding he was indeed a chip off the old block.

His sixteenth birthday fell during the following week and Lotte asked me if the party could be held in my garden so that the pool could be used by his young guests. I was more than happy to agree, and the party was well attended by dozens of other boys and girls out on holiday from boarding schools in England and other European countries. My husband was still away and Gunther was on a tour dispensing advice and condoms around villages in the bush in an effort to encourage birth-control methods and reduce the large amount of babies produced locally.

Under a burning African sun Lotte and I cooked dozens of chops, sausages, hamburgers and steak, roasting ourselves in the process over the glowing charcoal grill. The appetite of the youngsters amazed me, demolishing plates of food and washing it down with gallons of Coke, in between rushing about in their games, a deal of which seemed to be throwing the weaker boys and girls into the pool. Lotte and I wore bikinis out of consideration for the young ones present and their parents who came later to take them home. My hair, face and body seemed a cloying mixture of soot, smoke and sweat which trickled down between the tight cleavage of my breasts in the bikini bra, and ran on down front and back, sticking together the crease of my arse in the bikini briefs. Glad I was to see the last guests depart, leaving just Lotte and her boy, who were rescuing cups, glasses and plates from all over the garden. I announced I was going indoors to take a bath, longing to lay back and soak in warm sudsy water.

I took my time over it, luxuriating in being clean all over again, allowing myself a large gin or two as I lolled back in my bath. I would have to watch my intake, I decided, having had the odd gin during the barbecue too. With Harry away, I was drinking more than my usual quota, which was never very much and not very much could make me tipsily happy. I felt I deserved it after a hectic day. When I did at last get out of the bath and was towelling myself dry, Lotte came into my bathroom, shining clean and wearing a fresh floral cotton dress, a highly attractive woman.

'Quite a successful shindig we put on,' I greeted her. 'Was young Viggo pleased with his birthday party?'

As ever at the sight of me standing naked, her eyes lit up and she came close to me. 'You really are a beautiful woman, Diana,' she said, her voice thick with emotion. 'I have quite fallen in love with you. Do let me kiss you—' Her hand trailed down my back, over the mound of my bottom, smoothing, fondling. I attempted to move back but the side of the bath restrained me. Her hand splayed over the cleft of my cheeks, the middle finger curling and entering the divide, stroking my cunt lips and drawing back to apply pressure on the wrinkled serrations of my bum hole. Her fingertip entered me.

'Damn you, no, Lotte,' I tried to say sternly, surprisingly short of breath. 'It's not on. Not now or any other time. I'm a happily married woman—' It was all I could come up with.

Lotte gave a short laugh. 'Since when does that have to mean a married woman cannot have little extra pleasures? Did you not enjoy sleeping with your Lotte? What about making love with your house servant?'

'You said that would remain our secret,' I reminded her uneasily. Her finger probed me, making me arch my back in the tormenting pleasure of it. 'I thought I could trust you,' I complained. 'This is blackmail—'

'But such nice blackmail,' Lotte smiled. 'And I have arranged a special treat for you. There. Let me kiss you now. Your lips are so soft, so lovely and kissable.' Her other hand, palm extended, rubbed across my nipples. 'See, they cannot lie. How big and tight they become.' She held me tightly with the hand behind me, cupping my bottom and drawing me close. Her kiss was long and fierce, her tongue curling in my mouth. 'Turn,' she ordered. 'Turn around.'

I presented my back to her and she bent me over the bath. Feet apart, my buttock cheeks were parted and she drew her hand slowly up and down from my cunt to the tight puckered ring of my anus. She sensuously stroked my outer lips, slipped a finger inside, cocked her thumb and penetrated my arsehole. Finger and thumb seemed to meet, separated only by a thin membrane, making me squirm and moan in the extremity of reluctant pleasuring. 'Damn you!' I cursed.

'You don't mean that,' she laughed softly. 'You love it. I want to hear you admit you love it.'

'You know bloody well I do, bitch,' I said, shoulders hunched, gripping the edge of the bath to steady myself.

'Just a thumb and finger but how you wriggle on them,' Lotte said meanly. 'You cannot resist sexual enjoyment of any kind, Diana. You should not try. Are you ready to fuck for a new young lover? As a favour to him and to me? As a good experience for yourself—?'

'Certainly not!' I swore. 'I told you before, don't ever include me in your schemes. How dare you—'

Lotte continued moving her finger and thumb in me. 'It would be just for this once. You would be the perfect partner. I can assure you then it would be our great secret. Just as I would never breathe a word about your black lover Cato.'

'You crafty German procurer,' I said angrily. 'You've worked me up just to get your way with me—'

'Your clitoris is so pronounced, Diana. You are ready for sex.'

'I just can't fuck for anybody,' I argued, my will weakening as her probing had me rotating my arse on her wrist. 'Who is he? I won't if he knows my husband—'

'Come and see,' Lotte said. She led me determinedly

down the passageway to the living room. Lotte went through into the room but I hung back in my nude state. I heard voices, looked around the door to see whom she was so eager I was to make love to. I decided Lotte was the limit. If my mood had not been so heightened by the gins and her arousing me so well, I would not even have considered the matter. But as usual the unusual intrigued me. Standing in the centre of the room beside his mother, hair shining after a shower, wearing only clean shorts and flip-flops, young Viggo smiled broadly at the sight of my face.

'I wish to thank you for giving me such a fine birthday party,' he said, bowing his head mannerly. 'You were most kind.'

I shot an amazed look at his mother, who stood beaming beside her boy. 'Lotte, are you mad? How could you?' I said. 'What have you told Viggo? More, what have you promised him?'

'That there could be another birthday surprise for him. It could be the best gift you could give him, Diana.'

'Thank you very much, I'm sure,' I said caustically. 'And what might Gunther have to say about that, or Viggo himself? I'm sure he'd prefer a girl of his own age when he gets around to it—'

'His father and I agreed it would be the best initiation for Viggo; an experienced older woman to take his virginity; to guide him, instruct him in the correct manner of making love. You should be pleased to be his first.'

'Why not let nature take its course?' I said. 'In time Viggo will meet a girl—'

'And the sex will more than likely be a great disappointment to them both,' Lotte countered. 'The knowledge is so important. You know Gunther and I strongly recommend it. We have taught Viggo the facts, he's read the books, but has never experienced the real thing. Don't say you refuse, Diana. My lips would be sealed on this and all other secrets forever.'

'I'm glad to hear that,' I said, 'but really this is the most ridiculous conversation I've ever had.' I think I was beginning to see the amusing aspect of it all, and I had to admit young Viggo did look youthful and handsome. 'What does he say about all this?' I added from behind the shelter of the door. 'Wouldn't you prefer to have your first experience with some nice young girl, Viggo?'

For the first time Viggo spoke up on his own behalf. 'No. I would sooner have you, Mrs Saxon. I agree with my parents. It would be very nice. I want my first to be with you.'

That was definite enough. 'There,' his mother said. 'Surely everyone is in agreement. And do come out from behind that stupid door, Diana. I cannot talk to just a head.'

I supposed she was right. The situation seemed so agreed without my outright refusal that I found myself walking into the living room to join them. Undoubtedly Viggo had seen many a naked female on naturist holidays with his parents. All the same his interested young eyes ogled my body. His gaze travelled over my breasts approvingly and down to my thighs and the mound between with its returning bush of auburn hair. The front of his shorts bulged promisingly.

'Very well,' I conceded. A handsome youth and a virgin was mine to instruct and show the way. There were worse chores I could think of. 'As it's his birthday then. But I know I'll regret all this in the morning—'

'Oh, Mrs Saxon,' Viggo enthused. 'Then I am to be with you until morning!' He turned to his mother, speaking excitedly in German. She nodded her agreement.

'Yes, better the whole night,' Lotte said.

I hadn't quite meant that, but the cast was set. 'Then first of all he'd better stop calling me Mrs Saxon if he's going to sleep with me. Diana would be more in keeping. Any instructions from you, Lotte, seeing as how you've arranged all this?'

'He is in your hands,' his mother said, delighted. 'I'll leave and see you in the morning.' She kissed my cheek as if in grateful thanks. 'He will always remember you for this, *liebchen*. Even for you it will be memorable.'

Her going left Viggo and I at somewhat of a loss, her strong personality missing. 'Would you like something to eat or drink before – before,' I offered him, unsure how to phrase the next words.

'I should like to go to the bed, please,' Viggo said in his excellent school English. I'll just bet you would, I thought, standing beside him naked as a jay bird. I told him to go through to the bedroom at the far end of the corridor. It had its own door and I had already firmly decided he would be out before my housegirl came with breakfast. She had, I considered, seen enough people in my bed.

I needed time also to consider further the odd situation I'd once again found myself in, needing breathing space and another drink. Pouring myself a very large neat vodka at the sideboard I felt trapped, coerced into giving myself to Lotte's boy more for her own salacious pleasure than to teach him the joys of sex. I took a second drink with me and braced myself to go through to the bedroom and Viggo. He stood by the bedside waiting expectantly, still wearing his shorts, seemingly a nice well-mannered lad. As I'd gone along that far, I supposed I had better make a start.

'Firstly,' I said, making it up as I went along with my protégé, 'I think you'd better get acquainted with the important parts of a woman's body. The sexual parts, where she likes to be admired and touched. Kissed.'

'I have kissed girls, Mrs Saxon.'

'Yes, I'm sure you have,' I said hesitantly. 'I was thinking more of the – the breasts, vagina and such. Do you understand me, Viggo?'

'Of course. I have seen women naked but never touched.' He nodded eagerly at me. 'I think it could be very nice.'

'Would you like to feel my breasts?'

'Please may I?'

I took both his hands and placed them palms inward over my tits. He gave them a squeeze and jiggled them about, cupped them and pulled them apart, hefted them as if to test their weightiness. He seemed very confident, pinching my nipples and pulling them outwards. 'They are big breasts,' he said. 'So firm and nice to hold. I like this very much.'

'You've done this before?' I had to say. I liked it very much myself, his young hands on my breasts.

'No. I just did what I wanted to do. You do not mind?'

'Well, no. You played with my breasts very nicely. Some are not so gentle. You like to pull my nipples?'

'Do you like? I like.'

I admitted I did. 'They go stiff, grow bigger as a woman is aroused—'

'Like yours are,' Viggo said. 'These nipples are quite hard and long now. I have also read that to suck upon them is a pleasure to both male and female.'

'Suck them, please, if you wish,' I said weakly, my arousal such that I welcomed his suggestion. He bent his head and I cupped each tit for him as he suckled hard on my nipples. It seemed the whole preposterous act of tutoring the boy with my body was a tremendous turn-on such as I'd rarely known. He was as aroused it seemed, his hand going down to stroke me between my legs as I fed him, feeling at my cunt lips and beyond. 'Let us move on,' I found the strength to say. 'Would you like to see a vagina?'

He would, he announced readily, and I therefore lolled back across the bed with my legs parted and knees drawn up for his education. There is always a special salacious thrill for women like myself to flaunt their secret parts. He gave my lips and slit the closest inspection while I lay wordless. 'The English word for it is cunt, yes?' he asked.

'Yes.'

His fingers probed, held open the lips. 'This is the clitoris, is it not?' he asked, tickling it. 'I have seen pictures of it, of course.'

I found it the hardest thing to restrain a wistful sigh and move my hips to his inspection of my cunt, fingering it up so well as he did. His touches on my clitoris had me on the verge of a strong climax I sought to suppress. 'May I see you now from the rear side?' he suggested. 'Turned over. I should like to see you that way.'

I rolled over, on my hands and knees, my bum up and beginning to feel I was the one being taught a lesson. My cheeks were parted and my cunt well fingered again. 'Please,' I had to utter, starting to tremble as if my body was out of my control, trying to stop myself pushing back on to his busy hand. 'Please, dear—'

'Have I done something wrong, Mrs Saxon?' he asked.

'No, no! I – I'm getting ahead of you. I mean I shouldn't be,' I gasped. 'You're making me too excited. I shall come—'

'But that is what you wish to teach me,' the boy said reasonably. 'To bring a woman excitement. It is very good. I like to give you excitement—'

'Oh good God,' I moaned, letting it all go as I

orgasmed in involuntary spasms with his several fingers inside me, an explosive come that made my arse quake unrestrained against his hand. A glance behind saw him divest himself of his shorts, a moment later I felt a stiff young prick enter me to its full length, continuing my series of comes as it pounded my cunt. Shattering comes they were as he continued fucking me from the rear, straining against my rotating buttocks, buffetting them with his thighs. He reached under me, grasping my tits for leverage, his shunting cock as rigid as only the virile young can attain, almost splitting me in its urgency.

'Yes, yes!' I heard myself crying out in encouragement. 'Fuck me, fuck me harder. Don't you dare stop, boy!' And neither did he, his balls thudding below my cunt, his shaft hammering home its message. Then he was crying out too, in his native German, hoarse croaks while I brayed and whinnied in my ecstasy. I felt the jerks of his coming, the hot spurts drenching me, and his gradual easing of strokes before he fell off from above me and lay prone on his back on the bed. Our strenuous fucking, the huffing and puffing that followed, precluded speech. When at last he sat up over me his face was a picture of delight.

'Thank you for the lesson,' he grinned. 'Was I quite good?'

'Too good,' I had to say. 'I think I've been taken for a ride. You've done that before, naughty boy. No innocent inexperienced virgin fucks like that.'

'That will be our secret,' Viggo said proudly. 'My parents think I've never had sex. I kept silent because they promised one day they would find a woman for me. One like you I hoped.'

'Crafty boy,' I was forced to say admiringly. 'So who have you been fucking back in Germany?'

'Two cousins, sisters,' he announced proudly. 'Also some of the village girls. The nurse at the school

I attend. She is your age. I like the older women best.'

His hands fondled my breasts gently and he bent to kiss them. Then he kissed my mouth, long and lingeringly with his tongue exploring. 'We shouldn't be doing this, you and I,' I complained. 'You are such a sweet boy it's hard to resist you. As you seem to be the expert, what do you suggest we do next?'

'You have heard of fellatio?' he asked.

'It's the fancy word for sucking a penis.' I looked down at his young prick, still semi-erect, smooth and pale white with none of the gnarls and veins of older versions. I took it in my hand, felt it pulse in my fingers, thicken. Wordlessly I bent over and covered it with my lips, sucking it to full vigour. I cupped his balls, heard his pleasurable sigh. Then he had pushed me flat and was upon me again, embedded as I curled my legs around his waist. 'You could make me too fond of this,' I admitted as we fucked. 'Me, old enough to be your mother. Oh, but it's heaven, your young stiff prick. When do you have to go back to your school?'

'Not for a week or more,' Viggo breathed into my face. 'I shall call every chance to fuck you—' I had feared getting entangled with his parents; now it seemed the son would be my lover during his vacation. His fucking was slower, beautiful.

'Never a word of this to anyone ever,' I said in the final throes. 'If we are to meet—' A warning, I imagine, said by many a woman to a young fancy man who was bedding her.

'You want me to come to you?' Viggo cried delightedly. 'To be your lover?'

'Lord help me, yes, I can't help myself,' I promised him as I entered that helpless stage of not caring as I was coming. 'Only we must be careful. While my husband is away, yes do!'

I can hardly say we slept together, if sleep is what one does between making love all night. There were fitful dozes but his youth, eagerness and virility had him aroused time after time. If I lapsed into sleep I was aroused by his hands roving over me, his kisses on my mouth and breasts, his breath so fresh and sweet. To me it was like regaining my youth, a teenager pair exploring and experimenting with all the delights our bodies gave each other. I lost count of all the times he mounted me or I him. By dawn I reluctantly made him slip away, with many kisses and sighs. I could hardly believe it of myself, lying in the rumpled bed thinking back on a night of passion one rarely experiences. I slept to be awakened by the telephone's ring.

It was Viggo's mother, speaking excitedly. 'Viggo came home so pleased, I can't thank you enough, Diana. Was it as good for you? His first, and your first too—'

'What do you mean?' I said. 'My first virgin?'

'Yes. I also mean your first father and son. Gunther and now Viggo.'

I replaced the receiver to return to my bed to sleep off the effects of the night pleasantly, refraining from disillusioning Lotte. She was very mistaken on both counts.

Chapter Fourteen
ENGLAND

Lady Bellinger's idea of shopping was to stride into the most exclusive West End couturier's or jeweller's and demand the immediate and full attention of the staff. She invariably got it. I was fitted with coats and dresses for all occasions with the accessories to match: stockings, shoes and the most exotic underwear of silk and lace. She would then, with myself in attendance and Atherton loaded up to his chin with boxes, sweep imperiously out of the premises, everyone bowing and scraping and a liveried doorman saluting. It amused me to recall how this venerated being had bent over for her bare bum to be belted by her chauffeur prior to the pair of them fucking like wantons. The same chauffeur who stood respectfully to attention obeying her every order.

No money or the mention of it ever changed hands. No doubt her credit was as solid as the Bank of England. The way she lived, the way I now lived, suggested great wealth. My protected position in her household did not go to my head however. I remained my own person, such was my upbringing. While enjoying my new lifestyle and making the most of it, I imagined a time would come when Cynthia Bellinger tired of me, or more likely I tired of her. There were so many opportunities in life, avenues to explore, experiences to gain, especially for an attractive girl. Meanwhile I amused Cynthia both sexually and as a trophy. I was her kept girl, her toy, a pretty thing like the paintings, statues and ornaments in the Park Lane residence. She loved to show me off to her guests as her supposed ward. They admired my colouring, face and figure. The male guests eyed me as a desirable fuck, and the women cooed and petted me suggestively – such a sweet innocent sixteen-year-old!

Patience Bailey, the upstairs maid who tidied my room, made my bed, ran my morning bath and generally looked after me, was a well-built young countrywoman, unmarried and in her early thirties, a typical domestic of her time. From very much a working-class family like my own, attempts to make friends with her, to enjoy a chat with one of my own kind from the real world for a change, met with little response at first. I had to ask her what she thought I was doing in such a house? That I was as much a paid servant as she despite my exalted position. She was wary. Lady Bellinger's previous kept girls had treated the serving staff like dirt and been hated. However, once Patience had decided I was the genuine article, she loved a giggle and a chat with me. I learned a lot about the household, both upstairs and down, and found not all was as it seemed. Lady Cynthia's extravagances were not subsidised by family wealth so much as by her generous friends for whom she arranged parties. 'Famous for them, she is,' Patience told me darkly. 'Some of them going on all weekend. You wait and see,' she added ominously.

Of course when Cynthia was present Patience kept her place, but in our private moments we compared notes on our lives and I uncovered more of the secrets of our mistress. Porlock, the family butler, had revealed much to Patience when his tongue was loosened at times below stairs after imbibing too well of the Bellinger's wine and spirits. Lady Cynthia's lifestyle, it was patent, depended a great deal on her skill at putting on various entertainments for the rich and famous. Patience herself was a Dorset girl, daughter of a casual farm-labourer who drank his paltry wages, and her position in the Bellinger's employ, she admitted, meant witnessing and even allowing all sorts of 'funny goings-on' as she put it, 'embarrassed'. The salary received, sent home to keep the wolf from the door for her old mother and a village-idiot brother, made her stay and put up with unusual demands as and when required.

One of those demands I was to witness following a morning bath, sitting at my vanity unit in a silken robe with Patience in attendance. Lady Bellinger came into my bedroom in her negligee, admiring the auburn hair which fell down my back, shining from Patience's brushing. Cynthia bent to kiss my neck and sat beside me on the long padded stool, a hand slipping into my robe and cupping my left breast, a fingertip flicking the nipple. 'Shall we have a little amusement with Patience?' she whispered to me. 'It's quite fun to tease the country bumpkin.'

She smiled sweetly at the maid and asked her about her mother. 'Keeping well, is she?' Patience curtsied and said shyly that all was well at home in Dorset. She became edgy and I suspected well knew what she was in for. 'I shall send them another hamper from home farm,' Cynthia announced graciously. 'Some cured ham and a pheasant or two. Some fruit and such. Would your mother like fresh vegetables?'

'Thank you, milady, but my brother grows all the vegetables we need in the garden. He's good at that. But the ham and fruit would be most grateful—'

'Ham and fruit can't be grateful, silly girl,' Cynthia said. 'It's your mother who ought to be grateful. You too, I hope.'

'Oh yes, milady,' Patience agreed quickly, bobbing her knees. 'Ever so grateful. We all are—'

'Has your pubic hair grown back again, Bailey?' inquired Cynthia, speaking casually.

'I'm not sure what you mean, milady,' Patience answered nervously. She fidgeted from foot to foot, agitated.

'Pubic hair, the growth on your fanny, stupid girl. That which surrounds your cunt so luxuriently. Has it returned?'

Patience blushed to the roots of her thick dark hair under her maid's cap. She whispered shyly, 'Yes, milady.'

'I can't hear you. Speak up.'

'Yes, milady. Quite grown back—'

'Patience had her lower hair shaved at a party here that got rather boisterous and jolly,' Cynthia informed me. 'She served the *hors d'oeuvres* and the gentlemen present demanded to see how hirsute such a strapping country lass could be. It wasn't too bad for you, was it, Bailey?'

'No, milady,' Patience said with lowered eyes.

'The guests did make it well worth her while,' Cynthia continued to me. 'They were quite generous to you, weren't they?'

'Yes,' whispered Patience, greatly shamed.

'Quite a tidy sum as I remember. A collection was taken. Your mother would be delighted when you sent it home, I'm sure.' As Patience did not answer, Cynthia urged her to speak up.

'Yes, milady. Mother was very happy with the money I was given—'

'Then some good came of a little harmless fun,' Cynthia stated. Patience stood in an agony of shyness and embarrassment. She was a simple soul, village-school educated, and Cynthia described her exactly in her next words to me. 'Don't be so soft-hearted, Diana,' she reproved me, gauging that I was not amused by her teasing of her maidservant. 'The girl's a robust buxom village wench and it doesn't really affect her. Back home she'd be fair game for any local yokel to put her in the family way, probably after some farmer had taken her virginity if she hadn't lost it at home already. In those little labourer's cottages fathers or brothers have been known to do the deed. Almost an accepted country practice—'

Patience just hung her head but I had to speak. Cynthia obviously had the morals of a tomcat, or rather a bitch always on heat, enjoying her salacious talk. 'I was brought up in a cramped cottage,' I said. 'I know my parents wouldn't approve of you either. Leave Patience alone—'

'But she enjoys it, my dear. I know she loves it,' Cynthia assured me. 'You'll learn. People like her try to stand on their dignity or whatever. Think it isn't nice. But that merely greatly increases their total enjoyment. Really she doesn't mind,' which all was said while Cynthia kissed my neck and cheek, her hand resuming fondling my titties and nipples, always bound to lower my resistance. 'Watch now—' And Patience stood by uneasily, as if we were discussing someone else and awaited her orders.

'She's so hairy,' Cynthia went on, 'we had never seen the like. Her armpits sprouting great tufts as well. So let me see how the growth has returned, Bailey. Take off your clothes.'

'I don't want to, milady,' Patience whimpered.

'Nonsense. We are all female here. Do as you are told. I want Miss Diana to see you—'

Patience mumbled a further protest, glancing at me with burning cheeks. I had been annoyed at the teasing the maid was suffering but was curiously eager to see her naked, she was such a voluptuous figure of a woman. Her reluctance too, seemingly genuine, added to the expectancy of the occasion. Patience doffed her little lace cap, removed the short frilly apron, then slowly unbuttoned her grey maid's dress with fumbling fingers. All the clothes she removed she folded neatly on a chair beside my bed. She stood silent in a cotton vest that bulged with big full breasts, the prominent nipples almost piercing holes in the thin white material. The swell of her tits was so outstanding that the vest was drawn up revealing a white belly and a deep navel.

Below that were her elasticated knickers and grey lisle stockings held up by garters of black elastic. Where the stocking tops ended and up to the legs of her knickers was revealed several inches of very strong rounded thighs. I noted at her crotch how the tightly drawn cotton material of her knickers made a fine bulge, the fork of her legs prominent with a plump cunt mound.

'Hurry, girl,' Cynthia snapped.

Patience drew off the vest uncovering two large trembling tits, pointed and as shapely as full-sized rugby balls standing out from her chest. They drooped forward as she bent to draw down her knickers, fat tits becoming long tits and their mass and weight swinging them apart, thimble-like nipples pointing to the floor. I had a desire to fondle them, feel their rounds and weight in my hands, suck upon the teats that stuck out inviting a mouth. She stood, knickers divested. Between her ample thighs was indeed the hairiest quim I could imagine, a triangular mass of thick dark hair starting almost at her belly button and going on down to disappear between her thighs. Her armpits too had the same thick hair hanging in tufts.

'Keep your stockings on, Bailey,' Cynthia ordered. 'Have you ever seen such a hairy creature?' she asked me. 'Quite a shapely gal too, if you like them

Rubenesque. A lot of gentlemen do, don't they, Bailey? You've had your admirers here—'

'Yes, milady,' Patience whispered.

'Note the little semblance of a dark moustache on her upper lip,' Cynthia continued to me. 'That was the clue, the giveaway that she'd be hairy, one of my guests decided. Lord Bertie Willenhall actually, the devil. It was he who shaved you that night, wasn't it, Bailey?'

'I think so, milady.'

'It was, but I see it has all grown back into a veritable forest. Come here to me, girl.'

Patience shuffled forward as if unable to disobey, her big breasts trembling at her slightest movement until she stood before the seated Cynthia. 'Such udders on the girl,' said her mistress, lifting each one in her hands, releasing them and seeing them spring back to stand out proud on the maid's chest. 'Firm as marble, they positively defy gravity. And look how her nipples are tight and pointing up. Are you not aroused, Bailey?'

'I – I don't know, milady—'

Cynthia humphed as if in disdain, bidding the girl to stand still with her legs apart. With long fingers with vivid red nails she prised open Patience's outer lips, holding back the folds and revealing the pink interior of her cunt. 'Hardly a virgin's quim, eh, Bailey?'

'No, milady,' Patience agreed quietly.

'I should think not. Now turn around and bend over.'

The girl did as directed, facing away leaning forward with her feet spread. Her large plump arse was both rounded and wide, fully fleshed cheeks as white as cream. 'A fine bottom, made for corking if ever one was,' Cynthia opined. 'And for the whip.' She ran a languid hand over both mounds. 'Such cheeky cheeks. They ask for it. Have they ever been birched, Bailey?'

'Yes, milady. You know that—'

Patience's answers were mumbled so softly and shamefully that I had to strain to hear her replies, such as they were being merely agreements to Cynthia's leading questions. I was sure it was all a charade, almost a rehearsed dialogue between milady and the maid. Cynthia had a mocking smile on her lips, nodding at me as the routine proceeded to gauge my reaction. Here was a supposedly sophisticated woman, nearer fifty than forty, making sport with a naive and helpless servant. For my benefit as much as any, I guessed, bringing me into her fold, a circle of compliance. That in the near future I would be called upon to entertain her guests, I now had no doubt.

I wondered just how many gentlemen visitors had seen Patience put through this rigmarole. But there was an excitement about it, a heightened atmosphere of power and eroticism that was arousing me. The naked girl bent over, seemingly completely in her mistress's power, blushing, whimpering, obviously embarrassed and awkward, yet allowing it and perhaps highly aroused herself even if against her will. It was tempting to reach out and touch all the ample charms thus presented, but it was Cynthia's show and she was doing it very well. I watched fascinated. Sexually motivated creature that I couldn't help being, it seemed I was a mere beginner and had not dreamed of the variations of licentious behaviour possible.

'Part those cheeks, Bailey,' ordered Cynthia. Patience reached back with both hands and pulled each globe apart, revealing the darker skin of the deep cleft, the puckered ring of her arsehole and the secret place, the curved furrow so surrounded with tangled hair. 'Yes,' Cynthia said, using the self-same words Atherton had used about her. 'That's a well-fucked cunt.' She stroked the parted opening, inserted a finger and Patience at once stiffened her body, straightening her back.

'Over, girl! Stay as you were,' Cynthia said sharply. Patience resumed her position, presenting a fine target which received several sharp smacks, leaving pink imprints on both cheeks. Cynthia continued her fondling, two fingers now probing and stroking her maid's cleft. Patience let out a low moan and seemed to squirm against the hand working under her bottom.

'Aah, ooh—' went Patience.

'The horny creature is in wet flesh,' Cynthia smirked. 'She's positively drenched. Aroused and lubricating freely. Do you like this, Bailey?'

'Please, milady. Do stop—'

'Nonsense. Why, you tremble. Of course you are loving it. Bend over more.'

Patience bending so under the fingering had her backside giving little leaps and jerks before our faces. I was sure she could not hold out much longer, shaking as if she was having a convulsion. She gasped and Cynthia nodded with satisfaction. 'Her first climax. She always has several when we do this. What a large clitoris the girl has, I've noticed it before.' She continued stroking and probing the maid's cunt. 'Just a few touches and tickles and Bailey is quite set in motion. When were you last had, girl?'

In her throes, Patience positively stuttered. 'L-L-Last evening, milady—'

'Who did the deed? Was it Atherton or Robert?'

'No-ooo. Porlock. It was Porlock—'

'The old lecher,' Cynthia laughed. 'He's still at it, is he? Where was it? In your bottom?'

'Y-yes, yes—'

'Then you'll like my thumb up your bum,' Cynthia decided, inserting just that while her two nearest fingers continued to play on Patience's clitoris. The girl seemed to go mad, bucking and jerking even more. 'She's spending on my hand again,' Cynthia reported gleefully, while the girl's motions became a series of shivers and shaking from the knees upwards. She gave out a loud moan as Cynthia withdrew her hand, reaching out to support herself on the edge of my dressing table. Her bottom received a last friendly slap. It was all so exciting to watch, so perfectly conceived to make Patience come while we watched her in her helpless throes that I found myself clapping my hands in delight. I would have had Cynthia do as much to me.

'I couldn't help it,' Patience cried looking at me, as if apologising for her behaviour. 'I couldn't help myself, miss. She makes me come, she does—'

'You may go, Bailey,' Cynthia told her. Patience dressed hurriedly and fled the room. 'There,' said her tormentor. 'She loved it. How can one come like that and not love what you are doing to them.' She turned my head and kissed my mouth, pushing in her tongue, giving a fond squeeze to each of my tits in turn. I held her close in return, aroused and desiring sex with her, hoping she would continue but she held me at arms' distance. 'You horny little minx, that little exhibition has got you aroused too, hasn't it?' she teased. 'But we haven't time, dear. Lots to do this afternoon. Don't worry, there'll be satisfaction enough for you later.'

'I hope so,' I said pouting. I was really feeling neglected after Patience being serviced so well before me. Cynthia patted my cheek reassuringly.

'Be dressed by noon. I've an appointment at the art gallery, then we lunch at the Savoy before going on to a little party. You'll be meeting such nice people and they'll be glad to meet you. It doesn't hurt to leave you feeling so unsatisfied; you'll be all the keener for it, sweet child.'

She left me, her fingers trailing my cheek and leaving me rather annoyed. Much as a visit to the art dealer's, the lunch and a party to follow was something to look forward to, I was left in quite a state of unease. It was probable that Cynthia had arranged it all to have me left aroused for what she had planned for later. Cynthia's expert masturbation of her maid had certainly worked me up to a state of yearning – and I knew very well for what it was I really yearned. Sex play with Cynthia was good, a nice diversion, and the end result was satisfaction if any number of strong climaxes qualified as that. But I had not been pierced by a male prick since my last fuck with Geddes before leaving Scotland. I missed penetration by a good cock more desperately than I had thought. Sex with women was nice, but I knew I wanted a good fucking.

I sat dreamily, thinking back to Geddes and his rigid thickness filling my cunt, his weight upon me, the strength of his thrusts. I became awash with memories, my hand going down between my thighs to still the palpitations of a throbbing cunt. I remembered the excitement and anticipation of waiting in a deserted lane and Geddes' old car approaching. Then both of us getting out of our clothes in the cramped rear on the long seat, his eyes devouring my young charms, my so-well developed breasts and the cunt I flaunted to delight him and excite myself so much. The hot flush of lustful pleasure at the moment of being taken, urging him on with the talk we used to further arouse ourselves. There were the afternoons with Mr Saxon too, his more gentle and slower fucking which had also given strong orgasms. I wanted more of the same, I thought, staring at my reflection in the dressing table mirror wistfully.

A light tap sounded at my door and I called, 'Enter', expecting Patience to return to finish her work in my room. Instead it was old Porlock who came in furtively. 'Did she bring Patience off?' he asked conspiratorially. 'She's done it before—'

I nodded dully, emerging still from my thoughts. The fat old butler looked at me with lust staring out of his eyes. 'You're a young beauty, miss,' he croaked in his passion. 'God, but you are. You couldn't half do me a power of good—'

'Where's Patience?' I asked.

'Downstairs, she came down all of a tremble. Still shaking she was.'

'Lucky Patience,' I giggled.

Porlock cocked his head sideways as if considering what he was about to say. 'If you wants a good come like the maid had, miss, I would be happy to oblige.'

'Would you, Porlock?' I teased. 'Just for my sake? How kind you are.' Since he had licked me out so thoroughly there had been no further advances from him. Atherton had made none either, despite the lewd looks he always had for me. Cynthia or Patience was with me a good part of each day, and Porlock and Atherton had their duties to fulfill.

'Not kind, miss. You got such a lovely cunt on you, that's why. Lovely to suck out. Even lovelier to fuck, I'll be bound. I'd love to do you proper, a right pleasuring—'

'Old bugger,' I had to say, amused by his boldness. 'And you that had Patience only last night. Up her bum, too, I believe.'

'I does it that way to save the lass getting with child,' the old ram said gravely. 'She has an old mother depending on her wages—'

'Very noble of you,' I laughed at him. 'What would Lady Cynthia say if she knew you were talking to me like this?'

'When my prick's up begging for it, like as now, miss, I don't care. Seeing you gets me hard. Then I has to take Patience or cook to relieve myself. I go stiff as a poker thinking about fucking you, I do.'

Enough was enough, I decided. 'I must dress, Porlock. You'll have to run a cold tap over your cock, won't you?'

'I'd rather put it up your cunt, miss,' he said solemnly. 'Look at what you've done to me—'

I watched him unbutton his trousers and lower them to his knees. My hand went up to cover my mouth to stifle a laugh at the sight of his thick hairy legs, but the rearing prick he uncovered by lifting his shirt stopped me. Over a grand big pair of tight balls stood the long stalk of stiffened flesh, at least eight or nine inches, almost vibrating with rigidity. The pulsing in my cunt and lower belly was like it had a will of its own, drawn to the massive erection. I reached out to test it, curl my fingers around its girth, amazed at its stiffness. It was like an iron bar, yet warm to the touch.

'Go on, miss, that's right,' Porlock urged. 'Feel how it is. It hurts when its like that. Needs to shaft a nice cunt to find relief. Gives relief too, so it does, you'll see—'

'I haven't time, it's too risky,' I said, trying not to weaken. Tempting as it was, he really was too old, it would be like my grandfather fucking me. Was I that desperate? Besides, Cynthia was in the adjoining room.

'Take off your robe, miss,' he pleaded. 'Let me see your tits and quim. I want to see you all in the buff like before.'

I let the robe slip to the carpet, standing before him naked and trembling, my arousal mixed with fear of discovery. 'You must go,' I told him, not sounding very positive.

'Such lovely upstanding titties,' Porlock praised me. 'And that neat little cunt. Let me fuck you, miss—'

'Oh, Porlock, it's too risky—' I began. The last thing I wanted was for Cynthia to enter the room to find her butler fucking me, much as I wanted a prick up me right then. He in turn reached out to touch up my cunt and I let him, a thick stubby finger slipping inside. I could plainly hear it squelching about in my juicy state. My bottom resting on the dressing table, legs slightly apart, I began to move against his hand moaning my pleasure as he roved his finger in a circular movement around my clitoris. 'Yes, yes,' I told him. 'Hurry and make me come like that—'

'I can feel you,' he said, 'all warm and wet in there. You needs more than a finger-frigging, miss. You needs a good cock.' He took my hand and placed it around his shaft again. 'Come and sit on this—'

'What?' I asked.

'Squat over it. Long and thick does the trick. Goes right in all the way, it does.' His ruddy features took on a sly look. 'Why, you've never done it that way, have you, miss?'

I hadn't. Both Mr Saxon and Geddes had been 'mount the woman' men. My experience thus far of varying positions had been very limited. Only when viewing young Harry Saxon and his so-called Aunt Margaret fucking had I gleaned that there were other ways. Ways that looked intriguing as she had taken the superior position over the boy. Porlock, watching me, frigging me to higher arousal, sensed he had further lowered my resistance. He sat down on the edge of the bed and lay back, trousers down around his ankles and his shirt rucked up showing his thick-veined cock in all its proudness, the purplish plum-like circumcised helmet atop a shaft as straight and stiffly upright as a flagpole.

'Over me on the bed, girl,' he urged. 'Hurry now. It goes right up your belly to your throat it does—'

All thought of Cynthia being nearby disappeared. I climbed on the bed and shuffled forward on my knees until they were placed either side of his waist, poised with my cunt directly above his great stander. The glistening knob of it brushed against my outer lips. 'You put it up there,' he said excitedly. 'Just direct the head of it and sit down. There!'

This last was uttered as I held the knob to my cunt and lowered myself over it, feeling impaled on the whole shaft as it penetrated deep inside my channel, feeling its very hardness and shape in me, the head nudging I know not what. I groaned my pleasure at the intruder's length and girth, began moving on it slowly at first, then pushing down in a grinding motion as the delightful torment demanded. To prolong the exquisite feeling, denying the surge of a come rising from deep in my cunt, for a moment I sat with his balls tucked in the forked nest of my thighs. He lifted his body, urging me back to the up and downward movement over him, thrusting against me. 'Oh, Porlock,' I moaned. 'It's heaven—'

'You takes it well,' he praised me. 'Right to the hilt. It's a good nine inches up you there. Go at it, young miss, Porlock will watch out for you. He don't spunk until he wants to. You just pleasure yourself, you're safe with me—'

Being made pregnant by the lecherous old butler had been the last thing on my mind during such a fucking. That he should assure me he had considered that possibility, a likely one the way I'd thrown all caution to the winds in my wanton riding of his cock, had little effect on the heightened state I had reached. The surge returned to my innards, I groaned and grunted over him, my tits bobbing like wild things as I rode the last furious moments. I felt his hand go around my bottom, seeking between the cheeks, a finger pressing my tight ring and entering to the knuckle in my back passage, invading further as my frenzied up-and-down movements quickened. The noises I heard, the whimpering of a girl in an agony of bliss, I recognised as coming from me. How many times I came I could not count, a continuing ripple that at last ceased and I fell sideways gasping for air.

When I recovered somewhat I looked up to see Porlock leaning over me, kneeling, his still erect weapon before my face, before my lips. 'Such a randy little thing you really are,' he said, pleased with his effort and my response. 'It would have been so easy to have spunked up you, but we couldn't have that, could we, young miss? Now you finish old Porlock like a good lass. Where it's safe—'

Before I knew it he had breached my lips, forced entry into my mouth. Still recovering from such a draining succession of climaxes, I was hardly aware what he intended. His prick felt warm and alive, nudging my throat as I began sucking on it as if natural to do so. He stroked my hair, murmured his pleasure, and I put a hand to cup the heavy balls. It was what I had seen Margaret do to Harry Saxon, and I wanted to do the same. Soon Porlock was grunting, jerking, and I felt the gushing in my mouth. I swallowed, sucking and swallowing, still as if in a dream until the rigidity had gone and what was left slipped from my tongue and lips. I watched Porlock rise and adjust his clothes. I was still flat out on the bed when he drew the door closed silently as he left the room. His visit had added somewhat to my repertoire. I was left fully sated and stretched myself in the luxury of an afterglow reflected in a well-serviced cunt.

I slept, awakening naked on the rumpled counterpane to find Patience bent over me. 'Are you all right, miss?' she asked. 'Lady Cynthia is waiting for you downstairs. She said to go and see that you are ready.

'What do you think of Porlock?' I asked.

'He's a dirty old man,' Patience said spiritedly.

'Have little do to with him, Miss Diana. Now do hurry and get dressed, Lady Cynthia doesn't like to be kept—'

'She can wait,' I said. 'Tell me the truth, Patience. Has Porlock fucked you?' I smiled to reassure her. 'Was he good?'

Patience blushed, put her fingers to her mouth and could not suppress a giggle. 'He's had all the female staff. Lady Cynthia herself, too, so he claims. It's that big prick of his. It does fairly do the trick when he has you. There, now you know.'

I took another bath to refresh myself, dressed, and went down to find Cynthia sitting tapping her fingers on her knee with impatience. 'What kept you?' she demanded.

'It was what you did with Patience,' I invented. 'It made me feel all funny, you know. I had to play with myself after you'd gone, because you didn't do anything to me. I must have tired myself and I fell fast asleep.'

'Horny little bitch,' Cynthia smiled, almost using Porlock's words exactly. 'Did my little amusement with Patience arouse you so? Well, I shall forgive you this time. The wretched girl seeming so shy and embarrassed does add to the piquancy of teasing her, doesn't it? But you mustn't dissipate your strength so, Diana. There are other and better ways as you'll see—'

'I couldn't help it.'

'Oh, I'm glad you have such a nature. Perhaps you should be put to a man. Would you like that?'

'Perhaps. I don't know,' I said coyly.

'I have a special friend I want you to meet today,' Cynthia informed me chattily. 'Let's not waste any more time. I have so much arranged to do today. I want you to be especially good, Diana.'

I don't think that was the right choice of word for what Cynthia had in mind. Not 'good' as in good little girl, I was certain, but good at what Cynthia evidently had arranged for me to do. That I awaited to learn with great interest.

Chapter Fifteen
AFRICA

Harry's return from his trip to seek aid for his irrigation schemes by offering the same facility to an oil-rich desert kingdom in Arabia, thankfully coincided with our neighbours the Pohls leaving the area. They were posted to Zanzibar and their departure solved several problems I had been presented with during their stay. Foolish woman that I am, I truly believe I fell deeply in love with their son, Viggo. I know that nowadays 'toyboys' are an accepted thing; an older woman taking a youthful lover is no longer a cause for comment. But I was a married woman in a close community risking my reputation through a mad infatuation with a schoolboy. I should have stopped the affair after our first night together, but found I couldn't.

We met as often as was possible before he returned to Germany and college, furtive lovers inventing innocent reasons to be together to fool friends and his parents, lying as to our whereabouts at times, covering our tracks. I gave Ndegi my housegirl leave to go home to her village for a visit to her parents, thus avoiding one danger of Viggo and I being caught in the act, for with his youthful lust for sex, we fucked several times daily while his parents were absent on their medical duties. I know now it was a purely physical thing we shared, unable to get enough of each other and revelling in playing our sex games. But there were tender moments too, when we declared undying love during our kissing and fondling. Looking back it all seems very adolescent, more so on my behalf, so much his senior and supposedly wiser.

No doubt the infatuation I felt at the time heightened the sex. To even think one is in love is an elating thing. I do know during this short time the sight of him appearing at my door made my stomach flutter as if a million butterflies were inside me. He would enter and we would kiss like our mouths were fused together, still holding each other as we went on through to my bedroom, casting off the few clothes we wore en route. He was always gloriously iron-hard erect to fuck me anywhere – across the bed, in the bath, on the floor, at the sink while peeling potatoes, this last with me bending over gripping the taps while he penetrated my uptilted cunt from the rear. We went about naked and in our passing he would playfully grab at me, leading to love-making in whatever part of the house we might be in. On one occasion I drove him in my car to the new drive-in cinema on the outskirts of Kampala. During the whole double-feature programme of films we made love along the back seat of the car, fucking and sucking naked in the friendly dark, my breasts purple with love bites.

I knew all the time, of course, it would end and I would return to my normal state and get over the deluded besottedness I had for the boy. I loved my husband as much as ever and missed him, but I do think it is very possible to have strong feelings for others at the same time. Anyway, I considered that if I got away with yet one more adventure, as good as ever I'd look back on in my old age, it was as worth the risk. Viggo was a sweet boy, gaining experience too with every bout. But it was not only the son I had to contend with at this time. Both Lotte and Gunther had me on occasion, being always insistent, and I felt that by not refusing them it covered up the liaison I was having with their son. We thought it better to keep that item from them, a decision proved wise by the turn of events.

Viggo had made his usual morning call, thinking the coast was clear after his parents left for their work. As ever we undressed and by noon had enjoyed ourselves several times. We were actually fucking again after a bite of lunch, with me sitting up mounted over Viggo and nicely impaled on his upright prick when a scream of anger made me turn my head. Framed in the doorway were Lotte and Gunther, returned early and calling on me. Viggo was supposedly on a bicycle trip with young friends. To see him lying under me seemed to his parents the height of treachery on my part, despite their supposed strong belief in free love for everyone and their philosophy of 'get it where you can.' The furious couple descended upon us, pulling me off their son, screaming abuse at me and ordering Viggo out of the house. Alarmed, he grabbed his shorts and fled.

'Bitch, cow!' Lotte hurled at me in her anger. 'Filth!' She smacked my face, struck my breasts several hard slaps. I tried to hold her hands but Gunther gripped my wrists tightly, making me helpless before them. There was no doubt in my mind that the fury they displayed was the result of their jealousy, mad that I and their son were lovers in secret. I do believe in their twisted minds they would have liked to include Viggo in the romps they so liked to have with me. That this might well have been so I cannot claim, but her next scream at me was 'Why did you not let us know about this, filthy whore that you are?'

Lying back naked and feeling very vulnerable before them, I said, 'But it was you and Gunther who agreed to Viggo and me making love. What did you expect after that?' I was shouting my words too, such was the atmosphere. Turning to address Gunther, I expected some reason from him. 'You know these things can happen, Gunther—'

'We were here for you when you required sex,' he said grimly. 'You have dishonoured our trust. Taking the boy as a lover is not what we intended. He has his studies. The one time we agreed to was not meant to become an affair.'

'Well, fuck you then, and let go of me,' I demanded spiritedly. 'I didn't have to force your boy. Once he'd tried it he wanted more. Put that in your bloody sex manual that you're compiling. Don't blame him, he's a nice normal young man.'

'We do not blame him,' Lotte announced. 'So how often have you been together like we caught you?' Her look at me was pure venom. 'It was obvious there have been many times—'

'You started it,' I protested. 'Let's leave it at that.' Trying to be assertive as much as I could with Gunther holding me down by my wrists, I added, 'Leave my house now! Go and that will be the end of it—'

'Not quite,' Lotte decided. 'I want her punished, Gunther. Punished so that she will remember her treachery to us. I want her marked—'

'Don't you dare,' I started.

'Turn her over and hold her,' she told her husband. On my face and with Gunther's strong hands pressing me down on the bed, I implored mercy. Turning my head as best I could with a hand hard on my neck, I saw Lotte leave the room. When she returned she carried a bamboo cane of about two feet in length, the thin kind kept in our garden shed for tying up plants and flowers. 'I found this,' Lotte said with grim satisfaction. 'It will do well what I have in mind.'

'No,' I pleaded. 'Please don't. I'm sorry, sorry—'

'You will be more sorry,' Lotte promised.

Really, I'm too old to be thrashed like a bad child, but that did not save me. I have had fun smackings on my bottom before and quite arousing they proved. Lotte's punishment can only be described as a severe beating, the cane descending in her anger until I felt my bum cheeks sting as if on fire. I squirmed, howled, begged and cried out in agony. At last she threw the cane aside, regarding my red striped bottom with great satisfaction. This was the retribution for fucking her boy. I supposed I deserved it.

'Go now,' I blubbered through tears. 'You've had your revenge. Get out and I don't ever want to see you again.'

'You probably won't,' Gunther said. 'We called here to tell you Lotte and I have received a new posting and will be leaving tomorrow. Viggo will come with us until he goes back to Germany. After we have left you now, I suggest you bathe your buttocks and apply some soothing cream. You will probably have bruises for some days following.'

I certainly did, having a well-striped arse for a souvenir of my acquaintance with the Pohls, mother, father and son. I could not sit comfortably for days, glad my Harry was not due back until the weals had all but disappeared. I went to the airport to greet my husband and drive him home, but he appeared through the VIP gate in the company of a prince no less. A minor one, it seems, a cousin of the oil state's royal ruler, but important enough in his own right. All I got therefore was a glimpse of Harry being whisked off amid armed soldiers and the prince, a squat very broad man in pure white Arab robes. I was kept well back as the entourage went by, with Harry signalling to me that he would phone by holding his hand up to his ear.

Back home and on such a lovely morning I got into

my bikini and swam a length or two of my pool. I was improving my tan when the phone rang. It was Harry to say he was in Kampala but was leaving right away to join me. 'How are you getting here?' I asked. 'Shall I come for you in the car?'

'No need, my love,' he said. 'I have my secretary here beside me. She'll be using her car.'

'How did your talks go in that Arabian country? Did anything promising result?'

'It went extremely well, I think,' Harry replied. 'I know Prince Kalid Ameer is interested. He's one of the royal family in Kumar, and though it's small the place literally floats on oil. You no doubt saw him with his bodyguard at the airport this morning—'

'And hopefully he'll be instrumental in coughing up for your scheme in northern Uganda,' I laughed. 'He sounds worth cultivating, dear.'

'Very much so. His country could do with irrigating and if it works in the conditions in Uganda, he wants it for Kumar. We've been talking it over in his embassy all this morning. Now he wants all the plans, facts and figures by this evening. It's all the stuff in my office back home that I'll need. I should be with you in half-an-hour. Then I must work preparing the specifications for him.'

I was sorry to hear that, wanting Harry to myself. After his absence I was looking forward to a nice long unhurried session of sex with him that afternoon. 'Didn't you have all that with you in Kumar?' I pouted. 'I had hoped we could make up for lost time—'

'I'm sure we will,' Harry promised down the phone. 'What they want, now we have gone into it all, is a full estimate to complete both projects, here and in Kumar. Exciting, isn't it? More than I had hoped for. I can knock that out this afternoon at home with the papers I had prepared earlier with this in mind. Now that I've seen what I can do in Kumar as well as Uganda, I can come up with a realistic sum. Hopefully when I take it back to their embassy tonight, they'll agree to finance the whole deal.'

'And what do you get out of it?' I asked moodily. 'I wanted you to myself now you are back.'

'There's plenty of time for what you have in mind,' Harry chuckled. 'You are the limit, I'm delighted to say. As for what I get out of it, nothing but the satisfaction of doing something really worthwhile for people. Your satisfaction I'll see to later. Don't think I'm not as keen as you, Di.'

'You had better be,' I warned him, telling a fib for his benefit. 'I've been too long without satisfaction, as you call it. I don't suppose you did without while away, not with that secretary of yours there—?'

'Not a chance,' Harry laughed. 'I've saved it all for you, my love. But talking of my secretary, Samali is driving me home. I thought she might have lunch with us.'

'What doesn't she eat?' I asked. 'Is a pork chop or a slice of ham against her customs or religion?'

'Nothing like that,' Harry said. 'She is a very with-it young African woman. Business college in the United States, secretarial course in London. I'm lucky to have her.'

And I'll just bet you have, I thought, a twinge of malice as I added, 'She'll get chicken salad and like it.'

'This is not like you, Diana,' Harry said. 'Do you mind my bringing Sam home?'

So it was now Sam. I am not normally a jealous or possessive sort and in truth I was interested to clap eyes on this paragon of a secretary he thought so much of. 'No, I just selfishly wanted you all to myself,' I admitted. 'I had plans to lure you into bed all afternoon. To put it bluntly, I need a good fuck.'

'So what's new?' my husband chuckled. 'I won't need luring. It will be all the better for us not having had it lately, won't it?'

I could only agree, what else could I do? With the housegirl still away I laid the dining room table myself, using the best lace cloth and napkins, crystal wine glasses, best cutlery, the lot, even a centrepiece of flowers. My intention was to show this modern miss of a treasure that I was no slouch as a wife to her boss. I decided against getting dressed, calculating I'd impress her more with my full figure in the tiny bikini. To await their arrival I went back to my lounger beside the pool. When a car drew in the driveway, Harry approached with a very pretty young African girl. I judged her, as women do, as in her early twenties, and much too attractive not to be tempting to a man she spent so much time with.

Harry bent down to peck my cheek. 'Diana,' he greeted me. 'Is lunch ready? I've got a deal of work to do—'

I decided not to mention I thought his welcome cool to say the least. Whether because of his eagerness to get down to work or for the benefit of his pretty secretary, I was not too sure. One thing I was sure of, if they were lovers I was going to wheedle it out of him to satisfy my curiosity. I rose and shook her hand. 'Miss Kino,' I smiled sweetly. 'Or may I call you Sam, as my husband does? He tells me all the time just how useful you are to him.'

'And I've heard so much about you from your husband, Mrs Saxon,' the girl said pleasantly, offering a slim brown hand. 'Isn't it splendid about Harry's projects being considered?'

'Very,' I said, 'after all his work. Let's go inside,

I'm sure you both could do with a drink. Poor dear, don't you think he looks exhausted? He does overdo things—'

I noted the girl's eyes took in the fullness of my breasts, overflowing the tiny bra and revealing my tight cleavage, and the triangle of nylon covering my mound. Harry noted her stare too. 'Are you going to dress?' he said. 'I'm ready to eat and get down to work.'

'He's never complained about me being in a bikini before,' I told his secretary, smiling at her. 'Of course I'll dress.' I led the way into the lounge. 'Oh, Harry,' I said, as if just remembering. 'My damned wardrobe door is stuck again. Do come and open it. I think it warps or swells with the humidity—'

'What?' he said entirely surprised.

'The wardrobe door. It's stuck again. I've spoken about it before.' In the bedroom I stripped off the bikini and stood to face him as he followed me in, a pink gin in hand.

'What's all this about a wardrobe?' he began. 'I've never heard you mention it before.' Then my arms were about his neck and my breasts pushed against his shirt front. I kissed him with my tongue in his surprised mouth, rubbing my crotch suggestively into his groin. 'I might have known,' he protested. 'Really, Di, there's time for this later—'

'Now,' I husked against his mouth. 'I want you now.' My fingers drew down his zip, reaching inside his Y-fronts, grasping the limp warm curve of his long prick. I felt it give a little stir, start to grow in my hand. 'It wants it too,' I said.

'Bloody hell,' he said, growing agitated. 'Samali's out there waiting for us. She'll wonder what's going on—'

'Fuck Samali,' I said. 'You probably have, I'll bet.'

'Don't get that idea in your head,' Harry grinned. 'There's no chance. Samali prefers her own kind—'

'You mean,' I said delighted, 'she's a lesbian?' I still toyed with Harry's cock, feeling it thicken and stretch. 'Are you having me on? She's so lovely.'

'She's never admitted it to me,' Harry said. 'But I know she has a woman friend in Kampala. Also when we were in the States another female turned up and shared her hotel room. Now will you let go of my prick? It's not the time.'

'Nonsense,' I said, kissing him again. 'You come home to me without so much as a how-have-you-been or I've-missed-you, or kiss-my-arse, which I wouldn't mind right now. And don't deny that's a lovely hard-on you've got—'

I fell back on the bed, pulling him over me, covering his face between my tits. 'Come on,' I urged. 'Shall I suck you first? Never mind Samali out there; put it in me, darling. I've been longing for a fuck while you were away.' My hand now held a prick as stiff as an iron bar, drawing it between my thighs. When it nudged my cunt lips I raised myself and felt it enter me. 'Oh, yes,' I crowed. 'Do it. To hell with Samali, fuck me now!'

'A quickie then,' I heard Harry mumble, humping against me, his shaft going up with its knob reaching way back the way I love it, his balls pressed to the cleave of my raised cheeks. I captured him with my arms and legs about his back, meeting thrust with thrust. 'My God, that's good,' he mumbled into my neck. 'You really are the bloody limit. That hungry cunt of yours won't take a simple no, will it?'

'Never,' I said. 'You should know it now. So fuck it hard, pay it back!' I was giving an Academy Award performance; grunting, crying out loudly, demanding more. It was a ploy that worked, making me increasingly aroused and attracting a spectator. Harry's secretary, perhaps wondering what was keeping us, certainly not unaware of the noises coming from the bedroom, came to the door and peered in. I saw her face, eyes wide at our strenuous fucking, as I looked over Harry's heaving back. She at once turned and withdrew, leaving me highly elated. A moment more and she would have seen the lovely climaxes we had, my body lifting from the neck on the bed and Harry croaking out in his helpless state as he flopped about depositing his load into me.

I rose and dressed and served lunch. Samali hardly uttered a word, shocked into silence, I presumed. Harry excused himself and went off to his study as soon as the meal was over. I took the dishes to the sink and prepared to wash up. 'Have you no housegirl?' Samali inquired, coming out to help me, taking up a dish towel. 'It was such a nice meal you prepared. I thought European wives had it all done by their servants.' She gave me a brief smile, perhaps thinking back to the sight of Harry mounting me. 'I think you are not like the ones I have met, Mrs Saxon.'

'Call me Diana,' I insisted. 'Our housegirl is on holiday right now, but I have been known to do a little cooking and cleaning. I've even made a chocolate cake. What are you intending to do now, drive back to Kampala?'

'I should like to take a shower first, if I may,' Samali said. 'I haven't had a chance to wash or tidy myself up since last evening in Kumar. We have been so busy since, with the meetings and the flight, of course.'

'Of course, my dear,' I agreed. 'You look cool and very lovely to me, but I know how you feel. There's a shower in the bathroom that I use. It's just off my bedroom. I'll show you—'

I led Samali through to my bedroom, noting her eyes avoiding the rumpled sheet where Harry and I had fucked. 'Undress here,' I told her, 'while I operate the spray thing. It can be a bit temperamental. I find just lukewarm all right for the water temperature—'

'Lukewarm would be fine,' said the girl. She paused, as if waiting for me to leave, so I went into the bathroom and adjusted the water until the sprinkler was set right, spraying at the temperature I wanted. Back in the bedroom Samali stood as if embarrassed to be seen by me, her linen dress discarded and wearing a neat lacy bra and little briefs. She was a lovely creature, with smooth brown skin and neat breasts, the little bump in the crotch of her briefs showing a hint of a darling little cunt mound.

'What a beautiful girl you are, Samali,' I said sincerely. I fancied her fiercely. 'Take off your underwear and pop in the shower. I've got it just right for you.'

She unhooked the bra to reveal small but nicely rounded breasts, uptilted with dark purple nipples. Despite her very obvious embarrassment I hung about until she hesitantly drew down her briefs. The prominence between her thighs was sparsely covered with short and curly jet-black hair revealing a plump brown temptingly sweet little lipless cunt, a mere slit. I made a show of my admiration of her naked charms, my eyes roving from her tits to her tight quim. 'So sweet, Samali. You are a delicious creature. I wonder you are not married—'

'I've concentrated on my career—' she said shyly.

'Then you must have had lovers,' I said, deliberate in my leading her on. I wanted her, and not only because I found her body so mouthwateringly irresistible. There was the challenge of seducing her, plus Harry's claim never to have been her lover because of her lesbianism. If he hadn't had her then I would, I decided, running a hand from her shoulder down over a smooth arm. 'Your skin is so soft, like silk,' I praised her while she lowered her eyes bashfully. With my hand resting on the curve of her back just above the flare of her firmly rounded buttocks, I led her through to the shower cubicle. 'Take your time, dear,' I said as she stepped under the spray. 'I shall see if Harry needs anything.'

I made tea in the kitchen and took a tray through to my husband along with a slice of his favourite chocolate cake. He worked in his shirt sleeves, his desk laid out with the neatly sketched blueprints he produced, papers with rows of calculations, and maps. He sat up arching his back to ease the strain, a cup of tea in one hand and a slice of my cake in the other. 'I'll have it ready to take to the Kumar embassy in a couple of hours now,' he said in answer to my asking how he was getting on. 'This last bit concerns all the piping needed to get the water from the bore-holes to the strategic points I've marked on the map. Kumar fortunately has desalination plants on their coast to make fresh water.'

'So you'll be working in here for another couple of hours?' I said innocently. 'I'll see you are not disturbed.'

I went back through to my bedroom and into the en suite bathroom. Samali was still under the shower, her smooth brown skin shining wet. 'I'm not sure how to turn this off,' she said. 'I tried, but it got hotter, so I waited for you to return. I shall need a towel as well, if you don't mind—'

Of course I didn't mind. There was no towel for her because I'd deliberately made sure there wasn't one. I brought one from the bedroom and turned off the water. When she stepped out of the cubicle I enveloped her in it. 'Let me dry you,' I suggested. 'Just stand there and let me rub you dry. You must be tired. I'm sure my husband works you too hard. Now isn't that nice?' I rubbed her breasts as if caressing them, dried between her legs, applying pressure on her cunt.

Sex and Mrs Saxon

'Please, Mrs Saxon—' Samali said in a weak voice. 'I can do this for myself—'

'Diana. I told you to call me Diana,' I said, letting the towel slip. 'You really have such a pretty figure. Your breasts are so firm. Look how your nipples have extended. My, they're so stiff and long. I've never seen such nice long ones. Almost an inch, I'm sure.'

'Mrs Saxon,' she protested in anguish. 'You shouldn't—'

'You are shy,' I said sweetly. 'Such a beautiful girl as you. We are both women, my dear. You have nothing to hide. Only to admire.' I let the towel drop and ran my hands over her breasts, standing almost nose to nose, rubbing my palms in circular movements over her nipples.

'This is so embarrassing, Mrs Saxon,' Samali said quite tremulously. 'So disconcerting—'

'But nice,' I insisted. I kissed her mouth slowly, holding her face in my hands. 'Surely you have made love with another woman before, dear? I know I find you so very attractive, Samali. Do let me. You make me want you so.' I kissed her again, getting some response, her mouth relaxing, our tongue tips meeting.

'I never thought,' Samali breathed against my mouth. 'A married woman, I mean—'

'Why not?' I said, my own voice sounding throaty with the passion rising in me. 'One can have the best of both worlds. Come with me, my dear.' Taking her hand I led her through to my bed, lowering her on to it. She watched with eyes wide and startled like a trapped animal as I stood over her throwing off my dress and undergarments, neither did she protest again when my mouth went down to suck upon each nipple. Instead she smoothed a hand through my hair, sighed loudly and raised her breasts in her hands.

'Lick me,' I barely heard her say in a soft shy voice.

Sex and Mrs Saxon

When I lowered my head she opened her brown thighs and used fingers to part the tight slit of her cunt. I pressed kisses to the yielding mound, tasting the musty tang of her sex, made a stiff funnel of my tongue and probed into the bright red interior she offered. It brought a moan from her lips, a murmured word of gratitude. Her clitoris was a mere button but I sought it, found it and played on it with the tip of my tongue flicking rapidly. She gave a stifled cry before jerking against my face in her climax. When she quietened it was to look at me questioningly.

'How did you know?' she asked.

'I didn't, did I?' I said, never intending to mention my husband's suspicion about her sexual preference for woman love. 'I wanted you very much and took the chance. Do you regret it?'

'I don't know, it was so unexpected.'

Stretching out on the bed beside her, she came to my arms as I reached for her. The little kisses we exchanged grew in intensity. Usually the passive partner in such affairs, I suddenly felt very much the dominant one in our lovemaking. I rolled over her, my breasts flattening against hers, pubic mound to mound, making movements above her exactly like a male fucking a woman. Her legs encircled my waist and her cunt tilted to mine, clit upon clit, both rubbing furiously to attain the maximum pleasure. Coming together, we fell apart to gasp in air, drained in our exertions.

'We had better dress,' Samali suggested at last. 'What if your husband came through to find us—?'

I nodded, sitting up as Samali sought her clothes. 'Now that we know each other,' I said, 'we must meet again. Would you like that?'

'If it would not cause trouble, yes. I mean between you and your husband.' Her eyes lowered. 'I would like that.'

'He would never know, would he?' I smiled. 'Now you no doubt want to drive home. I'll tell Harry you left—'

'But I was going to drive him to his meeting this evening.'

'I shall do that,' I said firmly. 'On your way, Samali. I'm sure we'll meet again soon. Do keep in touch.'

'You seduced me deliberately, didn't you,' the girl suddenly said. 'Why?'

'To satisfy myself you weren't my Harry's lover,' I admitted. 'But once we were making love, it was because I very much wanted you. Couldn't you tell that?'

'When I was at college in the United States,' Samali said seriously, 'I had an affair with my tutor. She was a white woman older than I and I really loved her. You remind me of that woman. I do not want men, they demand so much. A woman is kinder, more understanding. I should like very much that we be lovers too.'

'If it can stay our secret,' I agreed, 'I'm sure we could meet.' When she left we exchanged a last kiss, and I went back into the house wondering if I had not got myself into yet one more entanglement. I looked into Harry's study and he was packing a bulky briefcase.

'Was that my secretary's car I heard leaving?' he said. 'I wanted her to drive me to Kampala now this work is ready.'

'I'll be taking you,' I said sweetly. 'Then I can drive you home tonight and put you to bed—'

'We may work very late,' Harry warned. 'You could be stuck up there for half the night.'

'So I'll have to wait,' I said. 'I won't mind. I'd quite like to see into the embassy. Is it fancy?'

'Like something out of the Arabian Nights, magic carpets and all,' Harry laughed. 'So doll yourself up,

Di, and impress them all what a beautiful wife I've got. What made Samali leave so suddenly, by the way? Did you two get on together?'

'Couldn't have got closer,' I assured him. 'We had what you might call a real heart-to-heart. Female stuff, you know.'

'I can imagine,' Harry said, but I was sure he couldn't. And so I went off to prepare myself for taking him to his meeting, already deciding to look a knockout for the occasion. As ever, light in step and happy in spirit following the afternoon's bouts with both Harry and his pretty secretary, I looked forward to what the night ahead would offer.

Chapter Sixteen
ENGLAND

Atherton drove us to Osmond's art gallery, where a selection of oil paintings were to be considered. I could not keep my mind on the business in hand despite my enjoyment of art, learned while I visited Mr Saxon for our sex sessions. Lady Cynthia could not make up her mind between a young modern artist's latest work, brought specially to the gallery for her inspection, or several post-impressionist oils.

'He's very good and barely known for his work yet,' she then informed me, 'and no doubt his paintings will become very sought after. Now could be the time to obtain one or two while the price is reasonable. What do you think of them, Diana?'

I couldn't think, although I readily agreed with her, for that is what she wanted to hear. My mind was full of the fucking I'd received from Porlock. Once mounted over him, I'd ridden his cock at full gallop, his surprisingly long thin rigid tool impaled deeper within me than any I had experienced. The randy old butler had brought home to me the truth that there was no substitute for a stiff prick, despite the excitement and pleasures of female love I'd been introduced to since my arrival in London.

Cynthia was more effusive than usual, fawning over me as if to get me agreeable to do her a great favour.

She had something in store for me that afternoon, I guessed, and wanted me in the right frame of mind to be fully obedient to her wishes. She purchased two of the young artist's pictures for delivery, then ushered me a few doors along the fashionable street to a jeweller's. The place was deep in carpet pile with brightly lit display cases filled with the most gorgeous and highly expensive tiaras, diamond bracelets, necklaces and rings. A morning-suited assistant bowed us in, oozing subservience.

After an exchange of words with Cynthia he led us with a curious gait of hunched shoulders, hand extended, to a glass counter under which a large selection of brooches were displayed on a dark velvet cloth. There he stood back a pace or two, beaming like an idiot, I thought, while two other human beings considered his wares. I was rapidly discovering why the rich and titled considered themselves so superior. They were made to feel so, or at least they were in those days, by the example before me. Obsequious, I think is the term. As for the jewellery, I was never one to set much store by it. As a Scot brought up the hard way, I considered hard cash more desirable.

'You may choose whichever brooch you wish, Diana,' I was told to my surprise by Cynthia. 'I was asked to bring you here for that purpose by a gentleman admirer of yours. Isn't that kind of him? Take your time, they're all so lovely, aren't they, dear?'

'Any one of them I like?' I said, determined to pick the most expensive one to keep against a rainy day. 'Do I know this – this admirer who wants to buy me this?'

'No, but he knows you, or at least he's seen you and is most impressed,' Cynthia cooed. 'Once you have made your choice you can wear it when you meet him later today. He will be charmed, I know.'

'What will I be?' I asked, getting an angry frown

from my companion. There were no price tags on the items, I noted, going on the assumption that if customers in that Alladin's cave had to ask how much, they couldn't afford it and shouldn't be shopping there. I saw a butterfly whose size might make it the more expensive, the wings and body set with rubies and diamonds perhaps, but I wasn't taking the chance. I crooked a finger at the waiting jeweller, had him bend to my ear. 'Which one is the most expensive?' I whispered.

He straightened, lips pursed as if to contain a smile, but his eyes told me he was in full agreement with my request. Going behind the counter he put his hand under the glass cover and withdrew a small brooch fashioned in the shape of a spider. I didn't fancy it much as he held it out for our inspection in the palm of his hand.

'What did you say to him?' Cynthia demanded.

'The young modom asked my opinion of the spider brooch,' the man said quickly, answering for me. 'She showed excellent taste. Exquisite, is it not, Lady Bellinger? The setting is an example of the finest workmanship. Quite a perfect little piece,' he added, meaning me, I was sure. Well did my estimation of him go up in large measure. 'Note the matched rubies for the eyes, the diamond setting of the body and legs—'

'Yes,' said Cynthia, bored with his talk. 'If that's what she wants. You know whom to charge it to. She can wear it now.'

I was handed the brooch and changed my opinion of it. It was beautifully made and even the pin was solid gold. 'I'd like the box for it too,' I said. 'I think its a lovely thing.'

'Give her the box while I pop back to Osmond's,' Cynthia said, as if a sudden decision had been made.

'I've decided to take another of that artist's paintings, the one with the dancers on the moonlit balcony—'

'The one I liked best of his,' I said in my good mood. 'Oh, I think you should buy it—'

'Milady could telephone from here and tell them to reserve it,' suggested the jeweller.

'No, I want another look at it,' Cynthia said. 'Diana, wait for me here while I pop back to Osmond's'

Left alone with the jeweller, he visibly relaxed. 'Come into my office and I'll find a nice suitable box for you,' he smiled. 'May I ask what relationship you have with Lady Bellinger, young lady?'

'She's my aunt,' I said boldly.

'Yes,' he said, not believing a word of it. He led me to a glass-fronted little office at the rear of the shop, almost every inch of it filled with filing cabinets. A spinsterish-looking typist clacked away at her machine on a desk cluttered with invoices and such. 'You may go for your lunch now, Miss Akers,' her employer said. He seemed a different person then, tall and dark with a thin moustache. I took him to be about in his late forties. I was still holding the brooch in my hand. 'Let me pin it on for you,' he offered. 'On your dress below the left shoulder, that would be best. Open your coat, young woman.'

I duly unbuttoned my tailored white linen jacket, opening it to reveal the pale primrose dress beneath with my breasts bulging the silk material. He stood so close his breath was on my face. 'Such pretty clothes and such a pretty girl,' he said, fastening the brooch. His hand stayed where it was, just above the swell of my left tit. 'You did a wise thing asking me for the dearest one. Over a hundred quid, the spider, well over. Taking the old girl to town, are you? The old bitch deserves it.'

'What's it to you?' I said, on the defensive.

'I fully approve. You're not the first girl she's brought

in her for some trinket, if the best one so far. You're quite lovely, you know.' His hand went down to cover my left breast, squeezing it temptingly. 'Look in some time and see me. I can be generous too. Diana, isn't it? We might come to some arrangement—'

He was a handsome man, I decided, scrupulously clean and smelling nice. 'I might do,' I said. 'You never know.'

'Exactly. I love your big tits. I should love to see them out,' he said, fondling them both. 'You've given me a hard-on now. Christ, I wish I had you for the rest of the day. Let me feel your cunt—'

'You're a quick worker,' I had to say, giggling. His hand went up under my dress and inside the leg of the so-called French knickers I wore. I leaned against the desk while his fingers stroked my cunt lips, one curling to probe inside. 'Warm and wet,' he observed. 'God, how I'd love to fuck you.' With his free hand he brought his prick out of his fly front. 'Let me put it in. I'll make it worth your while—'

True to say his fingering and the sight of his big bloated cock had me wanting to badly, but I was also well aware that Cynthia might reappear at any moment. 'There isn't time,' I said. 'I want to but there isn't time. She might come back any minute—'

'I suppose you're right,' he admitted reluctantly, still feeling my cunt. 'At least give this a quick rub,' nodding down at his stander. The things that I get into, I thought, the pair of us standing close, rubbing his prick while he fingered me up.

Looking out over the filing cabinets I saw Atherton loitering about. 'She's sent her chauffeur in for me,' I gasped. 'Just a little more and you'll make me come. Go on—'

I bucked my hips in my throes, coming strongly on his finger, my own hand wanking his shaft like fury.

'Christ, I'll flood the place,' he moaned, jerking about with his climax building. I remembered what I'd done for Porlock and bent over him, a strong urge within me to taste his come. 'Yes, bloody yes!' he said, realising my intent. His knob barely covered by my lips, the jets struck the back of my throat in strong spurts. When I stood again, swallowing hard, he handed me his handkerchief.

He found a suitable velvet box for me, putting a white five pound note inside it before handing it over. I went out from the little office with the warm glow inside me of doing business with pleasure, my cunt palpitating. 'Come on,' Atherton said. 'She's waiting for you in the Rolls.' He held the door of the car open for me to join Cynthia in the back seat. 'The Savoy, Atherton,' she said, and we purred away through the London traffic.

It occurred to me as we entered the hotel, Atherton dismissed for the day much to his annoyance, suspecting something was arranged for that afternoon that he would dearly love to be involved in, that in a morning I'd made more of value than my father could earn in several months of hard work. Now I was to dine in style and later meet the secret admirer who had lavished an expensive gift on me. I hoped he would be someone like my jeweller friend, whom I'd quite come to fancy with his outspoken words and demands belying a gentlemanly manner. No sense beating about the bush when you want somebody. Cynthia and I were shown to a table in the dining room and soon joined by a tall and very handsome young man with a military moustache. He was to be the one, I thought, pleased.

Cynthia called him Dorry as he kissed her cheek, introducing him to me as Major the Honorable Dorian Gurnard of the Brigade of Guards. He kissed my hand, muttering, 'Delightful' and obviously admiring me. During lunch he invariably kept his eyes on the swell of my breasts, and I felt his hand fondle my thigh under the tablecloth. He was in his early thirties, wore an impeccably cut suit and was very distinguished-looking. That summer of 1939, I imagine, was yet another nail in the coffin for the rich and aristocratic, as 1914 had been, when servants were still two a penny and life, customs and traditions in Britain were secure, guaranteed by an obedient population. Dorry, as he insisted I call him too, could summon waiters with a glance. The top-hatted commissionaire at the door saluted and had a taxi waiting on our appearance.

The taxi driver, instructed to take us to an address in Euston Place, set off with me settled between Cynthia and the young Guards officer. I felt replete with an excellent meal inside me and a glass or two of wine. Both my escorts began to fondle my thighs on either side of me. 'Your little companion is charming,' Dorry Gurnard praised Cynthia. 'Is she primed? Know what she's in for?'

'She's a dear and will be perfect,' Cynthia assured him, patting my hand fondly. 'We'll have a little chat when we arrive and I'll put her in the picture.' We drew up before a large imposing town house, shown in by a liveried footman, and Cynthia led me into a small side room. She sat me in a chair, kissed my mouth lingeringly and went to a cabinet to pour two large sherries. Beyond the door and across the hall I could see into a large room where a dozen or so men and women congregated around an ornate fireplace. They were elegant people from their dress, all with champagne glasses in their hands, talking animatedly.

I judged them all to be middle-aged, except for Dorry Gurnard who was deep in conversation to a man with grey hair, a heavy moustache and a paunch. 'Drink up, this is excellent sherry,' Cynthia encouraged me. 'We shall allow ourselves one more, my dear.'

'Who are all those people?' I asked. 'Is this a party?'

'It's a little get-together we've arranged for this afternoon. All extremely nice people and fun to be with. I want you especially to help the proceedings along, my dear. I'm sure they'll all love you.'

I'm sure they would, I thought, in the fullest meaning of the term. 'What is expected of me then?' I asked.

'To help entertain and amuse them—'

'How could I do that?' I said, purposefully naive.

'By being your own sweet self. As is your nature, what comes so naturally to you,' Cynthia flattered me. 'You know how aroused you get when we make love, well, those nice gentlemen and ladies too, I know, would enjoy the same with you.'

'All of them?'

'Perhaps not all, of course. Some like to watch, you know. Would you mind that? I think not. In fact I insist not, Diana. You are a very fortunate girl to be included in such company—'

The two large sherries warming my insides, I was game for anything she had in mind. An afternoon's romp, orgy, exhibition or whatever with the upper-crust crowd assembled in the salon both appealed to me and piqued my curiosity. 'Who goes with who and how and where?' I asked mischievously.

'Why, bless you, nothing is really arranged about who does what with whom. It just happens. Suggestions may be made and acted upon. There are no rules except one, that all who are present agree to participate freely in the spirit of the assembly—'

'Married couples?' I asked. 'Husbands and wives doing things with others?'

'Of course, silly girl. We have several married couples here today, and a mother and daughter. Why do you think they attend? One guest especially wants to meet you, so I have promised you to him first this afternoon. He can be most generous. It would be such a great favour to me if you would be nice to him—'

'Is it the major we had lunch with?' I asked, not minding him at all.

'No, but I'm sure he'll want you himself later. Actually it's his commanding officer, Toby Woodford-Halse. He's seen you with me at Claridges once and was quite struck,' she said as if imparting a confidence. 'It's quite a compliment to your youth and beauty, Diana my dear. Of course I shall be insanely jealous when you are with him, but I couldn't refuse such a dear friend.' She touched the spider brooch now pinned to my dress. 'Toby said I should see that you got something nice. Wasn't that kind of him?'

'That depends,' I said cheekily, 'how kind I have got to be to him. Is he a dirty old man?'

'Hardly that,' Cynthia said, shocked at my impudence. 'The gentleman in question commands one of the Household brigades. He has been an equerry to our dear King. Sir Toby is descended from one of the most ancient and noble families in the land.'

'He still wants to put his ancient and noble thing up my cunt, whoever he is,' I teased her, my effrontery a combination of a tongue loosened by drink and derision at Cynthia's talk to make procuring me for her friends sound like a favour I was being given.

'You little bitch!' Cynthia exploded. 'Behave yourself and stop that silly giggling! What has come over you? Do you know how lucky you are to be received in my circle, the cream of London society?'

'Perhaps they are lucky to have me,' I retorted, still impertinent. 'Someone young and nice for their rude games. I expect they have all fucked each other so often that they need new blood. Just to get it up—'

'Guttersnipe, wicked girl,' Cynthia stormed. 'You will not speak so of your betters.'

'Whose betters?' I sneered. 'A lot of stuck-up toffee-nosed sex maniacs?'

'And you,' Cynthia said icily furious now, 'what are you? What were you when I found you? Nothing. A cheap little slut.'

'But not so cheap,' I told her. 'I've moved up in the world, haven't I?'

'Ungrateful wretch. I should have left you with that Cole creature—'

'Then maybe she'll take me back,' I said, rising to my feet and collecting my shoulder bag. It was a calculated risk on my part, of course, a ploy to get my way. If present to be the main attraction, I felt I was in a good position to dictate a few terms. What was in it for me, for instance. Cynthia regarded me with a look of anxiety. Her assembled friends were gathered because she had promised them an added ingredient – me. I was therefore not going to perform without some lasting agreement.

Cynthia and I stood glaring each other out and were thus at a stand-off when Dorry Gurnard came into the room. He looked from one to the other, shaking his head. 'We're all waiting in there,' he said. 'Poor old Colonel Sir Toby is anxious to meet the young lady. What the devil's the matter, Cynthia?'

'It's this little whore. She's being awkward—'

'Not really,' I said. 'I just want to know I'm getting something for my trouble. Something more than a bit of jewellery—'

'Mercenary young cow,' said Cynthia.

'And you're doing this for nothing?' I taunted her.

'None of your business.'

'Come, now,' Dorry intervened. 'Cynthia, both you and I do well out of these little soirees in cash and kind, invites to country weekends and other perks. The bloody girl only wants something for her trouble. Assure her she'll be paid. Meanwhile we're all hanging about cocks in hand—'

'I've given her a home,' Cynthia said. 'What more does she expect?'

'How often do these arranged parties take place?' I asked. 'Is it regular?'

'You might say that,' Dorry answered. 'Both here in London and at weekends away in the best country houses.'

'Then I want a regular wage,' I said. 'So I can have my own bank account and a bank book. Be more independent.'

'I'd say that was reasonable, Cyn,' said Dorry. 'She's a pretty thing and will earn her salt. What say? Make it quick because the customers are getting impatient.'

'Most unusual,' sniffed Cynthia. 'Most of my young lady guests are content with living in style and receiving the occasional gift. However, if Diana wishes to be put on a payroll like any common employee, so be it. I want it understood she will do as I ask in future, and behave herself—'

'Behaving meaning being rather naughty,' grinned Dorry.

'Don't make it sound so sordid, young man,' Cynthia said with dignity. 'It is harmless amusement with the full consent of all. You have done well out of these arrangements, if I may say so, for a penniless officer with expensive tastes.'

'You don't do so badly yourself,' returned Dorry with spirit. 'Now that's settled between you and Diana, let's get her doing her stuff. Sir Toby is waiting and the old rake has an appointment elsewhere this afternoon. He's champing at the bit. The girl knows what he likes, does she? You've told her what to do?'

'What do I do?' I asked.

'Play the little innocent,' Cynthia instructed. 'Appear somewhat naive and inexperienced in the sexual variations the gentleman will demand. Be a little surprised and shocked, no doubt, but trusting too; certain that such a man of good breeding would never do anything outwith the bounds of accepted propriety. That whatever he does is all part of a young novice girl's training, what she can expect her husband to demand of her as a wife later. Be coy, shy, but compliant as to his wishes. In the latter stages allow the ultimate joy and pleasure you gain from his administrations to be very clearly expressed—'

'Like crying out, moaning and groaning, writhing in helpless throcs, that sort of thing,' Dorry advised laughing. 'It fairly gets the old boy going. If he thinks all of it is new to you, a respectable young girl put to the cock to introduce her to the way of things for females, so much the better. He's rich and can be most generous.'

I was ushered into the ornate salon by Cynthia, pleased as punch to introduce a fresh young girl for their approval. 'This is Diana,' she announced as a circle of a dozen or so men and women formed around us. None of them looked anything but very well-heeled, the men in well-tailored lounge suits and their women beautified with permanent waves, lots of make-up and expensively dressed. 'Remember, eyes down like a modest little thing,' Cynthia hissed. 'That's what they like. Say as little as possible to them.'

I lowered my head as the company discussed me. 'What a fine filly,' one man said in a loud aristocratic voice. 'I say, Cynthia old girl, you've outdone yourself with this young beauty. Sweet sixteen, what?'

'And never been kissed, not below the waist, surely?' one other man guffawed, a weak-chinned fop. 'I hereby claim that pleasure—' His wife, as plump as her husband was skinny, looked me over with what I'd call disdain.

'In which shop did you find this little trollop, Cynthia?' she said insultingly. For that I lifted my head higher and poked out my tongue at her. 'She needs to be taught a few manners, I'd say.'

'Actually she is a young cousin of mine and from a very good Scottish family,' Dorry Gurnard informed her. 'Now if you'll allow us, I've promised to introduce her to a friend of her father's—'

'Dammit, man,' grumbled a guest. 'You can't take her away now. I want to see what she's made of. Get the girl a glass of champagne, someone. Some fizz to encourage her, what?'

'She'll be back later,' Cynthia promised them. 'I suggest you entertain yourselves for a little while longer just now.' As she led me off the assembly were not fooled. Shouts of 'Who's the lucky devil?' and other ribald remarks followed us to a room along the passageway. Cynthia knocked and as we entered a tall broad man with a heavy military moustache stood up from a settee, his ruddy face lighting up at the sight of me. His suit was perfectly fitted to his portly figure, a fine dark worsted cloth.

'Lady Bellinger, what a pleasure,' he greeted her, kissing the back of her hand. 'This is the young lady, is it? Charming, I must say—'

'Miss Diana Mackenzie-Menzies,' she said, giving me the benefit of a double-barrelled name. 'In London for the season and presently my ward—'

'A cousin of mine from Auchterglennie,' Dorry put in to get his share of the acknowledgements.

'So I believe, Gurnard,' said his colonel. 'You may leave us. The girl will be in good hands.'

'None better, sir,' agreed Dorry, turning to leave as

if knowing his place. 'My cousin appears shy, but she has a good spirit. She needs to be brought out—'

'Diana,' Cynthia said as Dorry departed. 'This kind man is a very dear friend. Just do as he tells you and all will be well. He is going to introduce you to a very special kind of love, my dear. Something young girls should know about and experience for their future enjoyment.'

'She has never been exercised?'

'I can assure you no. That pleasure is yours. Let me undress her now, so that you can see her perfection of form.' Cynthia helped me off with my clothes, folding them neatly over a chair. I stood naked before Woodford-Halse and he walked around me on a tour of inspection.

'Jove, a splendid seat on her,' he approved, sitting back down on the settee and patting his thigh. 'Come and sit here, my dear,' he invited me. 'Tell me about yourself.'

I sat across his thick upper legs. 'What is it you want to know, sir?' I played up to him. Really, I thought, if he is going to fuck me, why all the rigmarole?

'Are you a good girl? Truly unspoiled?'

'I'm not sure what you mean, sir—'

'Over my knee, young lady,' he instructed. 'Don't be afraid. I can assure you it's quite normal. Now, over my knee and let me take a look at you.'

To comply, I rolled over and draped myself across his lap, bottom up. 'Good, good girl,' he said satisfactorily as his hand smoothed over my bum cheeks. 'I'm delighted. Such well-turned bouncy young buttocks. Sweet, sweet. Shall we see what we shall see?' He drew my cheeks well apart, pressing his face into the cleft and breathing deeply. I giggled, tickled by his large moustache. For my pains I got a sharp slap on the bottom which made me yelp.

'Behave, Diana,' Cynthia warned.

'His moustache tickled,' I explained. 'Anyway, it isn't very nice, is it, kissing my bottom?'

'You'll come to like it, I think,' Woodford-Halse promised. 'Young ladies acquire a taste for the tongue quickly enough once introduced to the practice. You have the nicest possible bottom to receive kisses upon. Such a delightful little brown hole too.' He pulled my cheeks even further apart. 'Tight as a mouse's ear, this one,' he declared, testing the puckered rosette with a fingertip. I clenched my buttocks and nipped the finger tightly. He withdrew his hand and gave me several more sharp smacks across both cheeks.

'Don't spare her,' advised Cynthia. 'She can be a wilful girl and obviously requires guidance and discipline.'

'Shows spirit though,' Woodford-Halse praised me. 'She didn't flinch, took it bravely. Stand now, girl,' he said. 'Stand erect and facing away from me—'

I did so and he rose from his seat to stand behind me, his hand going around to feel my tits, remarking upon their size and firmness for one so young. The hand continued down over my belly and toyed awhile in my bush, stroked my outer lips and then withdrew to caress my bottom. 'Lady Cynthia,' he said. 'Do sit and be good enough to steady the girl when she is bending over. Good. Now you, young miss, lean over Lady Cynthia,' he ordered. 'Feet apart and brace yourself.'

I did as bid, Cynthia holding my arms and my bottom raised, as ever intrigued as to what to expect and aroused by his touching, smacking and being exposed. 'Loose, girl,' he said sharply. 'Relax your bottom, do not clench.' To Cynthia he said: 'The cold cream, please, madam.' With my downward hanging head I could see between my dangling breasts and on down to the fork of my parted thighs with its hair and split mound. Beyond that I saw Woodford-Halse's trouser fly open and a thick standing cock and large balls freed from their confines. His hand then covered my cleft from cunt to arsehole, applying lotion.

The sight of his standing prick was tempting Cynthia to want some of it herself. 'It looks delicious, Toby,' she told him. 'Let me wet its head before you use it to fuck her.' Right before my eyes she sucked on it noisily, withdrawing finally with the rigid shaft glistening with her saliva. 'Now prepare yourself, Diana,' she said. 'Be still and do not make a fuss—'

It was thus I was taken, the ritual over, Woodford-Halse's thick member sliding up my cunt easily with the lubricant applied. I was more than ready to take it, tilting my rear to accommodate more. But after several in-and-out thrusts he withdrew completely. 'Don't stop, sir,' I dared say. 'I do like that and want it—'

'The little minx, the delightful baggage, I do believe she's in heat,' he chuckled. I felt his prick drawn back the inch or so and its crest directed to my arsehole, where it nudged to seek an entrance.

'Not there, sir,' I pleaded. 'That is not possible, I'm sure.' Cynthia gripped me tighter and I stiffened and drew in my breath as his fat knob forced a passage. For a long moment both my fucker and I remained still, then he eased an inch or two more into my behind. 'Ooh, ooh,' I grunted. 'It's too big, I'm sore.' I squirmed as if in agony but the warm full feeling I received was anything but unpleasant. Buttocks raised, I pushed back against the intruder and felt it go deeper, felt the cushiony warmth of Woodford-Halse's big balls nestle against my bum.

'You'll soon get the feel for it, girl,' I was told. 'Many prefer it in the tradesman's entrance once the taste is acquired.' His stiff cock, completely engulfed up my back passage, pressed to my stomach and I could feel its cylindrical shape perfectly. I jiggled on it, decided I liked the feel, moaned my pleasure.

'She has it all, to the hilt,' he told Cynthia. 'There's some movement too, she's moving against it now—' He began to increase his thrusting. 'Yes, she's definitely moving.'

I was indeed, tentatively at first with his length up me, but nevertheless working my bum to a growing sweet sensation. 'Dip your back, girl,' I was instructed. 'Raise your buttocks. Take it all. This one is a natural, Cynthia. She'll enjoy many a good corking.'

Toby Woodford-Halse, thus far so clinical in his approach as if his buggering me was a military operation, began to grunt and growl like a bear, his balls slapping my bottom as his thrusting increased its pace. My excitement mounted with his quickening penetration. I cried out and ground my arse back into him as I came, feeling his emission fly in a series of spurts deep inside me. Cynthia stroked my hair and congratulated me and I drank a small brandy from a silver flask kept in her handbag. Woodford-Halse straightened his clothes, excused himself, and left hurriedly, the taker of the virginity of my bottom hole.

'You did very well, my dear,' Cynthia praised me. 'Indeed I think you rather enjoyed it. I have no doubt that Sir Toby will want you again very soon and that will cost him plenty. Do you feel ready to join the others now? They'll have been anxiously awaiting your appearance—'

I was led through still naked to the assembled gathering in the salon, where much had gone on in our absence. The plump woman was naked and laid across a coffee table being fucked by a man who was not her husband. He and another man were sucking the nipples of a woman who had yet another woman kneeling between her legs licking her. My appearance was welcomed by several of the men, who led me off to lay me on a long table with my legs hanging.

It was late evening before Cynthia and I returned to Park Lane. I had, it seemed, performed well on my first appearance. 'Mercenary young bitch you may be, Diana,' Cynthia allowed, 'but you do give your money's worth. Such a little whore they had never met. They all want you for their parties.'

Chapter Seventeen
AFRICA

I drove the twenty miles from Entebbe to Kampala with Harry beside me engrossed in his papers and blueprints for the coming meeting with his prospective Arab backers. 'They've enough money to finance twenty such emergency irrigation schemes with their small change,' he said, 'but will drive a hard bargain before agreeing to a damn thing. What's in it for them will be the crunch point.'

'What is in it for them?' I asked, making conversation.

'A couple of good reasons at least. They could have market gardens in their urban areas growing fresh fruit and vegetables. Right now they have to import everything but dates. There'd be a few extra watering-holes for the nomads and their camel herds too, a man-made oasis here and there to improve their living conditions—'

'Would the Kumar royal family care about those things?' I queried. 'They do all right as things are, don't they?'

'Very all right,' Harry conceded. 'They rule like medieval despots. But times are changing, there's even an unofficial opposition party hoping for more democratic laws. They don't push their case too hard, of course, for even the professional and intellectual Kumaris can get their heads lopped off.'

'Charming,' I laughed. 'So how do you intend to push your case? They won't behead you, I hope.'

'Who knows, once you're in the Kumar Embassy it's a closed world to the outside,' Harry grinned. 'Could be my best argument would be that they could grow grass on their football pitches. They say the king is soccer mad, intending Kumar to win the World Cup eventually—'

'You are joking, of course.'

'Think so?' Harry said. 'I'll try every bloody way.'

'What about this Prince Kalid you're going to see?' I asked. 'Is he a medieval despot?'

'In Kumar, no doubt. In Europe he spends as much on expensive call-girls, gambling and his racing stables every month to pay for such as I hope to get. He's got a magnificent bloody great yacht moored at Monte Carlo that must set him back millions.'

'I'll bet his old grandfather was a herder who ran a small herd of camels and goats before they had oil,' I said. 'You've worked so long and so hard at this, it must surely be worthwhile, my darling.'

'I'll have a good try,' Harry determined. 'We could halt the spread of desert and rejuvenate the northern territory with a little financial backing. Even that I've cut to the bone. Locals would do the most of the work. Christ, it could save whole tribes from starvation in Uganda and even areas of Sudan adjacent. I must get that across.'

'Don't forget,' I reminded him, 'what's in it for them. Your own words. They'll be far more interested to know what you can do in their part of Arabia. Concentrate on that.'

'I will. I'll impress 'em that if the scheme can work in the conditions here in the drought areas of Africa, it's a piece of cake in modern Kumar.'

'What about the prestige angle?' I suggested. 'The

Kumar government, and that sounds like it just means the ruling family, can put it about that they are giving aid to the Third World. Willing to dip into their pocket and that it's just not the West that cares. And having your scheme in Kumar would be doing something for the ordinary people, improving their lot, keeping the opposition quiet—'

'By God, that's a good point which I'll use,' Harry said, nodding across at me. 'Dear Di, you always surprise me.'

'You mean I'm not just a pair of big tits and such,' I laughed at him. 'Aren't you glad you have me with you instead of your secretary Miss Samali this trip?'

'I believe you are jealous of her,' Harry teased.

'Not any more. I think you are right about her. She prefers her own sex.' I smiled at him innocently. 'Just a woman's intuition—'

'Wish I knew the best way to approach these people about the aid,' Harry pondered, his mind on the business in hand. 'I'll grovel as much as need be if that will help. It could take hours to decide. You may have a very long wait, my love.'

'Just get what you're after and we'll celebrate,' I told him, 'no matter how late. I've laid on some champagne in the fridge. We'll go to bed and drink a toast to your success.'

Harry nodded, reaching across to cup my left tit as I steered. 'You look particularly lovely tonight. Having you along with me will knock their eyes out. Arab men appreciate a good-looking woman. They'll probably want me to sell you.'

'For the money you need for your scheme?'

'Not even for that,' he laughed. 'Keep your fingers crossed for me. I shall be persuasion itself and clinch the deal. I'll talk 'em up a storm.'

At the wrought-iron Kumar Embassy gates, floodlit

and emblazoned with the royal coat-of-arms, we were scrutinised by fierce-looking Arab guards. Our identities checked, we were directed through grounds to a car park thick with Rolls and Mercedes. Marble steps and tall double-doors led into the foyer of the embassy, a ballroom-sized hall of cascading cut-glass chandeliers and the biggest genuine Persian carpet I thought imaginable. A major-domo bowed us through to a further magnificently carpeted room. Around the walls dark-visaged desert soldiers with automatic rifles stood motionless. The main area of the room was busy with guests both in Arab costume, dark lounge suits or the *kanzu* gown of African muslims.

I enjoy such scenes, looking around with great interest and catching the beady eye of the Prince Kalid, who sat on a fat pile of embroidered cushions under a huge framed portrait of his cousin the king. The prince squinted in my direction, perched like a squat toad, bored with the proceedings. More elaborate chandeliers lit the scene, the nearest thing to an Arabian Nights pastiche I was ever likely to see. Then Harry and I were confronted by a very tall hawk-faced man, handsomely dark with a scar on his cheek, impeccably dressed in a Savile Row evening suit.

'Jebel Aziz,' he introduced himself, taking my hand and bowing over to touch it with his lips. 'I met Harry in New York, of course. I am enchanted to meet you, Mrs Saxon.' His hand was cool, dry, and his clasp became a definite caress. All the time deep dark eyes searched mine as if to uncover any secrets hidden in them, his look calm and assured, too cocksure by half, I thought.

'How do you know I am Mrs Saxon?' I tested his confidence. 'I could be his secretary, or even his mistress.'

'Either way he would be a lucky man,' said Aziz, still

clasping my hand. I felt he was undressing me with his dark eyes, getting the measure of me. 'Harry told me he had a wife. He did not say she was a beautiful woman.'

'Don't try to get one up on this fellow,' my husband said. 'Jebel knows everything. As private secretary and adviser to Prince Kalid nothing escapes him.'

'I was informed by telephone at the gate that Mr and Mrs Saxon had arrived,' said the Arab diplomat. 'That is how I knew who you were. I have no crystal ball. Now I will present you to His Highness. He has expressed a desire to meet you, Mrs Saxon. Come with me, please.'

Harry and I followed the tall Jebel Aziz through the gathered people, noting I was the only woman present, hoping my hair was in place and smoothing my dress over my hips. We got in line, moving forward as the prince acknowledged the bowing and scraping of people led before one. Then we were directly before him. I wondered if I should curtsy or something, but then thought, no, why the hell should I? Harry bowed his head deferentially for his own reasons.

'Saxon,' said the royal personage. 'You have brought the full specifications as ordered?' I had a good look at him, seated cross-legged on his cushions like a medieval potentate, a fat caliph of ancient Baghdad. His Arab headress was circled with gold bands, his robes were pure silk. In his waistband was a curved ceremonial dagger. The overall picture was of arrogance and disinterest, however, a man going through the motions and not hiding his boredom.

'I have the specifications, drawings and costings here, Your Highness,' Harry said, bowing again and indicating the briefcase under his arm. 'I have the honour to present it to you with considerations for both schemes—'

Kalid waved a fat jewelled hand languidly. I judged the rings on his stubby fingers alone would have financed Harry's initiative to revitalise a large arid area in the northern Acholi territory. 'We have our own experts to evaluate what you have with you,' the Prince said. 'Also the Ugandan minister concerned, Okot Kidepo, to represent his government. Jebel,' he summoned his secretary and aide. 'Conduct Saxon and Kidepo to the conference room prepared.'

Harry left me with a last hopeful look and I gave his hand a quick squeeze for luck. Personally, for my own part, I did not give a tinker's cuss whether they accepted the scheme or didn't, except for the sake of my husband who had worked so hard in his own time to do a worthwhile thing. If these people were too disinterested, short-sighted or stupid to turn down a project that would improve the lot of their less fortunate subjects, so be it. As Okot Kidepo passed me, suitably dressed in his muslim cap and robe, he grinned and nodded his ebony face, no doubt recalling fucking me at the wedding reception. If that helped Harry in the coming discussions, fair enough.

Then the Prince was addressing me, stroking his small beard and regarding me with his narrow eyes. 'You are Saxon's wife, I presume, madam. I find your hair most unusual. What colour is that? Is it natural, or have you dyed it so?'

'Rich chestnut, I think, or auburn. It's all my own,' I answered. 'It's got darker as I've got older.'

'Older women improve in all ways,' observed the Prince, as if his word was law. 'With maturity comes the ripeness, the blooming. The ripeness has come to you very well. It is not uncommon with Arab females, but not so much with the European women I have noted.'

I smiled and inclined my head at his compliment, even if he made me sound like a pear or other fruit ideal for picking, plucking, or more likely fucking. At least he had shown some animation, some interest at something. I took it he liked voluptuous women with good tits and plush bottoms.

'You find me amusing?' he said, sounding angry.

'No, Your Highness,' I assured him hastily, not daring to aggravate his royal personage. 'I was pleased to be so appreciated by one so discerning. Not all men recognise that a woman can improve with age.'

At that moment we were rejoined by Jebel Aziz. He bowed to his master, salaaming or genuflecting, whatever they do to show respect. The prince crooked a fat bejewelled finger at Aziz and drew him close, whispering in his ear while still giving me his narrow-eyed stare.

'Come with me, please, Mrs Saxon,' Jebel Aziz said as he straightened up. 'There is a comfortable room where you may relax while you wait for your husband to conduct his business.' I followed behind the suave Arab, feeling the eyes of the men in the room directed at my body until we entered a thickly carpeted corridor. The room I was shown into was lavishly furnished. I was ushered to a deep couch set before a low table.

'You will find this a satisfactory place to wait for your husband, I think,' he said. 'There are refreshments, soft drinks. No alcohol, I'm afraid, as is our custom. Anything else you have but to command.'

He really was a smoothie, I decided, his bright dark eyes never leaving me. My surroundings were as luxurious as other parts of the embassy, carpeted with priceless Persian rugs, a chandelier dripping with light, wallpaper that was not paper but the richest embroidered silk. These people did all right for themselves, I decided. 'I shall be very comfortable here, thank you, Mr Aziz,' I said. On the low polished table inlaid with gold was set a silver box of cigarettes, turkish delight and marshmallows, soft drinks and crystal goblets. 'I really don't mind how long I have to wait if my husband's business is settled to his satisfaction.'

'You must call me Jebel,' he insisted. 'Remember, if you desire any extra refreshment, you have only to ask. Would you like a meal served, or coffee perhaps?'

I felt we were on friendly enough terms. 'Just one thing I'd like right now,' I said.

'Name it, madam. You impressed my Prince, you know. He insists nothing was to be spared for your comfort—'

'I'd like to kick off these shoes and rest my feet.'

Aziz laughed, showing gleaming white teeth. He knelt at my feet and removed my shoes, white kid leather with three-inch heels which he placed neatly together under the couch. Taking hold of an ankle, he massaged the foot, then did the same to the other one. His grip was firm yet gentle, his touch sensual, his hands light brown with perfectly manicured fingernails. The massage became a caress, went on up my leg to my calf. He looked up at me to test my reaction.

'You have wicked eyes, Mr Aziz,' I said.

'And you have such soft skin. We Arabs greatly admire beauty and you are beautiful. I told you to call me Aziz, and I shall call you Diana. That is right for two who will be such close friends.'

'How do you know that?' I smiled.

'Because you are not only beautiful but a friendly woman,' he said meaningfully, his hands now continuing the soft stroking movements above my knee. 'I was speaking earlier to Kidepo, the Ugandan minister of agriculture here for the aid programme discussions. He spoke most highly of your friendly nature.'

'No doubt he did,' I said coolly.

'You were representing your husband at a reception, I believe. You Europeans have a saying that behind every successful man there is a woman. Very apt in your husband's case, I think.' His hand was well above my knee, resting above my stocking top on the inside of my thigh. 'I feel you could help your husband's cause here, tonight. His Highness has expressed to me his interest in having an audience with you later—'

'If it would help to get my husband's schemes backed by your country's financial aid,' I said, 'then I would do whatever you recommend.' The hand on my inner thigh moved up insiduously, fingers stroking tantalisingly and reaching the crotch of my briefs, coming to rest on my mound.

'I'm sure some arrangement could be arrived at,' he promised. I said nothing and his hand moved again, long fingers stroking through the silky material against my bush. I shifted position, parting my legs enough for his access as if getting comfortable. Rub, rub went a fingertip up and down the lips of my cunt, a deliberately slow movement that brought a low moan from my lips as my slit pouted.

'Do you mean what I think you mean?' I asked, my voice thickening with arousal.

'You approve? His Highness would show his gratitude.' The finger pushed its way into the material of my briefs, inside my cunny lips. The itch in me grew stronger and I pushed my crotch against his hand, requiring to come off on the manipulation. An unusual, highly arousing thing for me was that he worked me up as casually as if he were scratching his chin. I gripped his wrist and pulled it to me fiercely.

He drew away, raising the finger to his lips, tasting the tip with his tongue. 'The scent of a very aroused woman,' he said. 'Unfortunately I must leave you now and see to my duties. You will be received by His Highness later, when his guests leave. In the meantime I have arranged a little entertainment for you—'

Sex and Mrs Saxon

'I was quite enjoying the entertainment you were providing,' I admitted. 'You stopped just when the best part was coming.'

'Patience, there will be all you need and more later,' he smiled wickedly. 'If you feel the urge for relief, however, I recommend these—' Aziz handed me two small weighty balls joined together with a thin chain. They were slightly smaller than table-tennis balls and smooth as ball bearings. I must admit having never seen such and asked what they were and what they were for.

'Some call them duo-balls or Ben-Wa, supposedly an ancient delight for Japanese ladies to amuse themselves with when their husbands were absent at the wars. They have long been a favourite toy for our Arabian women, too. Usually they are of stainless steel. These, of course, are solid gold including the little adjoining chain. Try it, and keep as a memento of your visit.'

'So just what do I do with them?' I asked, laughing.

'When inserted into the vagina almost any body movement produces very erotic sensations, so it is claimed. They give and maintain long periods of sexual arousal, with multiple orgasms guaranteed. You may find them amusing.' With that he bowed and left me. I was left with the balls in my hand and the chandelier above my head went out, leaving me in darkness. A moment later a beam came from above and behind me and shone on a screen that was lowered on the wall opposite. Projected on it I saw an ornate room with the floor covered with large cushions. I sat back realising I was to be given a private film show to pass the time.

Two young girls appeared, both amply curved as is the Arab ideal, dressed in what I considered the costume of belly dancers. They fondled and kissed, removing their scanty clothing, lying down among the cushions to suck each other's nipples, kiss cunts and generally make torrid lesbian love in close-up camera angles. Entertaining me with a highly pornographic show was no doubt meant to prepare me for what was in store later. There was a professionalism about the film that was evident by the colour, lighting, camera work, all bearing the stamp of a skilled film crew. The nude girls were gorgeous creatures, sloe-eyed, well-fleshed with pointed wobbly tits and plump shaven cunts. They seemed to enjoy their work as they touched tongues and masturbated, leering into the camera. One lolled back, thighs apart, while the other girl held open her cunt, the camera moving in for a vivid close shot of red-glistening innards with an erect clitoris as large as a thumb. Her partner swooped on it, sucking avidly.

Watching the sexual antics had me squeezing my thighs hard together, squirming my bottom on the couch. My hand went down to rub myself and I remembered the sex toy I still held in my hand. Now was the perfect time to try its effectiveness, I decided, slipping off my knickers. I pushed the balls inside me, an easy passage with the moistness brought on by Aziz and his expert touching up. They fitted snugly, touching the sides. With my first slightest movement they rubbed together and sent a flow of sensations through my cunt. I swivelled my hips and gasped at the surges of arousal that had me falling back and jerking my pelvis helplessly. I came once, bucking in the throes, and brought myself to an immediate second climax.

I moved more cautiously following that, realising their potency, enjoying the little ripples that pulsed through my cunt as the balls moved about inside me, keeping me on a delightfully protracted verge of another strong orgasm. The trick, I'd learned, was to control excessive motions, to luxuriate in the erotic feeling even the slightest movement produced, and be able to bring about yet another good come as desired. On the screen before me Jebel Aziz appeared, wearing a long cloak which he threw aside to reveal a naked tautly muscled frame and a massive erect prick rearing over a pair of heavy balls. He stood over the pair of girls so absorbed with each other, hands on hips as he awaited their reaction.

Both females immediately stretched out eager hands to grasp his huge stalk. It was indeed a prick to be proud of, stiff and stout and looking a good ten-inches long. The girls kissed it, licked along the shaft, tried desperately to share the great plum-like helmet in their mouths at the same time. Fascinated, I watched the tableau before me with an envious lust. My hips jerked to set the little golden balls inside me jiggling and exchanging places. I cried out, lay on my back along the couch and jerked as if mounted by a man and being fucked. On the screen Aziz was fucking one of the girls from the rear while she tongued the cunt of the other. Then the light came back on and I sat up dazed. Aziz stood before me wearing the cloak he had appeared in for his entrance in the film. He poured a drink of iced orange juice and held the glass to my lips.

'Did you enjoy our little film?' he said. 'There was very much more erotica in later scenes I should like you to have seen, but His Highness awaits your presence. I take it you found it of interest—'

'You knew damned well I would,' I told him, trying to gain my composure. 'You arranged that to get me primed for your Prince—'

'Well, I hope you are. We would not like to have an unprepared partner for the Prince's pleasure, would we?' he smiled graciously. 'Let us not waste time.'

'What if my husband comes looking for me?'

'He will not, I can assure you. His meeting will not end until word is given. That has been arranged.'

'Seems a great deal has been arranged,' I said. 'If I'm to go through with your Prince having me, can I be sure that my husband's schemes will be agreed?'

'You will ensure that by pleasing His Highness. He saw you and desired you. Go to him willingly tonight and your husband will get all he asks for.'

He escorted me to a nearby lift, noting my awkward walk with the duo-balls jiggling away inside me. 'I see you made use of my little gift,' he observed as we ascended in the lift. The door opened to a corridor where I was shown into a tiled room with a large sunken bath. Waiting were the two girls who had appeared in the film with him, dressed in their belly-dancing outfits, smiling a welcome.

'They will bathe you in readiness to go to His Highness,' Aziz announced, leaving us.

The girls came to me and unzipped my dress, stripping me with much giggling, especially when it was seen I wore no knickers. It was a relief to sink into the bath, the warm scented bubbles up to my neck. I used the chance to remove the duo-balls from my cunt, making sure they went into my handbag when I got out of the bath. The girls towelled me dry, passing comments in Arabic to each other and my breasts and cunt were no doubt objects of great interest. I was powdered and scented, and finally draped in a long white silk gown that tied at the neck and opened all the way down to my feet. Underneath it was just me.

If I felt like a sacrificial lamb at least I consoled myself it was all for a good cause. I could not say that I looked forward to being fucked by a fat frog of a man, royal or not. If I smiled wryly at the thought it was because I was thinking I had come some way from an affair with a coalman in Scotland to an assignation with a real Prince. The girls led me through to an adjoining room, a palace of a bedroom with the usual chandeliers, thick Persian carpets and ornate furniture including a mammoth bed with a tall canopy and hanging silk drapes. On it, sitting up cross-legged and looking more like a fat toad than ever was Princey. He was clad now in a single robe that was open and showed a large expanse of pot belly.

At my appearance he nodded his fat face as if satisfied with the look of the one he was to regale with a royal fuck. Jebel Aziz stood beside the bed, lifting his eyebrows at me as if to warn me to be on my best behaviour. Just what was that to mean, I wondered? My best seductively sexual behaviour while showing due deference to the royal toad, his lord and master? Should I be the one to make the first advances, or stand and await his pleasure? The two girls, I noted, had stripped off and climbed on to the huge bed, lying prone at the feet of their lord. Aziz came behind me and untied the thin silken cord that held the cloak-like robe I wore to my shoulders. It fell to the floor and I stood naked before the all-powerful one.

From behind me I heard Aziz's cloak slide to the floor, felt his broad bare chest against my back and the curved slackness of his prick rest in the cleavage of my bottom. His hands came around me to cup my tits, lifting both as if to offer them to his master for approval. 'Only as I instruct you to do, Diana Saxon,' he whispered into my ear, pressing his body harder to mine. 'The Prince desires an entertainment and visual stimulation prior to performing the act himself. I shall therefore do what I will with you to arouse you for his pleasure—'

I had to suppress a giggle. It appeared to me that the magnificent one, whom Allah preserve, couldn't get it up without others to titillate him by putting on a show. How he regarded my nakedness was hard to say, his hooded heavy-lidded eyes as expressionless as ever. Perhaps years of sexual excess with numerous wives and concubines, plus no doubt expensive call-girls on his visits abroad, had dulled his sensual potency. Or maybe I was doing him an injustice, being far too important or plain lazy to waste his royal time on dalliance, foreplay or whatever, so the sexual partners of his choice were brought to him already aroused and eager by the efforts of others.

Like Aziz. His huge cock, which I'd viewed with astonishment in the film, was now stiffening into an iron-hard cylinder and rearing against my posterior. I loved the feel of it, wriggled my bottom against it to show I would welcome its entrance. 'Join the other women on the bed,' he said firmly, so I climbed up beside them and they immediately closed in on me, directing me to lie flat on my back. One began caressing my breasts and giving my nipples little bites and sucks. At my other end I felt a mouth clamp over my cunt and a long tongue begin to flick away at my clitoris. Glancing down over my nose I saw the girl's head moving as she busied herself between my thighs. Her tongue moved down to lick wetly at my arsehole, the broad flat of it lapping and then the tip probing the entrance. Then Aziz was kneeling at my head, heavy balls draped over my face.

I was already a gone woman, moaning little sighs and moving my parted thighs to get the full enjoyment of being tongued so lewdly. The girl sucking my bubs left off to raise her head and I glanced up over Aziz's balls to see her take his prick deep into her vermilion-lipped mouth. My hand went up to cup the warm wrinkled sac drooping over my face, reaching out with my tongue to lick it, trying to draw the whole mass into my mouth. It was quite a tableau we presented, grunting our lust as four naked forms shifted position to get the most of each other. The girl between my legs began rubbing her mound against mine in simulated fucking, moving rapidly, getting my response in kind, which became wantonly wild as I realised I was actually penetrated. It was the girl whose thumb-sized clitoris I'd seen in close-up during the film. Now it was in me enough to feel its hardness prodding me like a miniature penis. I lifted against it, excited by being actually fucked by another woman. Crying out, I came in delicious spasms.

But then I was lifted, turned over by Aziz and my bottom raised and presented to him. Over my shoulder on my hands and knees I saw Prince Kalid stretch out an arm, his hand holding a joined necklace of gold chain set every inch or so with dark-red gems I took to be garnets. Was he rewarding me for being so lewdly uninhibited and wantonly integrated in the foursome arranged for his amusement? One of the girls took the necklace from his hand and, kneeling up with Aziz behind my raised bottom, undid the jewelled clasp.

The necklace was about eighteen inches in length when open and she drew it through her lips, wetting every gem stone thoroughly with her saliva. She then placed it in between the cleft of my buttock cheeks which Aziz held open for her. She pressed the first bit of chain and a stone the size of a grape against the puckered rosette of my bum and pushed it in me. More followed as I groaned a complaint, feeling both constricted yet excitingly depraved to be used so. My poor abused bottom passage bulged and burned. Then Aziz was on me, over me like a hound, his great thick penis up my cunt to the hilt.

He fucked me in hard quick strokes, the head of his prick seeming to nudge the necklace stuffed up my back passage with each deep thrust inwards. The sensation was like none I had ever known, having me clawing at the cover of the bed, raising my head and squawking out for mercy. There was no escape. Aziz clutched my hips in a vice-like grip and lunged away until my pain became pleasure and my cries were those of a woman in the throes of a tremendously body-shuddering climax. He too shouted in his orgasm, jerking and jetting his unction deep into my interior like a soothing balm. Before I had in any way recovered I was bodily turned around, my bottom now facing Prince Kalil. An inch or two of the necklace projected from my anus and it was withdrawn from me stone by stone. It was replaced by a prick, Kalil hunching over my back and pushing his long thin length up my arse, grunting his great pleasure like a lustful bear.

In my daze it seemed he was no sooner inside me than I was being lifted away and half-carried half-walked back to the adjacent bathroom. It would seem the Prince, brought to arousal by our exhibition, merely needed a receptacle to deposit his come in a matter of seconds. For myself, quite sated and exhausted for once, I was glad to be lowered back into the bath and be sponged of the sweat of my exertions by the two attentive Arab girls. When I had dressed, Aziz appeared again in his well-cut evening suit and escorted me to the lift and back down to the room where I had waited earlier. Both my cunt and arse tingled, but otherwise I felt none the worse for an extraordinary bout of group sex. Aziz handed me a tooled leather box of about six by four inches. I opened it to find the garnet necklace used upon me so intimately curled on a velvet bed.

'A little souvenir of this evening's audience with His Highness Prince Kalil,' he informed me graciously. 'It would give him great pleasure to know you would like it.' He then handed me a little card with a number printed on it. 'His Highness hopes you will keep in touch, as indeed I do. This number will reach me anywhere any time.'

'So we can carry on where we left off?' I reproached him.

'Why not?' Aziz reasoned calmly. 'It would be pleasurable, as you were seen to have found it so, and also to your great advantage. Prince Kalid finds you most pleasing. If your husband is busy with his irrigation work, you might enjoy a cruise on His Highness's yacht. As a collector of privately produced erotic films, he suggests you might appear in some—'

'Do all what we did on film?' I said. 'I don't think so.'

'You have already,' he informed me. 'This night. Hidden cameras captured our little orgy on film.'

'In glorious technicolor, no doubt,' I said dryly. 'Nothing you lot get up to would surprise me. What was that you said about my Harry being busy? Do you mean his schemes have been approved? For that I agreed to join in your little orgy, as you call it—'

'Signed, sealed and more than adequate Kumari financial aid granted to start your husband's work right away,' Aziz assured me. 'Let me take you to the conference room now, where all the parties concerned are busy congratulating each other. You should be congratulated too for your part, but that will be our secret.'

Driving back home later, Harry sat beside me in the car highly elated with the success. 'I did it, I did it, I bloody well did it!' he crowed. 'What do you think of your old man now, Mrs Diana Mackenzie Saxon?' He leaned over to kiss my cheek as I steered down the unlit dirt road hedged in by thick bush on either side. 'So, didn't I do well? To let me have what I wanted they agreed to do anything suggested—'

And so had I.

Chapter Eighteen
ENGLAND

Throughout summer I was very much part of a select London scene, living comfortably in Lady Cynthia's Park Lane house, a popular attraction in her circle of friends. I learned that many wealthy and aristocratic folk, the men and their women as well, had little to spend their money and energies on other than sex in all its variety of forms. This was true of the ones I met, whom Cynthia Bellinger catered to. At the arranged parties, in between their bouts of fucking or watching others at it, I did hear talk of Ascot, Henley, Monte Carlo and such, even occasionally mention of the threat of war with Germany. Meanwhile I had written home to my parents, telling them I'd found employment as a typist, studying shorthand and intending to gain promotion to secretary. That was to please them, as did the money I enclosed in my letters.

Cynthia came up with regular payments for my services. The dashing Dorry Gurnard escorted me to the best restaurants and night clubs, a lover skilled in all forms of lechery. Between times I enjoyed myself by myself in the bustle of London, window shopping, improving an enquiring mind with visits to the great variety of museums. I searched the antique shops and market stalls for bargains. My bank book showed a growing health balance, but I was still a canny Scots' lass at heart, spending on only what I cared to possess. My clothes, the roof over my head, the food I ate, all were provided by Lady Cynthia. If a prostitute – and indeed I was – I was hardly a common one.

On one of my lone forays to the market stalls of Petticoat Lane during a bright September morning I was tapped on the shoulder. I turned and was faced by Margaret Winthrop. She was the handsome woman I had admired for her chic in Scotland, the woman I had secretly watched making love with the young Harry Saxon. She smiled a welcome at me, as ever fashionably dressed, a Paisley silk scarf at her throat knotted to perfection. I was reminded how, on first seeing her, I had resolved to emulate her flair and confidence.

'Diana Mackenzie,' she said, offering a gloved hand. 'Do you remember me? You had us worried to death, you know, disappearing like that. Harry told me it was all his fault you had to bolt. We just hoped you weren't finding it very difficult, leaving home so suddenly. I'm delighted to see you look very well indeed.'

'I've got a nice place to live and a job,' I told her. 'Really I've done very well in London.'

'Obviously,' she remarked. 'So smart and quite a beautiful young lady too. Harry will be relieved to know you are all right. He was very taken by you, you know, and still talks of meeting you in Scotland. Will you join me for a coffee?'

We found a little café where the waitress, impressed by two such well-dressed females, cleared a window table for us and took our order. Poland had been invaded by German troops two days previously. The café owner turned on the wireless set on his counter and the booms of Big Ben preceded Prime Minister Neville Chamberlain's awaited speech. No reply had been made to our ultimatum for Nazi Germany to withdraw its army from Poland, he announced with unmistakable sadness in his tired old voice, and therefore a state of war now existed between Great Britain and Germany. All present were silent during the speech. At its end the bustle of the café continued.

The cockney waitress brought two cups of coffee. 'That's the balloon gone up then,' she announced cheerfully. 'Ninepence for the two coffees—'

Margaret gave her a shilling and told her to keep the change. 'Will you stay in London now?' she asked me. 'There's a good chance we'll be bombed here. Scotland might well be safer.'

'I'll stay,' I said. 'Who knows what will happen? I rather fancy going into the women's services. The navy one.'

'You'd make a pretty Wren,' Margaret said. 'Harry Saxon volunteered yesterday for the Royal Engineers. As I said, he oftens talks about you, wished that he'd known you better.'

'Well, I liked the look of him too,' I admitted. 'A very handsome boy, I remember. I had a crush on him myself. I liked the way he stood up to his mother that time.'

'You saw us that night of the ball at his father's house, didn't you?' she stated calmly. 'So you know we were lovers. No, not so much lovers as sharing a purely physical thing. Would that make a difference if you should meet Harry again?'

'Why should it?'

'Exactly. But many young girls might not think so. He'll be at my house this evening and I know would be delighted to see you.' She brought a little card from her handbag. 'My Chelsea address, Diana. Come along and surprise him. He'd be over the moon.'

'I'd like to. That would be lovely.'

'Good. Can I drive you to your digs?'

'No, it's not far away,' I lied. 'I shall look forward to tonight.'

The first air-raid warning of the war sounded out soon after we parted – a false alarm with the all-clear soon given. I took a taxi and arrived back at Cynthia's, my mind full of anticipation at meeting Harry Saxon again. I remembered how I had felt about him, the first stirrings of young love, I supposed, and realised that specially warm feeling still lingered. At the Park Lane house Atherton, Porlock and the footman and maids were loading a large van parked before the front entrance. Paintings, furniture and other items were being stacked into the van's interior.

As I entered the house Atherton gave me a conspiratorial wink as he carted out a Chippendale carver chair. 'What on earth is going on?' I asked.

'Rats leaving the sinking ship,' he grinned. 'Bolting. Heading for the highlands of Scotland and safety.'

'When was all this decided?' I laughed, seeing Porlock puffing as he went past with an antique roll-top desk, with Patience bearing most of the weight at the other end.

'The moment war was declared,' Atherton said cheerfully. 'My last day here anyway. I've been recalled to the Grenadiers. My only regret is that I never got a fuck at you, Scotty—'

'Chance would be a fine thing,' I teased him, going into the drawing room to find Lady Cynthia supervising the packing of her precious paintings.

'I'm leaving, Diana, leaving London,' she announced breathlessly. 'Leaving for my lodge in Inverburie this afternoon in the Rolls. Porlock will have to drive. Atherton has let me down—'

'Probably his regiment has more use for him,' I said. 'Am I included in this move?'

'Of course. London will be no place to stay in,

what with the blackout and God knows what to contend with.'

'Then I shall stay,' I decided. I went upstairs with a scream of 'ungrateful bitch, little whore' following me. Putting what clothes I thought suitable into a case, I went out into the street and walked away, ending yet another episode in my life. The taxi I hailed took me to Dorry Gurnard's flat, where I had occasionally slept with him and had been given a key. There was no answer to my ring so I went in.

The morning room showed signs of recent habitation, empty champagne bottles, glasses on the table, stubbed cigarettes in a large cut-glass ashtray. I put my case down and noted the bedroom door slightly ajar, cautiously peering in on hearing muffled sounds. On the floor, left as if hurriedly discarded, I saw the battledress blouses and trousers of two army uniforms. From my vantage point, looking in at the foot of a bed, muscled bare buttock cheeks were thrusting up and down. I recognised the broad back of the man in the superior fucking position as Dorry. The legs wrapped about his back were definitely not female.

I concentrated my gaze, looking hard between Dorry's legs and saw his shaft pistoning into the arsehole of the young man beneath him. It was obviously no place for me to find a night's lodging. One of the pieces of army uniform on the floor, I noted as I withdrew, had a bandsman's insignia on the sleeve. Another taxi took me to a small hotel, where I booked in for the week, long enough I felt to enable me to find a suitable bed-sit. I bathed, dressed and walked the distance to Margaret's house, not using the amount of make-up I did for Cynthia's arranged parties. It was a lovely September evening and I needed to walk to decide on my future.

Signs of being at war were all around as I walked the London streets, troops and civilians filling sandbags to place around public building and monuments. I would volunteer for the Women's Royal Naval Service the very next day, I decided. By then I was outside Margaret's Chelsea home, a neat three-storied Georgian town house. When I rang the bell the door was opened by a plain girl of about my own age in a lacy cap and apron. My mind still on my ambition to enlist, I said to her 'You should join the Wrens, I'm going to.'

Before the girl could utter her surprise, a tall sturdy figure bounded down the passageway, sweeping me up into his arms. 'Diana Mackenzie,' roared the handsome Harry Saxon. 'You'll never know how much I've wanted to see you again!' So saying he plonked a long kiss of welcome on my lips. He me led by the hand up a white stairway to a lounge as tastefully furnished as I'd imagined Margaret's would be. There he surprised me even more with his next announcement.

'Margaret and Dennis,' he said. 'This is the girl I am going to marry, if she'll have me. She will, of course, for I won't take no for an answer.'

Margaret sat with a little smile while her husband came to shake my hand. He was comfortably dressed in a checked shirt and cardigan, corduroy slacks, looking like the professor of music he turned out to be. Older than his lovely wife by some twenty years, I thought, I wondered if he knew she had fucked so eagerly with the young man beside me. 'What do you think of that sudden proposal?' he asked me.

'That he doesn't know what he'd be taking on,' I replied lightly. 'We hardly know each other.'

'Wait and see how serious I am,' Harry promised, taking my hand. 'I decided we'd marry when we first met in Scotland. Did I cause a lot of trouble for you at home?'

'I took the easy way out,' I said. 'All turned out well in the end. My parents know where I am.'

'Brave girl, taking off and making a new life for

herself,' Margaret said. 'Before dinner is served Dennis and I spend some time in the garden. Plants to be watered and such. You two stay here and get to know each other better. I take it you don't mind us leaving you alone?'

Left with Harry, I was struck once again just what a good-looking boy he was, beaming his delight to see me and be with me. 'That dress, it's perfect on you,' he said. 'The way you fill it, well, you could wear a sack and make it look good. Do you have an inkling how lovely you are?'

'We seem to have had this conversation before,' I laughed at him, teasing. 'Only this time your father isn't around, I hope. How is he, by the way?'

'In France with my mother, making each other miserable, no doubt. He sold the sand quarry and retired early. They live near Cannes and he hates it. You know, sometimes I think the old bugger had something going for him in Scotland. Some woman giving him what he wasn't getting from mother.'

'Would you blame him for that?' I ventured.

'Good luck to the old boy. Would you mind if I kissed you? I want to very much.'

He lowered me to the settee and I held him at arm's length. 'What makes you think I'm that kind of girl?' I enjoyed teasing. 'Wouldn't that make you want even more?'

'Undoubtedly,' he agreed. 'I remember our last time together and being so so rudely interrupted. I've never forgotten it—'

'And would you still want to marry me if I gave in to you so easily?'

'The more so. Tomorrow before I report to the army, by special licence, if you want.'

'I thought you were at university studying engineering.'

Sex and Mrs Saxon

'I quit on Friday when Hitler went into Poland. The Royal Engineers have got me for the duration. Doesn't that deserve a kiss?'

I liked his youthful humour, his exuberance, thinking how nicely normal it was to be flirted with by a young man of around my own age. It occurred to me I had never been courted or had sex with anyone much below middle age. His good looks and obvious admiration for me weakened my resolve. 'If you do want to go with me, I mean as a serious boyfriend, I'd like that,' I told him. 'With you away in the army it would mean exchanging letters mostly, I suppose, but that's nice too.'

'I want that very much,' he said, his arm going around my shoulder. I let him kiss me, fondly at first, then getting my response his mouth pressed hard on mine and I opened my lips to accept his tongue. We kissed long and passionately again and again, my arousal matching his. Little by little I was eased back on the long settee, his fingers clumsy in their haste as he sought to unbutton the front of my dress. Hardly waiting for him, I took over, undoing as far down as my waist. He held apart the dress top, his hands trembling as he lifted my breasts out of their bra cups. Lifted free and raised by the now underslung cups my tits stuck up like big melons, my nipples indecently erect and long, begging for a sucking.

So much for my determination to act the sweet little innocent to impress him! I had really wanted him to think of me as more than just a nice body and a good fuck. Girls are that way when they want to keep a boy. The last thing I wanted him to discover was that I was a whore. Yet no matter what I determine, my nature betrays me. 'Yes, yes,' I sighed as I held his head and drew him to my breasts. His lips closed over my nipples and sucked each in turn. 'Yes,' I repeated as his hands went under my dress and I lifted my bottom to allow him to draw down my knickers, raising my feet for him to pull them over my shoes.

His breathing was laboured as he went on his knees before me and I parted my thighs wide for him. 'I want to eat your sweet cunt,' I heard him mumble, his breath warm against me. His tongue lapped my outer lips, kissed them lovingly, then I felt entered and licked avidly, my clitty laved and sucked. Lolling back, I raised my knees, giving my all to him. His hands slid under my bum cheeks, lifting them, pulling me on to him. Margaret, whose house we were in, had taught him very well, I decided, not caring as long as his sweet tongue pleasured me so. I told him I was coming, my voice hoarse, my hips bucking. 'What are you doing to me? Making me do!' I groaned in the final throes. 'I shall come against your mouth! I'll come, I am coming! Oh God, I can't help it. Harry dear, go on—'

So did two young sexually oriented people begin their real relationship. I lolled back on the deep settee's cushions with that weakening but delightful feeling the aftermath of a strong orgasm gives. My breasts were still stuck up and I looked down between them to see Harry still on his knees admiring my cunt, a silly self-satisfied smirk on his face. 'I didn't half bring you off, didn't I?' he said proudly. 'Wasn't that great?'

'Don't boast,' I reprimanded him. 'You shouldn't have done it. What will you think of me?'

'That you are definitely what I want in a wife, a horny girl that enjoys a good come.' He leaned closer to kiss at the lips. My cunt seemed to pulse like a heartbeat. 'Nice hairy, hungry little quim,' he praised it. 'Do you know how much I'd love to fuck you? Won't you let me in right now while you are pouting so prettily for me?'

I sat up in some alarm, drawing my dress down over my knees. 'No! What if Margaret and her husband come back?'

'I suppose you're right,' Harry had to concede, 'but just look at this.' He stood, his fly open and from it projected a lovely thick and hugely erect young prick. 'All your fault,' he jested. 'What can we do about it?'

I pretended to cover my eyes in shock. 'You are the limit,' I told him. I was sorely tempted to suck the nice thing. 'Put it away,' I giggled. 'Run it under a cold tap.'

'What a waste,' he grumbled good-naturedly. 'Tell me you want it as much as I do.'

I felt there was no need to be coy. 'Yes, I do,' I said. 'I promise some other time, Harry. I'd want to—'

'That's all I want to hear,' he smiled. I put my breasts back into my bra and went to the open French windows that overlooked the little garden directly below. They had been left open to allow the warm evening air into the room, an evening turning to dusk. The balcony beyond was no more than a foot wide with an ornate wrought iron railing. By standing against it for support, one could look into the garden from above. I saw Margaret and her husband watering plants set in large ornamental pots. As I did so, Harry came behind me, his hands going under my dress, caressing the rounds of my bottom. I parted my legs slightly and he felt my cunt from the rear.

Margaret, looking up, saw me and waved. 'Won't be too long now and we'll have dinner,' she called up. 'I'm sure you must be ready for something inside you, Diana.'

Something inside me was what I knew I was about to get, Harry's erect stalk pressing between the cleave of my bum, its fat circumcised knob seeking out its target. Still looking down at Margaret, I leaned over the railing and tilted my cunt, directing it to the prick nuzzling into me. A press back and I felt my lips give and engulf his first inch or two. It felt so good up me I waggled my bottom in sheer delight at its warm alive shape entering.

'Where's Harry?' Margaret's husband called up, watering can in hand. 'I hope he's not neglecting you.'

'No,' I called down in a voice as normal as I could manage. 'I wanted to see your garden. It's quite sizable, isn't it? Bigger than I thought—'

'So is this, I hope,' Harry whispered from behind me, his tool in me up to his balls. I could not let myself respond as I would have wished, my flanks thrashing back to piston his prick into me, not without it becoming obvious to the couple below at least. I had to content myself moving my backside slowly and insiduously, using the slightest back and forward motions as his stalk filled my channel. Harry too was nobly restraining his thrusting to prevent me being pressed forward against the balcony rail. The constraint, tormentingly keeping our natural urge to fuck wildly in the heat of our passion from breaking loose, actually served to heighten our mutual arousal. To prevent being seen by those below, Harry leaned back from the waist, his hands resting lightly on my hips. Inside my cunt his prick moved the merest inch or two, a tantalizing taste of what could be when the freedom to fuck without restriction was allowed us.

Despite the limitation, or perhaps because of it, my arousal soon came to boiling point, the slight movements of my pelvis enough to bring me to climax. I came looking down at the garden in response to Margaret calling up to me, swallowing hard to disguise the strong surges flowing from cunt to belly. Harry was grunting behind me, holding back his convulsions as he shot a thick volley into my begging crack.

'You're shivering, Diana,' Margaret noted from below. 'Don't get cold. Close the French window and go in. It's almost blackout time, anyway. We're just coming back up.' Harry withdrew behind me, pressing a kiss to the back of my neck. Moments later when Margaret and Dennis joined us, we were seated together on the settee trying to look as if nothing at all out of the ordinary had happened between us. 'So, did you two make up for lost time?' Margaret asked innocently of us, but smiling as if she was not fooled.

After dinner the talk was on how the war would affect us all. All I could think about was how Harry had licked me out and fucked me on our brief reacquaintance. His eyes smiled at me across the table during the meal. I sat, still knickerless, my cunt twitching and pulsating with a wet warmth seeping to my inner thighs. As to the whereabouts of my briefs, I sincerely hoped Harry had gathered them up and they were not lying in wait to be discovered between the cushions of the settee. When it was time to take my leave, Margaret kissed my cheek and told me to call on her whenever I wished. A taxi was called by telephone and when it arrived Harry got in beside me. 'A hotel?' he said, hearing me give directions to the taxi driver. 'Do you live there all the time?'

'I gave up my flat as I'm joining the Wrens,' I made up quickly. 'I should be off wherever they send me in a day or two—'

'And I report to the R.E. base at Chatham first thing tomorrow,' he said. 'I just wish we had had longer together, that's all.'

'I think we made the most of what time we did have,' I reminded him. By the time the taxi arrived before my hotel we were kissing madly and passionately. Harry followed me in to the little reception area, his arm about me, both very reluctant to part. When I asked for my key, the old night porter looked us over with a friendly eye.

'The bar's closed but I can open it if you want a nightcap,' he offered. 'Or if you'd like tea, I can make a pot in the kitchen. What have you two young folks been doing with yourselves tonight? Testing the blackout?'

'Saying goodbye,' Harry said. 'We're both joining the forces so it could be a long one too—' He took two pound notes from his pocket. 'We *are* engaged. What chance of letting us say goodbye a little longer in her room?'

'Please,' I said. 'We don't know when we'll see each other again—

'Against hotel rules, more than my job's worth,' the old man said, holding up his hand to refuse the money but with a little twinkle in his eye. 'However, if I'm in the kitchen making myself a cuppa, I wouldn't see you two lovebirds going upstairs, would I?'

'No, you wouldn't,' Harry grinned, stuffing the two notes in the top pocket of the night porter's uniform jacket. I added my donation, a kiss on his cheek.

'Have to be out by half-past five, before the kitchen staff arrives in the morning,' he warned us. 'That long enough for you two?' He chuckled at his joke. 'Don't worry, I'll come and knock the door down if necessary.'

Harry and I entered my room, locked the door, and fell into each other's arms on the narrow single bed. How we undressed between kisses and fondles is an art that lovers always manage. Naked together, Harry mounted me and we were able to give full rein to fucking, going on well into the night and trying out every permutation of positions and methods of arousal to renew our lustful love. We slept at last, locked in each other's arms, until I awoke and saw the time was five-fifteen. Harry was sleeping on his back, his so well-exercised prick lolling slack in repose over his balls. I kissed his lips to awaken him but he merely stirred in sleep. That I loved him I had no doubt.

I took his cock in my hand gently, admiring its girth, kissing the plum head. Soon it stirred against my palm, pulsed with tumescense as I lowered my lips to cover it. As I sucked quietly it grew in my mouth and Harry sighed contentedly, a hand lifting to rest on my shoulder. My head bobbed up and down over him and his legs straightened, shuddered, and his hips rose off the bed. I got a load of his warm thick fluid at the back of my throat in strong spurts. Before I could swallow he had drawn me to him and kissed me. We were still kissing when a knock came to our door. I went to say we were up, speaking through the door. A muffled voice said there was a tray outside for us. I peeped out and saw the old man had gone.

He had left us a pot of tea, two cups, and a handful of biscuits. 'A veritable feast,' Harry announced, sitting up in bed drinking tea. 'Breakfast in bed with a naked girl supplying all my wants. What more could a chap ask going off to war?'

'Another fuck?' I suggested naughtily.

It was to be our last one for almost five years, because before I saw Harry again the war was over. He returned from service in North Africa, Sicily, Italy and Germany a major of Royal Engineers with a Military Cross and experience of building bridges across rivers under enemy fire, restoring electricity and water to shattered towns and clearing mines. Within a week of his return we had married, as he had said we would. He then returned to university to resume the studies to qualify as a civil engineer that would lead us eventually to life in East Africa.

My wartime experience as a member of the Womens Royal Naval Service for the five years I served deserves a book of its own, so I shall not detail the adventures and many misadventures that befell me in these pages. That is a story I shall keep for future telling, one serving woman's private war. It should make good reading, even though for services given above and beyond the call of duty I never got the Good Conduct Medal.

Chapter Nineteen
AFRICA

Word has come from London offering Harry a knighthood in the next New Year's Honours List. The citation says it is for his selfless services overseas in aiding humanity, work successfully completed in East Africa and Arabia, where his cost-effective irrigation schemes rejuvenated large arid areas for crop farming and grazing. His paper 'Making the Desert Bloom' has received worldwide acclaim since its publication and he has been offered a very senior post with the United Nations Organisation on a huge tax-free salary as an administrator of their food and agriculture policy for underdeveloped countries. For all of this I feel I can take some of the credit!

My husband is delighted, of course, and his new job means we will leave East Africa to be based in New York. I shall enjoy living in America and no doubt will find plenty to keep me occupied while Harry has to travel extensively to advise Third World governments in his capacity as an expert in his field. His knighthood and the title that goes with it doesn't mean a thing to him. 'But you bet I'll accept,' he roared with wry amusement on opening the official letter from London offering him the honour. 'The opportunity of making a lady out of you, my love, is far too good to miss. Lady Diana Saxon. How does that grab you?'

I'm no snob but it did grab me, finding it highly amusing myself to be officially a lady after all the ins and outs and ups and downs of my life, and no pun intended. No wonder Harry was tickled at the thought. 'I don't give tuppence for a title myself,' he went on, 'but I'm not going to refuse the chance of being married to a real lady. I always considered that I was anyway.'

I was glad he thought so. There had been so many lapses on my part during our marriage that if he had only known a part of them it might well have been different. Harry was dressing to go to a celebration party his colleagues were giving him to mark his honour awarded. 'You know,' he called through to me as I lay soaking in the bath, 'I've just had a thought. This will mean a trip to London for the investiture at Buckingham Palace. No doubt that means you'll be requiring a whole new wardrobe. Maybe I should turn down the offer after all—'

'You dare,' I warned as his head appeared around the bathroom door. 'If nothing else I want to be a lady just to make Midge and Molly green with envy.' He came into the room and sat on the edge of the bath, admiring what he saw, my breasts floating as I lolled back and my mound and its bush wearing a beard of soapy froth at water level.

'You deserve an award for having such great tits,' Harry observed. 'Really, Di, you've got better as the years have gone by. How do you do it?'

'Clean living and a pure mind,' I told him, 'and take your hand out from between my legs. You'll be late for your office party—'

'That can wait,' he said, pulling back the sleeve of his dress shirt with his free hand while the other one dipped into the bath, fondling my cunt. His finger entered me, stroking slowly, making me part my legs and tilt my crotch clear of the water. I jerked slightly with the first little thrills coursing through my lower belly building into the surge that leads to one climaxing. He flicked my clitoris, smiling down as my squirming about on his finger increased.

'Beast,' I told him. 'Is that the way to treat a lady?'

'Precisely the way,' he laughed, 'and look what it does to me.' With his free hand he had unzipped his fly, drawing out his rampant prick. 'Fair's fair, Di. I rub you, you rub me. Let's come together—'

I rolled half sideways in the bath, his finger still in me, reaching over with my right hand to grasp his stalk and wank it vigorously. Water sploshing around me in my spasms, I came unrestrainedly, crying out my pleasure as Harry's spurts flew out over my wrist to anoint me from my hair down to my tits. I used my face flannel to dab his cock dry on our recovery. 'I remember the first time I had that in my hand,' I recalled, giving the pink helmet a little kiss and seeing it returned inside his evening suit trousers. 'It was in the trees outside your father's house and we were caught in the act. We've made up for that since, haven't we?'

Harry laughed, thinking back fondly. 'Wouldn't change a minute of any of our time together, Di, even the hard times. It wasn't easy in our early days, but you were always cheerful and a bloody good wife in every way. I'm only sorry that my parents never accepted you, but that was their loss. I never got on with them anyway. Mother was such a snob. But for her I believe I could have got on with my father eventually. Water under the bridge now.'

He finished dressing, came to peck a goodbye kiss on me, and drove off leaving me enjoying my soak in the warm sudsy water. His words had me thinking of the years of our marriage. How at the end of the war we had married and I was pregnant when he resumed his university studies, independently refusing help from his father when a letter arrived with an offer of financial aid. We lived in a cramped one-bedroom flat on precious little. Harry worked at night as a barman to supplement a small student grant and I had worked in one of the bookshops that abounded in Oxford until so big and heavily pregnant that I had to quit. But being short of money and a few luxuries in no way prevented us from being the happiest couple alive.

And it was at that particular period of time that an unexpected visitor called when my husband Harry was out at his evening job one wintry evening. A surprise knock on the door, for we rarely had visitors, led to an even more surprising meeting. About to take a bath and in only my dressing gown, or rather Harry's army greatcoat which served as my dressing gown, I peeped around the inch or two of door that I opened and saw a face from the past, Harry's father whom I'd last seen a lot of eventful years ago in Scotland.

'May I come in?' he asked in the refined voice I remembered so well. He took off his hat and stood before me in a heavy Crombie overcoat, looking very refined and comfortably off. Handsome too, I thought, an older version of Harry.

'Of course,' I said, opening the door wider for him. 'When did you come back to England?'

'Yesterday,' he said, eyeing my very pregnant condition. 'Margaret Winthrop told me where to find you. I got no reply from the letter she forwarded for me—'

'Harry's decision,' I said. 'He's so independent.'

He nodded sadly. 'I thought that, so I'm here. It's been a long time, hasn't it, Diana Mackenzie?'

'Diana Saxon now,' I said somewhat defiantly, not knowing whether he resented my marrying his son after our past sexual history. 'You'd better come in before you let the cold in as well.'

He entered, looking about the room while I closed the

door, prepared to give as good as I got if he intended to throw our previous relationship in my face. I had, after all, been the young impressionable girl, albeit a willing victim, but he had been the seducer. He stood in the middle of the floor on our worn carpet and gave me a long look up and down, the army greatcoat dressing gown and the obvious swollen belly of an eight-months' preggy young woman.

'So how are you, Diana Saxon?' he inquired kindly.

'Bigger and better than ever,' I said, determined to be friendly unless otherwise deemed necessary. 'Would you like a cup of tea or coffee? We can't run to a drink, I'm afraid.'

'Tea would be nice,' he said, 'if it's no trouble—'

'None at all,' I told him, taking his hat and coat and ushering him to the one armchair we owned. 'I'll put the kettle on and join you. I expect you want to know everything about your son. He's well and happy.'

'I'm sure he is,' Harry's father said, looking around at our furnishings, the double bed in the corner of the room taking up so much of the space. At least the place was spotlessly clean and warm. 'Very happy with you, I'm sure.'

'We've got all we want, mainly each other. When Harry graduates things will improve. He hopes to work abroad in Africa or India—'

'Meanwhile you don't have to live like this, you know,' I was told. 'I have money. Harry seems to think it wrong to accept a little help—'

'We manage,' I said. 'There are no debts, even some savings.'

Mr Saxon looked around the room again. 'I could buy you a house; furnish and carpet it. I'd like to.' He was, as ever, a kindly man. 'And that army greatcoat you're wearing, surely Harry can afford to buy you a dressing gown?'

'It's warm and comfortable, and dressing gowns take valuable clothing coupons,' I smiled. 'As for the flat, it's really superior to the places students usually manage to rent. There's a kitchen and bathroom too. Both in the one space, I admit, but it's adequate.'

I went through to the gas ring to boil water for tea and he rose from the chair to follow me. 'I see what you mean,' he observed, looking at the narrow kitchen with its sloping ceiling and the bath tub set at one end. 'Adequate is the only word for it.'

'Cosy,' I argued, laughing. 'Nice and warm if having a bath while dinner's cooking. You've just missed your son, by the way. It's not ten minutes since he left for his evening job.'

'It was you that I wanted to see,' my father-in-law said. 'I thought Harry might resent my calling, so I waited across the street until I saw him leave. Margaret told me he worked evenings to earn extra money.' He shook his head. 'I could give you all you need, you know.'

'You should be proud of him,' I said, making the tea. 'At weekends he works on building sites too, making sure we don't do without.'

'I can see what it's like for you both,' he agreed, back in the armchair and accepting a cup of tea. 'He's a lucky man. Pretty little wife, baby on the way. I could wish it were me. For all my success as a businessman, mine was not a happy life.'

'So you noticed,' I teased him, 'noticed you are going to be a grandfather. Won't you stay and see Harry tonight?'

'No, I don't wish to interfere,' he said flatly. 'I'm booked in at an hotel here in Oxford and will return to London tomorrow morning, then leave for France. How,' he asked suddenly, 'do you feel about accepting money from me, especially with a baby coming?'

'I'm not so independent as Harry,' I admitted. 'It would be useful.'

'Good girl,' he nodded, taking an envelope from inside his jacket pocket. 'Then this can be our secret and Harry doesn't need to know a thing. Take this and I'll see that there'll be more at times.'

I thanked him, opening the envelope. The inside was thick with banknotes. 'Good God,' I said. 'There looks like hundreds here—'

'Five hundred. Get yourself something nice for you and the baby. Now I should go,' he said, waving aside my attempts to thank him. 'Perhaps I'm keeping you out of bed—'

'I was about to bath when you called,' I said. 'Hence the army-style dressing gown.'

'Can you manage to get in and out of that tub in your condition?' he said, concerned. 'You must be careful not to fall—'

'Are you offering to help me?' I asked.

'Please, Diana,' he said. 'I was not suggesting for a moment. No!'

Why is it these urges come upon me to exhibit and flaunt myself? There's a devil in me, I'm sure. Besides, I felt sorry for the man, was still overawed with gratitude at his generosity. I loved my husband, was heavy with his child, and the man before me was his father, yet still the urge to show myself to him was uncontrollable. 'It would help if you'd give me a steadying hand getting in and out of the bath,' I said, swallowing to disguise the thickening of my voice. 'After all, you wouldn't be seeing anything you haven't seen before, would you? Only more of me—'

He said nothing, standing perplexed yet unable to turn away as I unbuttoned the greatcoat and let it drop to the carpet. I stood in full frontal as they say now. In late pregnancy my breasts had swollen up like huge balloons, full and round as never before, hanging pulled apart by their weight and mass. My nipples seemed twice normal size, big as thimbles and reddish brown with their aureole surrounds stretched as big as saucers. The curve of my stomach bulged amazingly, rounding down to the fork of my legs, forcing my thighs apart and making my mound with its auburn growth and my cunt lips disappear down under for the duration.

My father-in-law stared at me with wonder in his eyes. 'I have never seen anything or anyone so beautiful,' he said in awe. I took his hand and placed it on my belly. 'God, I feel movement,' he announced excitedly. 'Quite strong movement in there.'

'Your grandchild kicking to get out,' I told him. 'Now I'll run the hot water and you can help me in. Wash my back if you wish.'

He stood by the bath while I soaped myself, then took my elbow and hand to assist me out of the bath when I had finished. 'I dry myself before the fire,' I said. 'Come and help me. It's not easy getting at the awkward parts like my back.' I handed him the bath towel warming before the fire when we went back into the living room. 'Don't be shy,' I urged. 'I'm not brittle. Give me a good rub.'

His eyes bored into my bloated tits and he towelled them gently, lifting to dry beneath them as I instructed. 'Can you remember drying me once before?' I reminded him. 'That day in Scotland when it rained and I went in swimming. I ran back to your Rolls and you wrapped me in a travelling rug. This is like old times, isn't it?'

'I made love to you that day for the first time,' he recalled. 'I wish it were that time again.'

Going to the bed, I sat up on it while he knelt before me drying my feet. I lolled back on my elbows, parting my legs, showing him my cunt. Between the opened thighs he looked directly at my hair-covered split mound. 'Touch it,' I told him. 'Feel it. I want you to. You won't harm me.'

He was hesitant so I urged him again. Then he placed a tentative finger tip to my lips, putting it inside me the merest half-inch. I told him not to be afraid, taking his hand and guiding it hard against me. The finger went right in. Aroused by my action, more confident, he stroked at my clitoris.

'That's lovely, lovely,' I said, writhing against his wrist. 'I still like to come, you know, even pregnant like this. Would you like to fuck me? I'd enjoy a nice go—'

'Is it possible?' he said. 'At your size?'

'Of course,' I told him. 'I want to, don't you? It wouldn't do any harm. Would you like to?'

'Yes,' he said hoarsely, rising before me. 'It's been so long, so long.' The front of his trousers bulged with the erection he'd gained and I wanted to see it. I told him and he brought it out, a good stiff erection rearing with arousal. Then he was moving between my thighs as if to penetrate me.

'No,' I said. 'Not on top of me. I can't do it the front way any more. Wait, I'll turn over for you.'

I rolled over, looking somewhat like a great white whale I can imagine, until my bared rump faced him, tilted up and on offer. I rested the side of my face on the bed and reached back with my hands, parting my bottom cheeks for his entry. What he could see I could guess, the divided buttocks and a crinkly anus with the hanging of my mound and the cunt lips awaiting his entry. He did not hesitate then, positioning his knob to the cleft and sliding into the moist nest, going on until I felt his balls against my raised bum. Once in he remained still as if afraid of hurting me.

'Go on,' I said fiercely. 'Poke me. Give me a good come. I do want one. Don't be afraid—'

He began fucking me, slowly at first and then hastening his strokes as the urge gripped him. We groaned our pleasure out together and my spasms began, making my bottom jerk hard against his thrusts. I told him he was making me come, I was coming, it was heaven, and then he was thrashing his pelvis into me and gasping as his load shot from him.

I lay back on the bed enjoying the languor of being brought off so nicely while he went to the kitchen to wash his hands and return with his dress adjusted. He kissed my cheek and left, pausing at the door to turn and say a simple 'Thank you, Diana.' I never saw him again although amounts of money were forwarded to me for several years. I suppose it fitting to end this story with the account of that night's sexual encounter with my father-in-law. He it was who opened the door to my life of sensual pleasure, who claimed my virginity. I owed him one, I felt, don't you?

More Erotic Fiction from Headline:

Lustful Liaisons

Erotic adventures in the capital city of love!

Anonymous

PARIS 1912 – a city alive with the pursuit of pleasure, from the promenade of the Folies Bergère to the high-class brothels of the Left Bank. Everywhere business is booming in the oldest trade of all – the trade of love!

But now there is a new and flourishing activity to absorb the efforts of go-ahead men-about-town: the business of manufacturing motor cars. Men like Robert and Bertrand Laforge are pioneers in this field but their new automobile has a design defect that can only be rectified by some cunning industrial espionage. Which is where the new trade marries with the old, for the most reliable way of discovering information is to enlist the help of a lovely and compliant woman. A woman, for example, like the voluptuous Nellie Lebérigot whose soft creamy flesh and generous nature are guaranteed to uncover a man's most closely guarded secrets...

More titillating reading from Headline:
AMOROUS LIAISONS
LOVE ITALIAN STYLE
ECSTASY ITALIAN STYLE
EROTICON DREAMS
EROTICON DESIRES

FICTION/EROTICA   0 7472 3710 7

A selection of Erotica from Headline

FONDLE ON TOP	Nadia Adamant	£4.99 ☐
EROS AT PLAY	Anonymous	£4.99 ☐
THE GIRLS' BOARDING SCHOOL	Anonymous	£4.99 ☐
HOTEL D'AMOUR	Anonymous	£4.99 ☐
A MAN WITH THREE MAIDS	Anonymous	£4.99 ☐
RELUCTANT LUST	Lesley Asquith	£4.50 ☐
SEX AND MRS SAXON	Lesley Asquith	£4.50 ☐
THE BLUE LANTERN	Nick Bancroft	£4.99 ☐
AMATEUR NIGHTS	Becky Bell	£4.99 ☐
BIANCA	Maria Caprio	£4.50 ☐
THE GIRLS OF LAZY DAISY'S	Faye Rossignol	£4.50 ☐

All Headline books are available at your local bookshop or newsagent, or can be ordered direct from the publisher. Just tick the titles you want and fill in the form below. Prices and availability subject to change without notice.

Headline Book Publishing PLC, Cash Sales Department, Bookpoint, 39 Milton Park, Abingdon, OXON, OX14 4TD, UK. If you have a credit card you may order by telephone — 0235 831700.

Please enclose a cheque or postal order made payable to Bookpoint Ltd to the value of the cover price and allow the following for postage and packing:
UK & BFPO: £1.00 for the first book, 50p for the second book and 30p for each additional book ordered up to a maximum charge of £3.00.
OVERSEAS & EIRE: £2.00 for the first book, £1.00 for the second book and 50p for each additional book.

Name ....

Address ....

....

....

If you would prefer to pay by credit card, please complete:
Please debit my Visa/Access/Diner's Card/American Express (delete as applicable) card no:

Signature ....Expiry Date ....